GENTLEMEN *prefer* MISCHIEF

EMILY GREENWOOD

sourcebooks
casablanca

Published by Sourcebooks Casablanca, an imprint of Sourcebooks,
Inc.
P. O. Box 4410, Naperville, Illinois 60567-4410
(630) 961-3900
Fax: (630) 961-2168
www.sourcebooks.com

Printed and bound in the United States of America.
VP 10 9 8 7 6 5 4 3 2

For A & S

One

IT WAS THE GHOST NONSENSE THAT STARTED IT.

Lily Teagarden had seen the phantom lights herself at night, flickering among the wide strip of trees that divided Thistlethwaite, her family's property, from the estate belonging to their absentee neighbor, Viscount Roxham. The trees belonged to him as well.

She did not believe in ghosts or spirits of any kind.

But most of Highcross village did, doubtless in part because as children they'd been told of the two people who'd met a dastardly end in the Mayfield woods fifty years before. Since no trace of the villain had ever been found, legend held that the crime had been done by an evil spirit—one who might still linger among the shadowy underbrush. Generations of misbehaving children had been warned that the barbarous Woods Fiend would find them if they didn't mend their ways.

That well-developed fear was doubtless behind what had just been delivered to the little stone building at the back of Thistlethwaite Manor, where Lily was currently standing with her hands folded tightly in front of her and frustration deepening her breath. Before her stood a large crate of neatly folded shawls over which she'd toiled with persistence and a deep sense of purpose. A note had been sent with them, which read in part:

> *I regret that I must return these unsold shawls, but I can no longer have them in my shop. Because of the situation near your property and its proximity to the sheep that produce the yarn, ladies no longer wish to be seen wearing them. Mrs. Croat was actually followed by a small crowd who forced her to take her shawl off and burn it.*
>
> *Doubtless things would not have gotten to such a state had Mary Wortham not been wearing one of the shawls when the little tree fell on her, but with the rumors circulating about the Thistlethwaite sheep, superstitious people can talk of nothing else.*
>
> *Perhaps in the future if the problem is resolved, we might again do business. Until then, I see no market for your shawls.*
>
> > *Yours,*
> > *Thomas Trent*

Lily folded the letter and creased it sharply. This was doubtless the reason Helen hadn't come to work for the last three days. Helen was the one who'd seen Parsley coming out of the woods—the sheep had been rolling her eyes and Helen had said, in a quivering voice, that Parsley had been taken over by the Woods Fiend. Lily had said it was midges.

Apparently, Helen had been talking.

The September afternoon carried late summer

warmth, and the back of one of Lily's sticky hands was covered with fluff from the wool she'd been picking through. As she considered the crate of shawls, she meticulously picked the fluff off her hands and gathered it into a neat puff that she put on the table. An unruly trickle of perspiration slid downward from the immaculate knot that kept her white-blond hair tidy and threatened to soak into the collar of her pale blue frock, but she brushed it away with a precise swipe of her index finger.

"So our sheep are possessed," she said aloud, giving vent to her frustration. "What, are they going to float into our rooms at night and *nibble* us all to death?"

"Oh, Li—ly," her younger sister Delia sang out as she rushed through the door of the little house, "I have the most amazing news." At fifteen, Delia never walked when she could rush. "Wait, what do you mean we're going to be nibbled to death?"

"Apparently everyone thinks our sheep are haunted or possessed or some such."

Delia let out a bark of laughter before clapping her hand over her mouth.

"I'm sorry, Lil," she said when she had collected herself, "it's just that Rosemary and Thyme would make such adorable ghosts." She saw the crate of shawls. "But what's all this?"

Lily found that she was clenching her teeth, and she made herself relax. This would be—surely it *must* be—resolved if only the Mayfield estate would do its part. She'd gone there last week when Helen had first suggested the Woods Fiend was responsible for the phantom lights, and Mr. Prescott, the estate manager, had listened and nodded, but there'd been no result. She'd even considered investigating herself, but if something nefarious were going on in the woods, she'd be ill equipped to respond.

She *couldn't* do without the money the shawls made.

"Mr. Trent sent them back," she explained. "Between Helen gossiping about evil spirits and what happened to Mary Wortham, our shawls are now very much *non grata*." Lily sat down at the table and dropped her chin onto her upraised palm and considered what to do. She forced herself not to dwell on the owner of Mayfield, even though it was no surprise that Roxham should be a neglectful landlord.

"Oh, dear. That *is* bad news," Delia said as she moved closer and perched on the edge of the table. Her blond hair was a few shades darker than Lily's—of the four Teagarden siblings, Lily had the lightest hair—and arranged in a pretty style that Delia had devised herself.

She reached for Lily's hand. "I know how much you like your clandestine shawl-making. All that special knitting, even late at night. And it's worked out having Helen as the public face of the business all these years." She squeezed Lily's hand as if to shore her up. "But now that every penny from the business doesn't need to be saved anymore…"

Oh, yes, every penny did need to be saved, Lily thought. But her plans for her proceeds from the business were her secret.

"The shawl business is important to me," she said, though she knew Delia didn't see why. Their brothers, Rob and Ian, didn't understand either why she persisted in making the shawls herself. The business had been started four years before, as part of the siblings' efforts to pay off the large debts that were discovered when their father died. The fact that Lily did much of the work herself had always been kept secret so it wouldn't be known she was engaged in trade. But now that the debts had been paid and Lily continued to work, her siblings looked on it as her odd secret hobby. Though Lily loved them, she wasn't ready to say why she needed to keep working.

"But it's not genteel," Delia said with a faint air of impatience.

To the devil with genteel, Lily wanted to say. Genteel was about papering over what really went on in people's lives. But it wasn't Delia's fault that she knew little of the unpresentable side of life, and Lily was glad that she didn't.

"Well," Delia went on, "with Mr. Trent not wanting to sell the shawls… maybe this is a good time to give up the business."

"Oh, I'm not going to give it up," Lily said, "and certainly not over this Woods Fiend nonsense."

"But what else is there to do if nobody wants to buy the shawls?"

"Nobody wants to buy them because they think they're tainted. But if someone from Mayfield would resolve the problem, people would want the shawls again." Lily stood up.

Delia stopped swinging her leg and narrowed her eyes. "You're not going to do something strident, are you?"

"Strident? It's perfectly acceptable to ask that our neighbor do the right thing."

Delia hopped off the table and took hold of Lily's sleeve. "But you can't do that! It's—it's unseemly. At least wait a few days, until Rob and Ian come back."

"I'm too annoyed to wait. Mayfield has been a careless neighbor of late, and something must be done."

"But what will Roxham think?"

"He won't think a thing—he's never there. As far as I can tell, he's washed his hands of the estate."

"But that's what I came to tell you," Delia said, giving Lily's sleeve an urgent shake. "He's here, with a party of ladies and gentlemen." She finally released the fabric and threw her arms in the air. "There's going to be a ball at Mayfield—and we're invited!"

Lily blinked at this gust of information. "What? After years away, the lord has come back to the manor? It can't be true."

"But it is! His sister herself came just now to deliver the invitation. And, oh, Eloise Waverly is unbelievably fashionable and charming."

"Of course she is."

Delia tilted her head. "Didn't you like Eloise when they used to be at Mayfield?"

"I suppose she was nice enough."

Privately, Lily admitted that perhaps she'd let her animosity toward Hal—no, Viscount Roxham, as she made sure to think of him now—color her feelings about his younger sister. She'd known his family from childhood—their families were neighbors and the two most important families in the area, even if the Teagardens were far lower on the social scale than the viscount's family.

"Well, *I* like her so far," Delia said. "And she's

sixteen, too—only a bit older than me, so I hope we'll be great friends."

"You'd be great friends with a kitten if she were sixteen, you're so starved for company. I'll just go and have a quick word with the viscount."

Delia's face fell. "Oh, Lily, no. I'm begging you not to go to him over the Woods Fiend. He's a viscount now, for goodness' sake—he needn't concern himself with something like this. Besides, they've just invited us to a ball, and it will seem ungrateful to complain."

"I *am* ungrateful if they're not going to be good neighbors."

Delia crossed her arms. "Rob wouldn't like it, your going over there about this."

Lily didn't exactly like the idea of approaching Roxham either; she couldn't think of the last time she'd seen him without shuddering from the bottom of her soul.

"Rob needn't even know."

"Oh," Delia fairly wailed, "but you are so uninterested in being pleasing to gentlemen. I still squirm when I think of how you wouldn't let Mr. Easton give you flowers last week at the fair."

"He was going to pick them from a bush where they were growing so beautifully. It was wrong."

"No, he wanted to do something gallant because he thinks you are pretty."

"There, you see. I don't want Mr. Easton to think I'm pretty."

"Argh, Lily. You always have to be so focused on things being *worthy*."

Lily laughed. "Very well, I promise to do at least

one unworthy thing in the coming week. See how agreeable I am?"

Delia sighed. "Well, if you really must go, put on something pretty first. That blue frock is so plain. You want to look your best if you are going to see Roxham. And be your most winning. He's—"

"Yes, I know. Lord Perfect. All the ladies adore him, *et cetera*, even though he's vowed not to marry until he's fifty-one. I know perfectly well what he looks like and that he knows how to charm," Lily said, cherishing a hope that he was getting fat by now, or was a wasted wreck of a man, or at the very least in constant despair over the fact that he was a shallow person. It would only be fair, really, if he'd developed a case of persistent boils.

Delia, gazing off into space, missed the scorn in her sister's voice. "First a dashing, brave army captain, and now he's a viscount. I can barely remember him, but he must be so handsome now, like Achilles."

"Achilles wasn't even real! Honestly, Delia. I just want him to see to his property so we don't all suffer."

And in fact, as she set out toward Mayfield with her dog, Buck, beside her, Lily was glad that she wasn't finely turned out. If she'd looked her best, she might have been tempted to try to charm Lord Perfect herself. But she was a different person now from the silly sixteen-year-old she'd been when last she'd seen him.

And she didn't need him to like her anymore.

❧

Under the domed, ornate roof of the small rotunda on the eastern edge of the Mayfield estate, Hal, Viscount

Roxham, crouched next to his young nephew, Freddy, who had eyes for nothing but the burning length of a slow match on the stone floor before them and the twist of paper in his uncle's hand.

Sitting on tall-backed chairs that servants had brought were Freddy's mother, Diana, and Hyacinth Whyte, a pretty widow. Occasional faint bursts of Italian, along with clattering sounds, came from a site somewhat distant where two men were at work amid a pile of stones.

"I really don't know that a child of five ought to be lighting things, Hal," Diana said.

"Nonsense," he said. "It's a rite of passage. Men love fire, don't we?"

"Yes!" Freddy said gleefully, doubtless thinking of his napping brother. "It's only for men."

The firecracker felt insignificant in Hal's hand; he was aware of an itching desire for something larger, like a rocket.

"Roxham is very good at setting things on fire," Hyacinth said suggestively. Hal could feel his sister-in-law lifting an eyebrow in his direction. The firecracker lesson had been partly motivated by a wish for less time alone with Hyacinth, which was shabby of him, as he was the one who'd invited her. He'd thought he might enjoy her silliness and chatter, but he hadn't. Which didn't necessarily have anything to do with her.

"So, Freddy," Hal said, "take the firecracker"—Freddy took hold eagerly—"and you're going to press the part that's sticking up on the slow ma—"

Freddy pressed the firecracker to the match before Hal could finish instructing.

"Throw it, boy!"

The firecracker sailed from the rotunda, emitting a loud crack. This was immediately followed by a sharp cry that came from behind the rotunda, along with a series of barks.

"Heavens," Diana said as they all turned to see Mayfield's butler approaching them in company with a petite, pale-haired woman and a black-and-white hound. "Who is that?"

At first glance, Hal didn't know—and then, as she drew closer and the detail of the prim set of her mouth could be added to the near-whiteness of her hair, recognition dawned, along with a spurt of gratitude at the diversion she would represent.

"Miss Teagarden to see you, my lord," Johnson said. Hal was already walking toward her.

"Lily Teagarden." He bowed. Teagardens... he'd forgotten all about them. It had been ages since he'd seen any of them.

"My lord." Her curtsy was a sketch, a brisk reference to what was owed a viscount. He wouldn't expect formality from such close neighbors as the Teagardens, and the last time he'd seen her he'd been merely a captain in the Foot Guards and the younger brother of a viscount. Still, there was no warmth in her greeting either. Her eyes flicked to the floor of the rotunda, where the still-burning slow match was gradually disappearing.

"I'm sorry about your brother," she said. "He was a fine man."

"Yes, he was," he said, an inadequate reply he'd made countless times in the last six months since acceding to a title that never should have been his. "And how is your family?"

"My sister is well. Rob and Ian are away at present."

He was about to ask after her father when he remembered that Mr. Teagarden had died some years ago—of drink, it had been rumored, though he didn't remember the man being a sot.

He presented her to Diana, Hyacinth, and Freddy.

"We're lighting firecrackers," Freddy informed her.

"Yes, I heard."

"Wasn't it splendid?"

"Splendid."

"I should think you'd like a demonstration up close," Hal said. Her primness was irresistible.

"N—" she started to say, but caught sight of Freddy's eager face. Her stiff smile softened into quite a kind look and she said, "Certainly."

"Oh Hal, he needn't do more," Diana said. "It *is* rather loud."

"Nonsense, I'm certain there's nothing Miss Teagarden would like better."

Hal handed Freddy a firecracker; Freddy pressed it immediately to the slow match and flung the burning twist of gunpowder away. The satisfying crack was followed by an equally satisfying yelp from Miss Teagarden.

"Well done, Freddy," she said a little tightly. "Most diverting."

Turning to Hal, she said, "Might I have a word with you in private, my lord?"

A private word with him? "Certainly, Miss Teagarden," he said, wondering why they were being so formal when it had been Hal and Lily when they were younger. He excused himself from the others and led her toward the shade provided by a copse of trees. Her dog followed them like a furry chaperone.

"It's about the woods between our properties. The villagers think the Woods Fiend is back."

"The Woods Fiend?" he said. "By Jove, I'd forgotten about him." As children, he and his elder brother, Everard, had gone on raids of the woods looking for the Fiend. Everard had always led the way, with Hal his faithful lieutenant.

If only Everard were still here, he thought for the thousandth time.

"People are saying that he's possessed our sheep, or haunted them, or some such." She made an impatient gesture as she uttered these bizarre words. "Thistlethwaite is known for the shawls made from our wool, but the rumors are hurting the business. So I ask that you find out what's going on in the woods at night so this silliness can be cleared up. Please."

He absorbed this slightly breathless request. Since he'd become viscount, many things had been asked of him, but this was certainly the strangest. "The Woods Fiend is believed to be possessing your sheep?"

"I'm not surprised you know nothing of this," she said with an air of accusation, as if to suggest that this trouble was his fault. "I've spoken to Mr. Prescott, but to no avail."

Ah. Prescott had managed Mayfield for decades, and as Everard had relied on him, Hal had known he could, too. However, since arriving at Mayfield yesterday, he'd become increasingly convinced that the man was going deaf, despite trying to carry off a charade that he could hear. So that was something else to contend with.

Since becoming viscount, Hal's respect for his brother had only grown as he'd seen the effort it took to meet all the needs of the role. Everard had been perfect for the task; all his life, Hal had known that his brilliant, unselfish, dedicated brother was the ideal person to be viscount. Hal hadn't even minded knowing that he himself was lacking in comparison—Everard was such a good man that he'd always wished him the best.

And, damn fate for the cruel idiot that it was, Everard had been carried off by a fever six months ago. Leaving Hal—the unsuitable brother, the one who made mistakes, the one who had so much trouble being serious—in a role that never should have been his. If he could have given the viscountcy to his steady younger brother John, he would have. But hereditary titles didn't work that way.

He cleared his throat. "Why do people think the Woods Fiend is in the neighborhood? And… tampering with your sheep?"

The flicker in her eyes dared him to laugh about the problem she'd brought to him. They were pretty eyes, of an intense if surprisingly soft blue.

It was funny, he thought, how you could forget a person entirely, and then years later meet that person again and there was that feeling you got from being around him or her. The feeling he'd always gotten around Lily was amusement tinged with irritation; she could be a killjoy.

But one thing had certainly changed in the

intervening years. She used to be odd-looking. All the Teagardens had blond hair, but hers had been the palest, a white-blond that had made her seem fragile, a little unearthly, and not in a charming, pixie-ish way. Compared to the rest of her family, she'd been different, because her brothers were handsome and tall. She'd been too thin, which had doubtless been much of the problem with her looks, because the whole effect had been a sort of sickly almost-colorlessness.

That had all changed. Her blue dress was not fashionable—he would have described it as adequate—but it skimmed a very fine figure that started with a set of shoulders held decisively upright. Her face had acquired an interesting definition, and he felt rewarded for his attention by something unique. Those sharply intelligent cornflower blue eyes, which had not seemed remarkable to him when he was younger, now struck him as compelling. In truth, she was a beauty.

"Lights have been observed in the woods at night," she said, "and people take that for a sign he's there. Though why a spirit should need lights, no one stops to think."

He would wager the foolishness of adults believing in spirits would annoy her—she had such a determined air, as if she had things to accomplish and the Woods Fiend was in her way. "Who knows, really," he said, "how well specters can see in the dark?"

She did not dignify that with anything more than a glare. Even her dog was glaring at him. But what a farce, and undeniably the only truly amusing thing that had been brought to him since he'd left the brotherhood of the army.

A heavy clatter came from the folly site, drawing her attention, and she squinted into the distance at the half-completed building. "What are you building over there?"

"A folly." The builders were a father and son, Italian mercenaries his men had captured in Portugal. The duo were soon deemed rather tenderhearted, and in the way that his troops often adopted stray dogs, the Italians had been adopted and trusted with small jobs. Not knowing how his replacement would look upon the two men, Hal had brought Giuseppe and Pietro with him when Everard's death had made him viscount. "It's to be a miniature ruined amphitheater."

"Doesn't Mayfield already have a folly by the lake?"

"Yes, but I can't see it from the manor."

She sniffed. "Another folly."

Her lips pressed together in disapproval; she seemed to have rather a lot of exasperation with him already. It was almost as if he'd offended her beforehand, which was ridiculous, since he hadn't seen her in…

A smile tugged his lips as he remembered. Her fair brows drew together.

"You know very well, my lord, that there's no Woods Fiend. It's obvious someone is up to something in your woods. I would appreciate it if you would please see to this problem as soon as possible."

"I'm surprised Rob and Ian haven't gone after the Fiend themselves."

"The problem developed after they left."

She was waiting for him to agree to help, and then she would turn on her heel and stride back to Thistlethwaite with her hound. But he wasn't ready for her to leave yet, perhaps because her acerbic presence was so interesting—he never got acerbic treatment from females, of any age.

"You know, Lily Teagarden, now that I see you here, I'm reminded of the last time I saw you. Because it was here at Mayfield, on the terrace, wasn't it? You can see the spot quite well from here. Look." She refused to turn her head, but he'd had his reaction in the spill of pink now suffusing her fair cheeks. A keener alertness sharpened the cornflower eyes.

"It was a fine summer evening, as I recall," he said. "There I was on the terrace, chatting with friends, not even aware of your presence. Understandable, in that you'd concealed yourself in the bushes." The color in her cheeks deepened.

"I'm not as entertained as you by memories of that night," she said tartly.

"Oh, come, it's amusing now, isn't it? You're all grown up, and you can have a laugh about your younger self."

"As you say, it was a long time ago. Now, if you'll promise to see to the woods, I'll be on my way."

But a commotion by the rotunda drew their attention; it was his brother John returning from a stroll with their sister, Eloise, and Hal's friend Colin, the Earl of Ivorwood. Everyone was looking at Hal and his visitor, no doubt wondering what they were discussing. Eloise, ever exuberant, came over, trailed by Freddy and the others.

"Why, Lily Teagarden!" she said. "How good to see you. It's been years."

Warmth softened Lily's heretofore stiff features.

Cool, small, collected—with her white-blond hair, she was like a petite, pristine snowdrift. "Miss Eloise Waverly, it's—it's really quite lovely to see you again."

"Can we know the secret you were talking about?" Freddy asked.

"Secret?" Eloise said.

Hal could see Lily wanted to keep this Woods Fiend business quiet, but that would be closing the barn door after the horse was out since apparently the rest of the neighborhood was already atwitter with it. "Which secret did you mean?" he said innocently.

Eloise's eyes lit with interest. "Is there more than one?"

"Perhaps," Hal said. "What do you say, Miss Teagarden?"

Two

LILY SUCKED HER TEETH AS ROXHAM'S GUESTS GAZED AT her with interest. She'd wanted to avoid making a spectacle out of her problem, but nothing, obviously, could have pleased him more. Beyond him, the magnificent presence of Mayfield Hall glowed pale yellow in the afternoon light, a stately, lavish counterpoint to the endless rolling green of his ancestral grounds.

"There's no secret," she said, forcing a smile. "Just a little problem with the woods."

And a problem with that wretched old journal of hers, if he truly still had it. *Would* he mention it? He was enjoying having the advantage, but what else should she expect when he'd always so loved to tease?

Most disappointingly, he had not become a disgusting wreck of man. No, he was even more handsome now. She'd forgotten the way the flecks of green sparkled in his blue eyes, and how his dark blond hair shone as if gilded. His coat, a vivid green, was distinctively tailored; it whispered of emeralds and glittering ballrooms and gleaming coaches, of luxury and indolence. And yet the easy, athletic grace of his posture bespoke a man of action, and his soldier's straight, broad shoulders hinted at command.

But something in his eyes said mischief.

Did he still have her journal?

"A problem with the woods?" John said.

"Apparently," Roxham said, "Mayfield's resident bad spirit—you remember the Woods Fiend—has made a return. People have seen lights among the trees at night, and it's rumored that he's up to no good."

"A ghost!" Mrs. Whyte said in a breathy voice. Her large blue eyes widened in her pretty, round face so that, with her golden sausage curls, she looked like a doll. "I hope you will protect us, Roxham."

"I assure you we shall all be quite safe," he said in reply to Mrs. Whyte's ridiculousness. Lily felt smug to see the sort of female companions he chose for himself.

"I forgot about the Woods Fiend," Eloise said. "But it was just nonsense—it wasn't a *spirit* that killed Great-Uncle Edmund fifty years ago."

"Unfortunately," Roxham said, though he didn't sound dismayed, "not everyone has outgrown belief in the Fiend. Thistlethwaite's proximity to our woods has caused many of our neighbors to believe the Teagardens' sheep are… possessed by him."

"That's dumb," Freddy said.

"Still," John said, rubbing his son's head affectionately, "it's not an advantage to be neighbor to the haunted woods, is it?"

John always had been more considerate, Lily thought. But then, unlike his brother, he wasn't a veritable feather of a man, morally speaking. He raised his eyebrows at Roxham.

Roxham's lips ticked up, and there were those dimples she'd forgotten about, tucked into the hard planes of his cheeks; they used to make her insides flip over. She looked away.

"Miss Teagarden," he said, "nothing will give me more pleasure than to solve this mystery. I envision a night camped out in the dark, doing battle with whoever is disturbing the peace of Highcross."

"Ha," John said, "you think it will be so easy, do you? The war hero, ready to take on a new enemy? I wager it will be more difficult than you think to catch a villain in a dark wood at night."

"I'll take that wager. Let us say that I'll unmask the Fiend within, oh, two weeks, or you shall have my new hunter."

"That is confident!" John said. "Very well. If you succeed, I shall order you ten cases of sherry from our cousin James's Spanish sherry vineyard."

"I must insist," the Earl of Ivorwood said, "on joining this adventure."

Roxham turned to Lily. "There, you see, Miss Teagarden. Two gentlemen pledged to solve the mystery. We shall make an attempt this very night."

Mrs. Whyte laughed giddily and clapped her hands. "It sounds like a game! Can we all bring blankets and watch?"

"Perhaps that wouldn't be a good idea," Roxham said with indulgent amusement.

Lily gnashed her teeth at the way her problem had been turned into an entertainment, but she wouldn't dwell on that since they were committed to helping. Though now if Roxham did succeed, he would be rewarded with a prize, a thought that annoyed her deeply.

"Thank you."

She was about to take her leave when he said, "And I'll take a look around for that little book of yours as well, Miss Teagarden."

She froze. Unwanted memories pressed in on her, a remembrance of that old *sickness*.

"I'm sure I have no interest in it," she said as casually as she could.

"What book is this?" Roxham's sister-in-law asked.

Lily tried surreptitiously to read his face. Did he truly have it?

"Oh," he said, "just a book Miss Teagarden left here some years ago."

"A journal, wasn't it?" said Eloise, squinting her eyes as if trying to see into the past. Eloise would have been perhaps twelve at the time. "Wasn't there some incident…"

Lily was certain she couldn't stand there while these elegant people probed her for a second longer. She thanked them for their hospitality and commended the gentlemen for their pledge to try to apprehend the ghost that night.

She set off across the lawn with Buck at her side, almost certain that she heard Lord Perfect chuckling. Blast the man.

Hal watched Lily's departing figure, disappointed that she was leaving.

"What do you say to a swim in the river, Ivorwood? John?" he asked.

"Oh," Diana said, "not a good idea. Freddy and I were down there earlier, racing leaf boats, and with all the recent rain, it's running very fast. You'd much better swim in the lake."

"Sorry, can't," Colin said. "I've a few letters that must be sent off to my secretary."

"And I've some affairs to attend to myself," John said.

There were things Hal was meant to be doing as well, but they could wait. Mayfield was, as far as he could see, in fairly good shape, even if Prescott was not in top form.

"I'll just have a look round," Hal said. "Assess the state of things."

Diana frowned as he turned to go, but he merely winked. He was fond of his sister-in-law and relieved that the birth of his nephews had eliminated the need for him to set up a nursery himself.

The river was high, he saw when he reached it, perhaps thirty feet across at the point where he stood assessing the water. Its rough swirls indicated strong currents. Just the sort of thing he wanted.

He tugged off his boots and stripped off his coat and shirt and dove in.

The rushing water pounded him instantly, driving against him. Fear and courage rushed up in that battle he'd missed, and his furious thrashing through the current was the cannon he shot into the void.

If he surrendered, he'd be carried away, with no one the wiser for some time. The thought gave him an unexpected, pure sense of connection to men hundreds of miles away striving on battlefields, to others on fighting ships submitting to the surgeon's knife.

Pushing through the water with all his might, his mind tightly focused, he welcomed the struggle. When he finally reached the opposite bank, he hauled himself out and lay in the grass with his chest heaving and his heart pounding.

As soon as he'd caught his breath, he dove back in.

By the time he got out again on the opposite bank, the river had carried him some distance, onto Thistlethwaite property. He lay in the grass for several minutes, staring up at the sky and feeling the water running off him and his soaked breeches sticking to him.

He ought to ride out and visit some of his tenants that afternoon. Everard would never have been swimming when there were tenants to visit. But Everard had never seemed to need what Hal needed. He'd always been content with his lot and happy to be viscount. Hal had even secretly thought, when he'd become a captain in the Foot Guards, that soldiering was the one thing he did better than his brother. Camp life was useless stretches of time to fill with horseplay that took his men's minds from their wounds and troubles. The battlefield was smoke and noise, glory and agony—life in all its intensity. Surging to meet the enemy, dispatching him any way he could—Hal had been good at that.

Not a talent that much lent itself to being a viscount.

He got up and started walking upstream toward his clothes.

❧

Lily craved the solace of her favorite thinking spot by the river.

Roxham meant to look for her journal. What if he found it?

She tried to push away the memory of the silly fabric decorations she'd affixed to its cover in the throes of besotted affection, but she couldn't. That book glowed in her memory with the power of shame. In it, she'd set down all her adoration and desire—desire, dear God!—for Captain Hal Waverly, the man who was now Viscount Roxham.

Even now, at twenty, she could hardly bear to think of that summer evening four years ago when she'd slipped into the bushes around the Mayfield terrace in the hopes that he'd appear. And when he had, with a party of friends—for he was always with people— she'd begun sketching him in her journal. He'd been almost unbearably handsome in his scarlet uniform.

It seemed so inevitable now that he'd discovered her there. He'd snatched her book and playfully refused to give it back while his friends laughed, and she'd had to stand there with her face, her whole being on fire, pretending it was something she'd done for a lark.

At least the incident had begun to make her see him for what he was: a shallow golden fellow only interested in having a good time.

Deep in thought, she rounded the edge of a stand of trees near the banks of the river—and almost crashed into Roxham.

She yelped in surprise, then drew in a gasp.

His chest was bare, and he was soaking wet.

"Why, Roxham, did you fall in the river?"

"Just went for a swim."

"A *swim*?" The river, swollen with recent rains, swirled behind him dangerously.

The expanse of his naked chest tempted her eyes to move downward, but she kept them on his face. Though that was hardly better, since his tousled wet hair and skin gave him the intimate look of someone who'd just emerged from a bath, a very handsome someone with a strong jaw and glittering blue-green eyes.

She reminded herself that good looks were just a wrapping, that if what was inside was no good, they were empty. She could almost feel sorry for him.

"Concerned for my safety?" he asked.

"Certainly not. Anyone foolish enough to jump in there deserves whatever befalls him."

He laughed.

It was annoyingly awkward standing there with him in his wet, half-dressed state and finding herself far too interested in learning more about the muscular contours teasing the edge of her vision, but since she had this chance for a private word with him, she must take it.

"About that book of mine you mentioned—should you discover it, I ask that you return it to me immediately."

"Your journal, you mean?" he said in a lazy tone. The dark mockery glinting in his eyes unsettled her. She sensed he was aware that she was trying to look anywhere but down. "I seem to recall there were drawings of me in it. I'd say that gives me a certain right to examine it."

"It does not!" she said far too forcefully. She mustn't let him see how badly she wanted it back. At least she'd written it in code, so it was entirely likely he'd never even read it. She was in fact fairly confident that he hadn't, because he seemed to have forgotten about it until now, and it would have been hard to forget if he'd read it.

"I meant, even if it *did* have a drawing of you in it," she said—and it had far more than drawings of him—"it wouldn't matter because it doesn't belong to you. So you have no right to look at it. You never should have taken it to begin with. But I would think that now you are a viscount, you'd feel yourself called to a higher standard of behavior."

Something shifted in his eyes. "It seems you have me confused with other viscounts."

With those puzzling words, he left her. As if she knew any other viscounts aside from him and his brother Everard. Though if he was referring to his brother, she knew Everard would never have kept her journal. But then, he never would have taken it either.

In the early evening, Lily took a few supplies and set out for the large flat rock beyond the orchard, which the Teagardens called Table Rock. Mary and Anna Cooper were already there.

"We only have half an hour tonight, Miss Teagarden," Anna said after Lily greeted them. "There's a heap of sewing to be done for our brother before he goes to school."

Tall and thin and a little grubby about the hands, the sisters had alert expressions and sensitive lights in their eyes.

"I see," Lily said, that familiar impatience stirring

in her. Many would say it was unnatural of her, but she couldn't accept that girls—even poor ones—weren't meant as much as boys to use the gifts of intelligence they'd been given. Mr. Cooper certainly saw little purpose in his daughters' meetings with her to learn reading and writing and arithmetic. Even Lily's brothers and sister thought it little more than an amusing hobby for her.

"It's generous of you to make the effort," Rob had said, "but those girls will be needed to cook and clean and sew. What difference will it make if they can read and write?"

"All the difference!" Lily had said with a vehemence that had made Rob's brow rise.

"Suit yourself," he'd said with a careless shrug. "Though I don't understand why you want to spend your time on that and on the shawl business now that the debts have been paid. You're wasting your youth in toil."

She'd bristled. "It's not wasted. And it's not toil for me."

She didn't expect him to understand—how could he? As a man, his life was too different from that of the Cooper girls, and even from that of his own sisters.

Anna and Mary were fourteen and twelve; hard-working, bright, and poor, they had everything before them, and Lily didn't intend to stand by while their potential for a richer life—for something *more*—was squandered simply because they were girls.

She smiled. "Then we'd best get to work."

Reaching into her pocket, she took out two sticks about six inches long and handed them to the girls.

Mary and Anna crouched down in the smoothed dirt at their feet, sticks poised.

"Begin with your full names, please," she said, and as they formed the letters in the dirt, she observed with pride how much neater each girl's penmanship had grown. If only they had desks and papers and pens and ink.

Patience, she told herself, *one step at a time*. She'd saved quite a bit of money already from the shawl business. Once the ridiculous Woods Fiend problem was resolved and the shawls could be sold again, she would be able to save the rest of the money she needed to realize her dream: a school for all the girls of Highcross.

Three

"Perhaps you ought to have asked Miss Teagarden if there was a particular time this Fiend favored," the Earl of Ivorwood said quietly to Hal as he shifted to lean against a tree at the edge of the strip of woods between Mayfield and Thistlethwaite. "It's been a good two hours already. Not that it isn't romantic, old boy, standing about with you under the moon."

Hal tipped the gold watch at his waist at an angle to catch some moonlight. He'd been thinking about Lily, and how perversely pleasing it was to rile her.

He'd found that journal of hers in an old guest room, though he hadn't had a chance to look at it yet. She certainly wasn't happy about him having it, and that made it all the more interesting. If he suffered a twinge of remorse about being in possession of her journal with the intention of reading it, he quashed it with the knowledge that it was obviously to do with him, and also that it was from four years ago and thus practically a history book.

"It's getting on for midnight," he said. "Isn't that the standard time for evil spirits?"

"So they say. Almost like the rush of battle, is it, waiting for him to show?"

"Almost." Hal had been in Spain, at the forefront of the battle against Napoleon, when he'd gotten the news about Everard's death. The news had possibly saved his life, because when the letter arrived, he was sitting in a makeshift jail awaiting punishment. His crime: riding drunk through the conquered town, which wouldn't have been notable except that he'd finished by performing a bitter, mocking serenade under the window of the house his colonel had commandeered.

Hal had been drinking with some other officers, all of them angered by the summary execution of one of Hal's enlisted men, who'd stolen a small piece of salt beef from the colonel's personal stores. The enlisted men were all starving, literally, because of much-delayed provisions, and had been growing agitated in the preceding days. The conquered town had yielded nothing but some barrels of sour wine, and any fool could have seen that, out of desperation, men might be driven to meet the needs which the army that had brought them to Spain could not. But Colonel Burke wouldn't hear of extenuating circumstances, and he'd marched the soldier in front of the troops and shot him as a lesson to all.

The letter revealing Hal's sudden accession to the viscountcy had resolved the question of what was to be done with a well-liked captain who'd shown disrespect to his superior, and had doubtless been a relief to Colonel Burke, who'd already done much to make himself hated.

Since then, Hal had tried to behave in a way

that would have made his brother proud, but the viscountcy had been Everard's passion, not Hal's. He hated the blathery, horse-trading world of Parliament, keeping track of the family's three estates made his head swim, and the social whirl that had once entertained him now felt dull.

So what did it say about him that he was looking forward to tussling with a fake spirit?

All had been quiet so far, save for the rustlings of forest creatures. If it weren't for the fact that his staff was anxious about the Woods Fiend, Hal might have suspected Lily of tricking him into standing around like a fool near his woods solely for her own amusement, though she seemed unlikely to do things for her own amusement.

The snap of a twig a short distance away made the two men instantly alert. They stilled, listening as the sounds drew closer, a whishing of something against the grass and dry leaves, the sounds of a very inept Fiend if this was their quarry.

"Who goes there, and what is your purpose on the viscount's land?" Hal demanded.

"It's Miss Teagarden," a feminine voice whispered.

"Oh, I say," Colin muttered.

"I really think, my lords," she murmured when she reached them, "that you should lower your voices if you don't want to alert the Fiend to your presence."

Hal sucked his teeth. "Lily, what are you doing here?"

"Why, I've come to see you gentlemen at work."

More like checking up on them. And she'd come alone, apparently, which was interesting. He wouldn't have thought her capable of something so scandalous.

"Is this wise," Colin whispered, "with the Fiend afoot?"

"But I knew I'd be safe here, with you gentlemen watching over the woods. And if you're wondering how I found you in the dark, it was the moonlight glinting on your shiny buttons."

"Blast," whispered Colin.

"Lily," Hal said in a low voice as the men reversed their coats, "your brothers would not be pleased to think of you out at night like this, in a possibly dangerous situation. The earl will see you safely home."

"No, thank you. I should like to see who the Fiend is if you catch him. I have quite a bone to pick with him. Or her."

"But look," Colin whispered. "Our quarry."

A light had appeared in a section of the wood about fifty yards away.

"I suppose you shall have your wish then, Lily," Hal said. "If you can keep your skirts quiet."

"I can." A brief rustling as she arranged them.

They began to creep quietly toward the light along the edge of the wood. Hal thought he heard a soft thunking sound ahead of them. When they were perhaps thirty yards from the light, he sent Ivorwood ahead to flush the Fiend toward him. He told Lily to stand back at a reasonable distance for safety.

"And miss everything?" she said. "Certainly not."

Her insistence reminded him of how she'd accompanied him and Ian and Rob on childhood escapades, often wanting to be included but then getting nervous about danger and consequences.

"If you change your mind, I'll have to worry about abandoning you in the woods while I go after the ghost."

"I'm all grown up now, my lord," she said tartly. "I never change my mind once it's made up."

He thought about the purposeful set of her sharp little chin. "Very well then. Quietly now," he whispered, and they moved into the pitch-black woods. As they drew closer to the glow, Lily stuck by his side, and he kept being distracted by thoughts of how she must look with her frock pulled tight against her legs and likely tugged above her ankles. Lily Teagarden, of all females.

Ahead of them, the light began to dance around.

"He may realize we're onto him," Hal whispered. "Give me your hand."

"What?"

"So we don't get separated." He stuck his hand out in the darkness and felt her reaching for him. She swiped at his coat first, his elbow, and, what made his eyebrows shoot upward, his rump, where she lingered a moment before snatching her hand and thrusting it to the side to find his hand.

"Stop smiling," she said.

He *was* imagining the prim blush that must be creeping over her cheeks. But her hand felt small and warm and dry in his; quite nice, actually. He couldn't think when last he'd simply held a woman by the hand.

The light went out and there was a shout and a heavy rustling in the wood—the ghost being flushed. Hal tugged Lily with him as they picked their way past the trees toward where the light had been. Crashing sounds came from various points, some doubtless the trespasser, some the earl. And then the noises were only coming from one area, at some distance off.

They moved up a small, steep hill and Hal slowed their pace at the top as they came to the edge of a clearing. Bright moonlight picked out stumps and bushes but nothing else as he surveyed the area. He'd been certain someone had been near, but now there was nothing.

And then, unaccountably, he stepped on something that moved—something hard, like a hand—and he heard a grunt. A streak of moonlight coming through the clearing picked out a dark head writhing under a screening pile of leaves.

"Got you!" he cried just as Lily gave a funny sort of yelp.

And though he was bending over, he didn't have hold of the Fiend yet, and then—what the devil?— Lily grabbed him around the waist. She knocked him backward down the hill.

They rolled and slid down the incline, sticks and brush scratching them, until they came to rest at the bottom, with her on top. Hal could hear the diminishing sounds of the enemy escaping, and farther away what was doubtless Colin giving chase.

"Let me up," he said quickly, trying to move under what seemed a dead weight. "I might still catch him."

She didn't reply.

"Lily? Are you hurt?"

She gasped against his chest and moved jerkily, and he realized she was trying to breathe. Her pointy elbows dug into his ribs.

"You've had the wind knocked out of you," he said, keeping the disappointment out of his tone. He could hardly throw her off him, but unless Colin was quick, the Fiend would escape.

"I'll lie still while you try to breathe slowly." He put an arm over her back to steady her so she wouldn't roll off him and silently gnashed his teeth.

They lay there in the dark woods as she gasped shallowly. A rock pressed into his back, hard with her weight added to his. A few feet away, a small creature moved about in the dry leaves.

Her breathing became more regular. Just below his chin, her head lay against his neck, and the fresh scent of her hair teased his nose. Violets? Did violets have a scent?

Dear God, but having her lying across him was working upon him. It had been months since he'd known the receptive softness only a woman could offer.

She shifted and pressed against his hips, and he almost groaned. Under his forearm her rib cage seemed fragile, made on such a smaller scale than his own. She was a petite, tightly wound, governessish woman whose attitude toward him was far from warm. But she was also refreshingly *apart* from what his life felt filled with: compromises, gossip, vacancy. Could a life be filled with vacancy? He was overcome with the urge to bury his face in her neck, to kiss her and touch her and do everything.

"Oh," she muttered, apparently now able to speak.

She pushed herself off his chest, grinding him further onto the rock as she shifted onto the ground. He sat up next to her, his mind refocused on their purpose. Or at least, on his purpose, as he was now very suspicious about hers.

"Do forgive me," she said as they stood. "I tripped."

He brushed at the leaves and twigs stuck to his clothes and hair. "That was an odd sort of tripping. You had me by the waist."

"The Fiend startled me, being right there. That caused me to trip against you, and I tried to catch myself."

"And then it was just an accident that you and I ended up rolling down the hill."

"Exactly." She seemed eager to confirm this version of events, especially for someone who so far had not agreed with him about anything.

"That's odd, because from the sound you made when I stumbled on our man, I thought perhaps you'd recognized him."

A pause. "How should I have seen anything in the darkness?"

"There was some light in the clearing. I saw dark hair."

"Well, if I knew who the Fiend was, why wouldn't I have gone to that person myself and insisted he stop?"

She was being purposefully obtuse. "No doubt you would have. If you had *known* that you knew the person."

"That is so nonsensical a statement I can hardly follow it."

A shout came from not far away—Colin looking for them.

"Here," she shouted, practically in Hal's ear. "We're coming."

He would bet she was grateful for any reason to end their conversation, but he could hardly insist they stand there in the night woods and finish it. They made for the sound of Colin's voice.

Lily was grateful to step out of the darkness of the woods and into the moonlit meadow on the Thistlethwaite side as they followed the earl's voice.

Already a foolish part of her wanted to relive the moments of feeling Roxham's muscle and bone and energy underneath her. He smelled very, very good— some kind of wonderfully scented and doubtless costly soap. It had felt so good to rest her head in the curve where his neck met his shoulders. She suspected herself, disgustedly, of lingering there longer than she'd needed to.

He… did something to her.

Of course he did: he was handsome as sin and the king of charm.

But she couldn't think about that right now, because *oh dear oh dear oh dear!* The Woods Fiend was Nate Beckett! Moonlight had illuminated his dark hair and the distinctive missing top of his ear, which he'd lost in a woodcutting accident years before.

The Becketts had a small farm near Thistlethwaite, and Mrs. Beckett had been a help to the Teagardens after Mrs. Teagarden died. Lily had thought of the Becketts' home as a sort of refuge during that difficult year when she was twelve. She used to sit at their kitchen table with Mrs. Beckett. She *knew* Nate, even if she didn't see him much anymore. What on earth was he up to in the woods?

Oh, what if Ivorwood *had* captured him in the end, she thought sickly as they moved closer to the sound of the earl's voice. It would be a disaster, and one she'd helped bring about by insisting that Roxham investigate.

The earl hadn't caught him, they discovered when they reached him. *Thank God.*

But she would have to get to the bottom of what Nate was up to as soon as possible.

"Very well," Roxham said. "That's it for tonight, then. If we haven't scared him away for good, we will have to catch him next time. Why don't you head back, Colin, and I'll see Miss Teagarden home. Obviously, we can't mention…"

The earl's grin flashed in the moonlight. "I never saw her."

"Thank you," she said in a small voice.

She and Roxham started walking toward Thistlethwaite. In an effort to find him less appealing, she decided she would think of him as the Old Duffer, a term her Scottish nanny had used for silly, aimless men. She'd keep an image in her mind of him as being older than her and thus closer to the years of baldness and bad teeth. Surely it would help.

They'd been walking for a few minutes in silence when he said, "You are very comfortable wandering around by yourself at night. Have you no fear of the harm you might come to?"

"It's the *country*," she said. "There's no one here but cows. It's not London—there are no footpads with whom to engage in fisticuffs, no fashionable shops. Though I suppose if you were to ride about drunk on horseback, you wouldn't be the only one."

"Heard about that, did you?"

"It was in the newspaper."

"Keeping track of me? I'm charmed."

"It's impossible not to hear tell of your doings since

my sister reads all the London news and Lord Perfect is a frequent topic. Anyway, being put in jail for serenading your commanding officer isn't something to be proud of."

"I beg to differ; I was extremely foxed at the time. It's a wonder I was able to keep my seat, never mind performing a serenade."

His outrageous words made her lips start to curl, but she pressed them together and whispered *Old Duffer* to herself.

"I suppose life in the army was just another game to you."

"Perhaps it was," he said after a moment. "In any case, you ought to be careful—only consider what happened to my great-uncle and the young lady he was trying to rescue: the Woods Fiend did them in. And here he is, abroad again."

"Of course he isn't—that was fifty years ago. He'd be at least seventy."

He chuckled. "Very well, I grant you our current Fiend may not be on the same order as the original. But danger aside, only think about your reputation if word got out that you were here tonight with me and Ivorwood."

"But word won't get out, will it? Only you and the earl saw me. Unless I can't trust you to keep a secret?" She realized that, as much as she knew him to be shallow and an accomplished tease, she didn't believe he was so lacking in integrity that he'd expose her harmless part in the evening. Well, mostly harmless. She found herself not wanting to admit that he might have a virtue or two.

"You can trust us to keep your secret," he said tightly. "But you're forgetting about the Fiend. *He* might gossip about your presence tonight."

He was being coy. He'd already guessed that she'd recognized the trespasser and that that was what had made her knock him over. Well, he could guess all he wanted—she'd never admit it.

"I don't suppose I have to worry about him outing me," she said, "as he would then be outing himself. Whoever he is."

"Yes," Hal said. "Whoever is he?"

She made no reply.

"Oh," he said, "this may interest you. I managed to find your journal. I'd forgotten about it being in code, which was why I must have put it down to begin with. But now that I've found it again, I have a new patience for code-cracking."

Her stomach took a deep dip at these words. "I can't believe you're thinking of not returning it to me. It's the gentlemanly thing to do."

"Ah, but a gentleman might not return it if he felt it belonged to an adversary. If he felt it might be needed for a little friendly persuasion. My new hunter is riding on this wager. You tell me what you know about the Woods Fiend, I'll return the journal."

She pressed her lips together unhappily, grateful for the darkness that kept him from seeing how bothered she was that he had her book. He'd been so very good at mischief when they were children, swapping out adults' medicines for Dr. Pitt's loosening drops, putting toads in people's wardrobes. He was doubtless enjoying teasing her now, but the idea that he would read about her youthful passion for him—good God. To get it back, though, she'd have to betray Nate.

"I have nothing to tell you about the Woods Fiend."

But she had to get that journal back as soon as possible, no matter what.

"Nothing you *want* to tell me, evidently."

Thistlethwaite Manor was a dark bulk ahead of them—it must have been well after one. She stopped by the rosebushes that flanked the walkway to the manor.

Roxham sighed. "Can you really get in without waking anyone?"

"Yes," she whispered back. "Now go away."

Hal walked into his bedchamber and tugged off his cravat. He was glad the ladies hadn't waited up for him and Colin, as they—or rather Hyacinth—had threatened to do. It wasn't so long ago that he'd found Hyacinth's empty-headed chatter and deep fascination for all things fashionable diverting, but he didn't want it tonight. For once, he wanted no one's company but his own.

He went over to the small desk on which sat a brandy decanter and poured himself a generous measure. Lily's journal was lying there, where he'd left it earlier.

It was her private book. He really should not read it. Everard certainly would never have done so, but then, he would never have taken it to begin with or done most of the other things Hal had done.

He wasn't his brother. He took another sip of brandy and opened the book.

The first few pages were a nonsensical text of coded words. And then, a few pages in, was an illustration of a cravat tied around a neck. It could have been his, or someone else's.

He turned over another page of text to find a sketch of a man's hand resting on his knee. Hardly a sensual picture, and yet he felt something from the attention to detail in the hand and leg. He was tempted to think that it was *his* hand and *his* knee. Unless this journal were a collection of various gentlemen's parts, a thought that drew a dark chuckle from him.

He used to go to cozy old Thistlethwaite for tea often, finding it a break from the grander, more formal world of Mayfield. She might have been sitting across the room, ostensibly writing letters while in fact sketching him. It was not as if he hadn't known back then that she'd had a secret affection for him—he'd felt her eyes on him many times. But the odd, pale, thin Lily Teagarden had merely registered as another in the always flowing stream of young ladies who'd admired him.

The last sketch was the one of him on the terrace at Mayfield. She'd obviously been in the process of filling in the details when he'd discovered her.

A woman might well have felt violated to find a man hiding in the bushes, sketching her. He hadn't felt violated then, nor did he now. The drawing had been made out of adoration, and how could he mock that? He'd never felt something so pure as what had made her create the journal, and he marveled at this sign that such innocence existed.

It took half an hour, but he finally saw the pattern

in her code, and he had to admire the discipline that had gone into using it. The first paragraph was not at all what he would have expected.

> *I am going to write here about Hal, with whom I think I should like to lie. No, that is not true, and I will only tell the truth here. I do want to lie with him. He fascinates me, and I want more than anything to touch him. And to have him want to touch me.*

Well. Well, well. He sat back in his chair, a little breathless at the bold and intimate words.

He slung back the rest of his brandy. These words had been written by a younger version of the woman who had, not a few hours past, been lying across him. By Lily, the tart and smart neighbor of his youth, who had turned, like a caterpillar emerging from a cocoon of years, into a beautiful woman.

She intrigued him, though she was not his type of woman. He could only imagine what she'd say if she knew about all the drinking and carousing he'd engaged in over the last few years, though perhaps she'd approve of the killing, being that it had been in the just cause of dispatching Napoleon's troops.

It was late, and he sat there, staring over a guttering candle, and considered that this journal that promised to recount young Lily's sensual journey would be very good leverage in finding out what she knew about the Woods Fiend, and what she was up to. Not that he truly intended to show it to anyone. There was some force in it: innocence, the pure passion of youth.

Qualities that, had he ever had any claim to them, had long been washed away.

He wanted to decode the rest of the book, but first he would rest a moment. He crossed his arms over the closed book and rested his head on it—this made him smile, to think how excited the sixteen-year-old Lily would have been to know his cheek was on her book—and that was how he awoke the next morning.

Four

BUCK WAS SNIFFING HER EAR.

Lily dropped a hand drowsily onto his furry head and murmured at him with her eyes still closed. Visions of last night presented themselves—the glow of a lantern and men and darkness. She shifted, and a note of Roxham's fabulous, expensive-smelling scent came to her, apparently having been imprinted on the skin of her neck.

Doubtless that was why she'd dreamed of him.

She pushed thoughts of him away and focused on what was important: what had Nate been doing in the viscount's woods?

She opened one eye to find her dog gazing eagerly at her, waiting for her to get up. Her bedroom door was ajar, and the modest, tidy room, with its unadorned white walls and plain wooden furniture, was suffused with a late morning brightness that felt like an accusation. Normally by this time of the day she'd already be at work on yarn dyes, or knitting a shawl in her room, but that was hardly necessary at the moment. However, now that she knew the Woods

Fiend was Nate, it was possible the problem might be solved this very day, as she intended to speak to him and convince him to stop whatever he was doing in the woods.

Buck gave a discreet yip, mindful of the need to not make a nuisance of himself in the house.

"I suppose you and Malcolm have already seen the sheep into the pasture," she said. Buck nudged her hand with his soft snout, and she sat up and petted him a little before gently shooing him out.

Some minutes later, dressed in a simple, butter-colored gown, she was stepping into the hallway.

"There you are, Lil," Delia said, poking her head out of her own chamber. Her nose wrinkled as she took in Lily's attire. "Such a plain gown. Can't you at least put on a necklace?"

"Perhaps later," Lily said.

"Which means never." Delia was ever-aggrieved at her sister's lack of interest in adornment. "Listen," she said in a serious tone at odds with the merry look of the pink bow tied in her lemony hair, "Roxham's ball is only a few days away, and I can't think what either of us is going to wear. All those fashionable people will be there, and we'll look like bumpkins."

"No we won't," Lily said. "We can find something among the gowns from my Season."

"Oh! I'd forgotten about your Town clothes. You never wear them."

True. She'd put those clothes away years ago, wanting to put away any reminder of that time. Father had died soon after their return from London, and it had then come to light that the estate was straining under debt—a debt to which her Season had only added.

"The gowns are in a wardrobe in the guest room. Choose one, and I'll help you make alterations."

"Oh," Delia said excitedly, "this is going to be such a treat! And you'll pick one out, too."

"Mmm," Lily said vaguely.

"Lily, how *can* you possibly be so unexcited about the most thrilling thing to happen to us in ages?"

Delia's despairing tone made Lily smile as she walked down the stairs.

Breakfast had already been cleared away, and she passed through the kitchen and took a roll on her way outside. She and Buck stopped briefly by the high pasture, where the sheep were contentedly grazing, then set off on the path to the Becketts' farm.

Their place was about half a mile away, just off a path used by the local farmers. George Beckett had died several years before, leaving the farm to Nate, his oldest, who was in his late twenties. He lived there with his mother and three much younger siblings.

It had been a long time since she'd talked with any of the Becketts. She felt a bit bad about that, considering all the cheering cups of tea she'd consumed with Mrs. Beckett when she was younger. But Lily hadn't had much time for visiting with anyone in recent years.

She wanted to speak to Nate alone, and she found him at the edge of the property, fixing a fence. He was hammering a crossbar to a post, and he stopped when he saw her and greeted her.

At a little distance behind him, the familiar

farmhouse looked oddly forlorn. A downspout pitched forward off the front of the house, and the white paint that had once freshened the door and window frames was little but streaks on weathered wood. At the side of the house, little Liza—shoeless—trailed after a thin-looking cow.

Concern pricked her. Why did things look so shabby?

"Well, Lily," he said in that perpetually gruff voice of his, "what brings you here?" He held the hammer loosely in his deeply tanned hand.

She pulled her attention away from the farmhouse. "I've come to talk to you about the Woods Fiend. I know it's you."

He cocked his head as if her words could only be silly, but wariness had crept into his brown eyes. He was a sturdy man, and handsome, with brown hair and a strong jaw. Even when he was younger he'd never been much for conversation, and seeing him now, toughened from seasons working the fields, she wondered if he ever stopped to laugh.

"Come now," he said, picking at a splinter on the hammer's handle and not meeting her eyes. "I'm far too young to have done anything to the ill-fated sweethearts."

She didn't comment on the word "sweethearts," though the reason those two people had been in the Mayfield woods years ago had always been a matter of dispute. Nate's family had more reason than most to give a romantic slant to what had happened on that night fifty years before, because the young woman had been his great-aunt, Anne Beckett. And the gentleman found with her had been Hal's great-uncle. But to polite society the only reason Edmund Waverly had been there was to rescue a woman who was being attacked. Since the Woods Fiend had never been discovered, no one could say for certain why the two had been found together, cruelly slain.

Nate was stalling for time, she guessed, not certain he could trust her. After all, she'd all but neglected his family in recent years. "Nate, I was in the woods last night. I saw you, and I knocked Roxham down the hill so he wouldn't catch you."

His eyes were definitely wary now. "You? In the woods at night? Why?"

She explained about the supposedly possessed sheep.

"Your... sheep?" he said with raised eyebrows.

"Yes—their yarn is now believed to bring bad luck. Nate, you know you can trust me. I'm not going to reveal it's you."

He crossed his arms and leaned back against the fence with a frown. "Very well, it was me."

"And?"

"And what?"

"*And* what are you doing in there?"

He frowned. "I didn't know about the trouble this has caused for Thistlethwaite, and I'm sorry. But what I'm doing is secret."

"I can keep a secret. Come, we are old friends. And I've already confessed to being in the woods at night myself. Besides"—she fixed him with a piercing eye—"remember that I never revealed who it was that broke your mother's favorite vase."

A rueful smile briefly teased the edges of his stern mouth. "Very well. I've been digging. There's something of value buried there that belongs to my family.

If this thing could bring a significant sum of money, we need it now to pay some debts."

She felt a pang that they'd apparently been struggling and had received no help from the Teagardens. But he was too proud to want her compassion, and he didn't linger on that part of his story.

"It was just happenstance," he went on, "that someone saw my light and started the rumor that the Woods Fiend was back, but it's worked to my advantage, since no one's wanted to see what I was doing there. Until now."

She blinked. "A buried treasure?" How fascinating, like a pirate story. Except there was nothing amusing about his family's evident need for money.

"Of some sort. We found a letter last year in the attic, written to my great-aunt fifty years ago. It was signed by Edmund Waverly."

Lily sucked in a breath. "So maybe they were sweethearts!"

"Of course they were sweethearts."

"What did the note say?"

"That he'd hidden something valuable for her under their favorite birch tree—some pledge of his love. And how he would soon come to her."

"Perhaps they were to be married."

"So it would seem. But I didn't dare look for this valuable thing because of it being in the viscount's woods. Now we don't have a choice."

Well. This changed things considerably. While she needed the Woods Fiend to go away, Nate badly needed to find this treasure. How could she stand in his way when his need was so urgent?

There ought to be a way to work this situation to benefit both of them. After all, if she helped him, the Woods Fiend would go away. And she would be thwarting the Old Duffer's efforts to win his bet. Next to restoring the shawl business—well, was it so bad that she wanted to pay the OD out for taking her book four years ago and refusing to return it now?

"I want to help you find what you're digging for. If I help you—say, if I let you know the viscount's plans regarding the Fiend—then you can find the gift faster, and the Fiend can go away sooner."

He considered her plan. "But how will people ever believe he's gone?"

"We'll plant some evidence that he's been scared off or something, so it can all be laughed off."

"That could work," he said slowly. "But there's not much time—the debts must be paid in two weeks."

"Then here's our plan: you must stay away tonight, because I know he plans to watch again. And perhaps your absence will lull him into thinking he's scared you off. And then, since he expects you near midnight, if the next night you came at a much different time—"

"Right. I'll come at half-past four. His lordship won't want to stand around that long waiting."

It took some doing to get Nate to agree that she should come to the woods and stand sentry, but in the end he saw how desperate things would be for his family if he were discovered. Their signal would be the hoot of an owl repeated three times.

Walking back to Thistlethwaite with Buck at her heels, Lily felt satisfied with the plan. She also admitted that, however idiotic it was, she would enjoy her secret battle against Roxham.

But. She could feel herself wanting to daydream about him just as she had years ago, as if that part of her were a muscle that had gone too long unused. She wanted to remember how it had felt to have his muscular body underneath hers on the forest floor, and how his breathing had changed as they lay there.

No. No! She knew him, could *see* him, now that she was older, for the wealthy, careless rogue he was. She was too wise now to be seduced by his handsome exterior and his limitless charm. She was going to get the best of him this time, and then she'd be able to forget him for good.

⁓

That afternoon Lily was in the little stone house behind Thistlethwaite, which the Teagardens called the yarn house, when Delia rushed through the open door.

"Make haste, Lily! They are here!"

"Who is here?"

"Oh, step away from that pot and take off your apron. Roxham and Eloise are here. They've come for a visit—and they want to see you."

"Me?"

"Yes, any moment—and they are coming out *here*. Lord, what is that vile smell?"

"It's only some moss boiling." Lily stood up and brushed powdered green and brown bits from her apron and sleeves. "No one will think it amiss that I occasionally experiment with the dyes."

Delia's only response was a long-suffering casting upward of her eyes over such an unconventional sister. Behind her, voices signaled the approach of their visitors.

"Ah, Lily Teagarden," the viscount said, ducking his head as he entered the small house.

The sight of him—tall and golden, his chocolate coat hinting at his beautiful proportions—made her cringe as she thought about him reading her journal. Had he deciphered the code yet? She couldn't think about it or she'd be a wreck.

"My lord." She inclined her head. "And Miss Waverly."

Eloise Waverly came forward with an open, friendly expression. She looked fresh and lovely in a cream-and-gold-striped gown, her glossy brown hair curled prettily to frame her face.

"Oh, but we are Eloise and Lily, are we not? Can we not be familiar as we used to be? Oh, do say it's all right."

Lily smiled. "Of course it is."

"Yes," Roxham said, "let us not stand on ceremony, Lily." As he was nearer to her than any of the others, she was the only one who saw his mouth creep back in a one-sided smirk that brought out the fascinating slash of a dimple in the plane of his cheek. It played up the dark light of mischief in his eyes that said he knew better than anyone how *familiar* she'd been.

He sniffed the air. "Making potions?"

"It's a yarn dye."

He moved to the table and picked up a dish of dandelion flowers she'd gathered and peered at it speculatively. "You look so scientific here, Lily, with all these little cups and spoons and liquids. I hope we're not interrupting anything."

"Not at all," she said. "I merely like to dabble with the colors used in the Thistlethwaite shawls."

"How creative," Eloise said.

"And this is where the shawl work would be done, if people weren't afraid of your horrifying sheep and their evil yarn?"

Delia giggled. Lily gave him a dry look. "Yes."

"A pity."

"It really is such a pity," Delia said, "since Lily knits—I mean since the knitting is so different and pretty."

Delia shot Lily a horrified look, but their visitors seemed not to have noticed what she'd started to say.

"We've come to tell you," Eloise said excitedly, "that Hal and Ivorwood nearly caught the Woods Fiend last night!"

Lily relaxed at the change in topic. The last thing she needed was for Roxham to know she was engaged in trade, for how might someone who so loved to tease use such damaging information?

"Did they?" she said. A twinge of conscience prodded her for pretending that she hadn't been in the woods the night before, but she was Nate's ally now, and what else could she do?

"Yes!" Eloise enthused. "Hal and Ivorwood went out together and watched and waited for hours by the wood."

"Oh," said Delia with shining eyes. "How persevering and brave of them."

The viscount was looking ever so nonchalant while

his praises were being sung. *Old Duffer, Old Duffer,* Lily chanted to herself as she took in the interestingly boxy way his brown coat sat on his lean, broad shoulders.

"I'm certain they must have been *so* uncomfortable," Eloise said, "but they were rewarded when they saw the lights of a torch in the trees."

"No!" Lily said.

"Yes!" Eloise clasped her hands excitedly. She seemed like such a sweet young lady. Lily wondered what it was like for her, having Lord Perfect for a brother. Being so much younger, she probably idolized him.

"Hal was just about to capture our trespasser when a small tree fell on him."

"Surprising, a little tree just falling in the woods like that," Lily said.

"Yes—it was some sort of trap." Eloise shook her head. "And though Ivorwood gave chase, the Fiend escaped."

"Goodness!" Delia said. "I hope you weren't hurt, Hal."

"Fortunately I wasn't injured by the… trickery that prevented me from catching our trespasser," he said. Lily could feel him looking at her with an air of accusation.

"So fortunate, so brave," she said, at which point the Old Duffer made his eyes into slits meant to let her know she was overdoing it. She gave him her most serene smile.

"In any case," he said, crossing his arms and giving her the kind of look he might once have trained on an enemy spy, "I mean to win that wager. I've done some investigating and discovered places in the woods where our spirit has been digging. One can only wonder why. Is something being buried? Or is our Fiend looking for something? What do you think, Lily?"

She forced a smile—he mustn't see how worried his probing was making her. "Possibly. Though perhaps it's best not to spread it around, about the digging. People might think the Fiend is preparing fresh graves."

Delia and Eloise thought that quite funny.

"Do you think," Eloise said, dabbing at a tear of mirth, "that I could see these sheep that are supposed to be possessed?"

"Oh, let's do!" Delia said, taking Eloise by the arm. "If you and Hal don't mind, Lily?"

"Of course we don't," he said, not giving her a chance to reply, and the girls departed, heads already bowing together as they chattered.

"I don't appreciate your speaking for me," Lily said.

"Viscount's prerogative. So tell me," he said, reaching out and giving the spinning wheel a spin, "how much time do you spend in here?"

"A little." Her stomach took a dip. *Was* he suspicious?

He began wandering around, and she felt he was taking pleasure in invading her space. He took his time, lifting the covers of the dye buckets and asking her how the dyes were created, as if he truly wished to understand how it all worked.

He paused over the crate of shawls Mr. Trent had sent back; she'd refolded them and put the top on, and she told herself it didn't look suspicious, but it was her work in there, and she was afraid something about the shawls would announce her involvement. But he moved past the crate and peeked into the pot where the moss was boiling.

"And will this be the new color for spring?"

It did look fairly disgusting. "Perhaps not one of my more successful efforts."

He moved on to the carding paddles, which he examined as though they were some intricate foreign object. Probably for a man like him, they were. This hut, these tools—all of this was inconsequential and mundane compared to his world of liveried servants and echoing halls.

"I've never seen these in use," he said. "It must be fascinating."

She gave him a skeptical look.

"Show me how to use them," he said.

"Why? It's not as if you'll ever have need."

"Because I'm curious." And he stood there with such an innocent, pleasant look on his face that she didn't want to refuse him.

"Very well." She took the carding tools from him, pulled out a tuft of wool from a nearby barrel, put it on one of the stiff brushes, and dragged the paddles against each other.

"Ah, I see," he said. "Ingenious. One feels grateful to one's ancestors for devising tools that can accomplish such things as the turning of sheep fluff into yarn."

"One feels that viscounts are too removed from the small realities of life."

His laugh was a deep rumble. "You forget how I've toiled in the muck as a soldier."

Though his tone was light, there was truth in his words—he would have seen and done things of which she couldn't conceive. Still, he had been born into a life of silver dishes and velvet cloaks.

"I can't think there was so very much muck for the brother of a viscount."

"Only the very best muck."

But something about his flippant manner niggled her. She cocked her head. "Was the army—the war— what you expected?"

Her question had evidently surprised him; he looked a bit off-kilter, which pleased her. "Was it what I expected?"

"Yes, when you bought your commission—I suppose you must have been twenty-two or so?"

"Twenty-three, and why do you ask?"

"I just… I imagine it must be such a different life, especially for the son of a viscount."

"It's not that different in some ways. I had servants, good horses."

"Do you miss it?" she said.

"Pardon?"

"I was just wondering whether it was hard to exchange soldiering for viscounting."

"It's far safer being a viscount."

"That wasn't what I asked. I asked if it was hard, exchanging one life for another."

"Only a fool would prefer being shot at to running an estate."

"Or someone who needs to be thrilled frequently. I remember you at twenty, making your own fireworks and setting part of Mr. Lovett's fence on fire. But I suppose such exploits weren't half so thrilling as almost getting court-martialed."

His eyelids lowered in a lazy, dangerous way. "You seem interested in my serenading episode."

"I only wonder what made you do such a thing."

"I was drunk, Lily. People do things like that when they're foxed. But as I suppose you've never over-indulged, you would find that hard to imagine."

She'd seen her father foxed countless times, which had given her ample acquaintance with the foolish things drink could make a person do. But she was hardly going to reveal any of that to Hal. "Drunk people are commonplace," she said. "I can easily imagine how foolish you looked."

But now he cocked his head. "Can you? I was angry. I'd lost a good soldier, a good man who was desperate. He stole—only a little—from the colonel's stores, and was discovered and shot in front of his mates."

"Oh. How horrible. I…"

"Wouldn't have ridden drunk and singing through town. No, of course not. It's not an appropriate action."

She frowned. "I'm sorry about your soldier. What happened to him was wrong."

He shrugged. "Ultimately it's the price of war. Each of us knows that when he signs on."

"I think it admirable that you served in the army."

He laughed. "Perhaps, but you don't think *me* admirable."

How could he so blithely put such words in her mouth, even if they were true—and care so little whether people had an unflattering opinion of him? "I think you have often preferred diversions to serious undertakings."

"Lucky for me, then, that viscounting is providing unlimited diversions this week. Like the very interesting words written in a young lady's journal."

She forced down the wave of panic and shame that threatened to engulf her. She'd never wanted *anyone* to read those words, let alone him.

"Ingenious code, by the way. I was only able to read a bit, but I'm looking forward to more. Unless, of course, you'd like to trade it for information?"

"I've already told you I have nothing to offer you."

"And yet I don't believe you."

She let the silence stretch out.

"So," he said finally, "you make shawls."

He'd noticed Delia's mistake. "I like to knit," she said vaguely.

"Is that so?" He ran a hand over a partially completed blue shawl that lay folded at the edge of the worktable. "Fine work indeed, the work of a careful, dedicated hand. It makes me think there was a personal reason you asked me to get rid of the Woods Fiend: the business is yours."

Oh no.

He could make things very uncomfortable for her family. For her. She would lose standing in the community if it were known she was selling her work.

And yet this had always bothered her: that she might contribute to pulling the estate out of debt and make something worthwhile that might allow her to help girls who had so little—and that she would be looked down upon if it were known she earned the money to accomplish these things. Women of her class weren't meant to be useful but decorative. And she couldn't bear the thought of a life of being decorative.

"You don't know what you're talking about."

"You're a terrible liar, Lily. It makes you go all stiff. Well, stiffer than usual. In fact, you're looking more rigid every moment."

"I don't owe you explanations."

"You know," he started to say, but laughter sounded outside the door just then, and Delia and Eloise appeared in the doorway, much to Lily's relief.

So the Old Duffer had made some guesses about her involvement in the business. He had no proof, and even if he did, why should he bother to spread rumors about her being in trade? She told herself that the only person's good opinion she was likely to have lost through this conversation was his, and she could hardly care about that.

She smiled at Delia and Eloise. "Why don't we all adjourn to the garden?"

Once outside, they passed the crab apple trees that grew at the edge of the garden, the lingering warmth of September occasionally giving way to little wafts of cool that presaged October, and followed the stone path among delphiniums and larkspur. The back of Thistlethwaite, which was more of an overgrown cottage than a manor house, made a pretty picture of stone walls overrun by pale pink climbing roses and ivy. Overhead, a flock of starlings frolicked in the endless bright blue of the sky.

Eloise talked about a recent visit to Spain, where she and Hal had visited their cousin James and his new wife, Felicity, at their vineyard.

"Felicity and James met when he won her family's estate in a card game. And now they're blissfully married. Isn't that just like a fairy tale?"

They'd then journeyed on to France and Italy, which made Delia cry, "Unfair!" with cheerful frustration, as she'd never been much beyond Highcross.

The Thistlethwaite estate manager passed through the garden then, and Roxham asked if they might discuss a stream the two properties shared. The ladies continued strolling the garden without him.

As soon as the men were out of earshot, Eloise linked her arms with Delia's and Lily's and leaned her head in close to theirs. "I must tell you," she said, "that I shall probably, before the autumn has come to an end, have broken my heart for Ivorwood."

Delia blinked at this poetic confidence. "You mean the earl?"

Eloise sighed exquisitely. "I do. Oh, he is divine. Handsome, debonair—even his voice is heavenly." She gave a heavy sigh. "But I'm afraid he has yet to really *notice* me."

"But, Eloise," Delia said, "I don't see how any man could not admire you."

A twinkle lit Eloise's eyes. "I will confide that I enjoyed some enthusiastic attention this Season from certain gentlemen. I'd rather hoped Ivorwood would take notice of them, and me."

"You mean that he would be jealous?" Delia said. This talk of enticing men was slightly wicked, compared to what life in the country had been like for Delia and Lily. "How thrilling! It's just like a novel. Did it work?"

"Unfortunately, no. But I haven't given up."

Listening to their chatter, Lily was amazed at how free Eloise was in discussing her attraction to Ivorwood. Lily had never breathed even one word to anyone in her family about her feelings for Hal, and though he might have said something to her brothers years ago, she didn't think he had, because neither of them had ever said a thing to her.

She realized that Eloise was squeezing her arm. "I was hoping to do you a favor, Lily."

"A favor?"

"Yes. About that journal of yours."

Lily blinked. Well.

"What journal?" Delia said.

Eloise looked surprised. "Don't you know about how Hal took Lily's journal when she was our age?"

Delia looked at Lily with something bordering on accusation. "No."

Lily sighed. "That's because I wanted to forget about it. It *was* four years ago."

"Yes, but your personal journal! It had to have been embarrassing."

"Rather," Lily said, wanting only for the subject to be dropped.

"Anyway," Eloise said, "it's been forgotten all this time at Mayfield. But I think he's found it, because I saw him coming out of one of the guest rooms with a volume. I could tell it upset you, his reminding you about it yesterday."

"Well, I suppose I can get him to give it back to me soon," Lily said, though she believed nothing of the sort.

Eloise bit her lip. "My brother has the best heart in the world, but I'm afraid he's always been a terrible tease. And I rather think he might not give the book back if you asked. But I thought that *I* might secure it."

Lily wasn't willing to allow that Roxham had anything like a good heart. But the thought that Eloise might get hold of her book—well, she didn't know if it was better or worse than Roxham having it. It was so private, and Eloise was so... not. She forced herself to be casual. "So have you had a chance at it?"

Eloise's pretty lips pressed together in disappointment. "Unfortunately, no, because the door to his room was locked. Which it never is. But," she said with a little grin, "here's what's amusing. There's a nest in the tree outside his window, and I saw a bird fly into his room just as our carriage was pulling away to come here. So it will be only what he deserves if desperate things have happened in there because no one could get in to chase the bird out."

Delia gasped with naughty glee, which caused Roxham, still speaking with the manager, to glance their way. The ladies quickly stepped to the side of the path to inspect a white rosebush.

Lily whispered her thanks to Eloise for trying, but she hardly knew what words she used because she was so excited by something Eloise had just revealed.

"Well," Delia said, "I suppose you'd like to have the journal back without any blemishes, Lil. But just think that if the bird has spoiled it, no one will want to read it anyway."

Which supposition caused both girls to collapse in giggles. Lily, meanwhile, was consumed with plans, which occupied her as Roxham and Eloise took their leave amid promises to keep the Teagardens apprised of any developments with the Woods Fiend.

Eloise had mentioned the old tree next to Mayfield, and Lily knew just which one she meant; it grew close to the walls of the manor. And now she knew that the room it was near belonged to the viscount—who would be gone to the woods for much of the evening.

Making tonight the perfect opportunity for her to take back what was hers.

On his return to Mayfield, Hal was met by his butler, who was wringing his hands. "They've gone, my lord. The Italians—the folly builders."

"Giuseppe and Pietro?"

"Apparently they heard about the Woods Fiend and it scared them."

"How could it? They barely speak English."

"I think that's part of the problem, that they don't quite understand. It's been illustrated to them with wild gestures and looks of fright—the stable boys amusing themselves. The Italians packed up their things while you were gone and left."

Damn that man, whoever it was that was masquerading as the Woods Fiend. Hal had been hoping the folly would be finished well before Guy Fawkes Night; he meant to have an enormous bonfire at Mayfield then, with ladies clad in togas wandering about the folly. Some of his fellow officers were to be there as well, on leave.

He sighed. "Do you know where they've gone?"

"To the village inn."

"Send someone with funds to tide them over."

"Very good, sir. I did try to get them to understand that the Woods Fiend is undoubtedly just some local rascal, and that you and the earl are close to catching him, but they made it plain they couldn't return until he was captured."

"Which will be tonight, if I have anything to do with it," Hal said, advancing up the grand staircase with determination growing at every step.

Five

LILY WAITED IN HER ROOM THAT NIGHT WHILE
Thistlethwaite settled down, her knees bumping
together nervously as she sat at her vanity in the
dark and went over her plan. She was wearing an
old black pair of Ian's breeches, along with a dark
waistcoat of Rob's. A bag slung across her body held
gloves for climbing.

The snugness of the pants across her bottom felt
like a warning for what she was about to do, which
was certainly far worse than hiding in shrubbery to
sketch a gentleman. Her common sense had already
tried talking her out of her plan; she knew the risks
of being discovered by Roxham or a servant or guest.
But she couldn't seem to make herself want to stop,
and she had to admit that the pleasure she might have
in besting Roxham was irresistible.

A faint chiming sounded in the drawing room, the
notes of the grandfather clock marking half past ten.
It was time.

All was silent as she slipped out of the house on
tiptoe. It was a brisk twenty-minute walk to Mayfield

Hall. The moon was hidden by clouds, and she hoped to be well concealed by the dark. Not that there ought to be anyone about, except Roxham and Ivorwood in search of their quarry. Please God they wouldn't see her.

She kept away from the woods, skirting them so widely that she tripped over a pile of stones near the half-built folly. So like him, she thought as she crawled over the rocks until she was clear of the site, to want a building whose only purpose was pleasure. Reaching the back of Mayfield Hall, she hid herself among the dense hawthorn bushes that grew along the terrace, the very ones where she'd hidden four years before. All the rooms on the second floor were dark, as was his—she saw it near the tree.

Across the terrace, the drawing room doors were open. Eloise, Diana, John, and Mrs. Whyte, all dressed in evening clothes, stood talking. As Lily watched, Diana went over to the piano and began to play, and Lily recognized a sweet tune that had been popular during her Season.

Longing pierced her unexpectedly, though she couldn't understand why. They were just a group of fashionable people whiling away the evening with carefree entertainments.

And yet it was that very carefree quality she so scorned that made her yearn. Her life at Thistlethwaite was good; she loved her siblings, and she felt fulfilled by her shawl business and her secret plans for the school. But she never felt carefree. She didn't think she knew how. She'd always been the responsible one, whether she'd wanted to be that or not.

Even her father had called her that. *You're my serious one,* he'd say when, drunk from a boozy luncheon, he'd lean on her as he climbed the stairs to his room. *Just like your mother, God rest her soul.*

When their mother had died, he'd taken Lily aside and said, *Your sister is only seven, and she still needs a mother's care. Nanny has to go, so you'll have to do your best with Delia.*

Nanny's departure was the beginning of the economies they'd had to make to enable Papa's investments. Lily had never minded helping with Delia, but a sore part of her had wished that a twelve-year-old might be expected to miss a mother, too.

Go over to Dimble's for me, he would say, words that had made her quiver. Dimble was the wine merchant, and the father of her childhood friend. *He won't say no to you.*

And Mr. Dimble never had, but she saw each time in his eyes that her family paid their bills too slowly. Her father had been a good man, but when their mother died, he surrendered to drink.

With her older brothers away at school, she, as the oldest girl, was the one who'd had to oversee the household. She was the one left to take care of many of the details of life for herself and her father and Delia. Along with duties like keeping the household accounts were never-acknowledged ones, like providing explanations for her father's sometimes odd behavior to neighbors and servants.

She'd vowed back then that she'd never let herself become like him: out of control, muddled with drink, dependent. Even now, through the blurring of years, she still hated the waste and the shame of that time, which had been crowned with the utter foolishness of giving her a Season they couldn't afford.

She made herself look away from the scene in the drawing room because she realized that the sight of Eloise—young, beautiful, and cheerfully falling in love with gentlemen—was threatening to engulf her in envy. Why should she envy Eloise when she had a very good life now? Why should she want anything else? What was *wrong* with her?

She trained her eyes resolutely on the viscount's window and focused on her plan. It was after eleven and the men had to be gone. Aside from the drawing room, there was no sign of activity; most of the servants would have retired, though some would still be about, and she would have to be very quiet. She moved toward the knobby old tree outside Roxham's window and put on her gloves.

The climbing was harder than she'd imagined it would be, and it was quickly borne in on her that the last time she'd been up a tree she'd been ten. But the thought of Roxham reading her journal was enough to force her past trepidation, so that without quite knowing how she'd gotten herself there, she had reached his tall window. All was silent, except for the tiny sound of the distant piano. She put a foot on the windowsill and stepped inside.

It was very dark in his bedchamber, and she pushed the curtains wide to let in the little moonlight there was and allowed her eyes to adjust to the thicker blackness of his room. Traces of his scent teased her, the cedar notes of his soap coupled with the expensive smell of an immaculately cleaned room full of beeswax-polished furniture. A luxuriously thick rug under her feet absorbed the sound of her movements.

She suffered the despairing thought, which she'd previously refused to consider, that her journal might not even be in his room. But she moved into action and started her search at the small table by his bed. There was a book on it, but it was too small to be her journal. She moved on to the desk, sweeping her hands lightly over it, keeping the journal's square shape in mind, and the memory of the little strips of fabric she'd glued on it... and there it was.

She slipped it into her bag. At the window, she took a deep breath and put her foot onto the branch just outside. And then she was working her way down the tree, feeling unstoppable.

She returned across the dark grounds wearing a smile of triumph. Back in the safety of her room, she lit a candle and opened the book and read again for the first time words she'd written at a very different time in her life. By the end of the first paragraph her face was burning, and she slammed the cover closed and shoved the book as far as she could in the back of her desk drawer.

Still, she thought as she collapsed onto her bed, she was satisfied with her night's work. She'd finally gotten her wretched journal back.

❧

In Mayfield's breakfast room, the late-night darkness relieved by the light of four artfully placed candles, Eloise was waiting with the door to the hallway ajar so she'd know when Hal and Ivorwood got back from hunting the Woods Fiend. It was after one in the morning, and she'd been there already for an hour, but she didn't mind—it was part of the excitement.

She'd been secretive, not setting things up in the breakfast room until the manor was quiet so nobody was around to say she was being inappropriate or any of those other things boring people said when a person tried to do something interesting.

She was wearing her midnight silk gown—she thought it made her eyes look deep and mysterious— with her pearl drop earrings as just the right accent. She'd made the sandwiches herself, filled a jug with ale, and arranged the items on a pretty platter on the breakfast room table along with the candles. When she'd lived at Mayfield, the small breakfast room had never been used at night, and she thought it would be the coziest place for the evening surprise she'd planned for the men. Of course she'd done it all for Ivorwood, but obviously they'd have to include her brother since the men would come back together.

Being together tonight was going to be so dreamy and perfect, just like it had been when the three of them had gone to the Opera in Town. That was the night when she'd first realized how very special Ivorwood was. Best of all, since everyone else was asleep, Hyacinth wouldn't be around. Eloise wished Hal hadn't invited the widow to Mayfield. She was always dragging the conversation around to herself, and she seemed to think Ivorwood found her feather-brained conversation and endless gossip fascinating, when any fool could see he was only being polite.

A small commotion sounded in the hallway that led from the back entrance—they were coming!

She moved to stand in the doorway so they'd see her as they drew close. Lit candles had been left out for the men's return, and the play of light and shadow in the corridor made her think of how she'd never done something like this before. Little thrills danced around inside her.

"You still up, Ellie?" her brother said when he caught sight of her. Ivorwood was right behind him, yawning adorably. His teeth flashed white in the semi-darkness as he came to stand next to Hal. They were both tall, and of course her brother was disgustingly handsome—she sometimes felt with irritated affection that it was wasted on him, like the water that overflowed a cup if you kept pouring when it was full—and they looked extremely well together, like some kind of masculine force. A matched pair of handsome, the dark and light versions.

But Ivorwood, *oh* he was special. How dear was his gorgeous face, with his black hair all windblown around it from standing outside. She knew the exact color of green his eyes were, even if she couldn't see them in the dim light: clear, silvery green, exactly the look of sunlight when it dappled the Ionian Sea at dusk.

"Yes," she said a little more breathlessly than she would have liked. She smiled in what she hoped was a sophisticated manner. She knew Ivorwood thought of her as his friend's younger sister, but she was determined to make him see her as a man sees a woman. "Did you catch the Fiend? I want to hear everything!"

"Nothing to tell," said Ivorwood with a rueful grin. He had the most knee-weakening grin. Almost, the sight of it now was enough to take to bed with her and dream on. "The fellow never showed."

"Not surprising," Hal said, "as he knows we're onto him. I shouldn't be surprised if we've seen the last of the Woods Fiend."

Ivorwood covered his mouth as he yawned again, and Eloise sighed inside. She loved his long-fingered hands, the hands of a sensitive man.

"Though I rather think," he said, "that I'll be disappointed if he's never caught and brought to justice. And there's Hal's wager to consider."

"Yes!" she agreed. She always agreed with him, even when she didn't exactly agree—she couldn't seem to help herself.

"Well," she said in her best gracious voice, "there are sandwiches in the breakfast room. Won't you come in and refresh yourselves?" Even as she said them, the words sounded stupid, like something an elderly lady would say to weary travelers. Her smile felt a little stiff.

Hal's eyes settled on her in a kind look, and the compassion in them made a lump start forming in her throat. "That was thoughtful, Ellie. But I think we're both for our beds."

"Right," said Ivorwood. "Most thoughtful of you, Eloise. I'm afraid I'm just about dead on my feet, what with all the standing about." He gave her a sweet smile that almost made up for the disappointment pinching her heart. So stupid of her, to think they'd want a snack when it was so late.

The lump in her throat threatened to make her

mouth quiver, and she swallowed hard, forcing it down. "Of course. It was just a trifle. I couldn't sleep anyway, and it gave me something to do."

She refused to meet her brother's eyes because she felt certain they were looking on her with pity, and she wouldn't have it. She quickly blew out the four candles in the breakfast room while Hal extinguished the ones in the corridor, and she followed the men up the stairs.

There had been, anyway, another reason she'd stayed up late, and after Ivorwood bid them good night and entered his bedchamber, she followed her brother down the corridor toward the family rooms.

"I want a word with you, Hal."

"Yes?" Hal said, making sure to keep the exasperation out of his voice, because the frustration wasn't with his sweet, love-struck sister but with the Mayfield trespasser. Perhaps the man had been scared away by them last night, but Hal was annoyed that he'd been prevented from capturing him, especially now that work had been stopped on his folly because of him. Too, there was the possible loss of his new hunter, since the terms of the wager had specified he must catch the Fiend within ten days.

And he'd had not a free minute all day, what with his hosting duties, and then there had been an awkward conversation with Prescott, who'd refused to acknowledge hinted suggestions that his hearing was going. Everard would doubtless have handled the situation better.

So he hadn't yet had a chance to poke around in that journal of Lily's, which was, actually, the thing he was most looking forward to at the moment.

His sister bit her lip. The poor thing obviously had a tendre for Ivorwood, never mind that the man was a good fifteen years older than she was and rightly saw her as merely the charming sister of his friend.

"It's about that journal of Lily's," she said. "But before I say more, Hal, I want you to swear you won't speak to her of it again or tease her about it."

He blinked. "Eloise, my dear, I can't think why any of that should concern you."

"It concerns me because I like her very much, and she's not happy that you have her journal. And, really," she said, drawing her slim form up stiffly in a way that made him want to smile, "I find it most uncomfortable that my brother has in his possession something private that belongs to a lady which he is not returning."

He cocked his head. "Did she put you up to this? I wouldn't have thought—"

"No! She wouldn't be happy that I mentioned it to you. But she doesn't know you like I do." Her face softened and she reached for his hand. "I know you are good."

No, I'm not. His sweet, indulgent sister would never acknowledge that in the copybook of life, his pages were well blotted. "El, you needn't worry about Lily. This is a trifling matter."

She frowned. "I'm not so sure. Why don't you give it to me, and I'll return it for you so there won't be any awkwardness?"

And what would be the fun in that?

"I'll think about it," he said, intending nothing of the sort. "Good night."

He kissed her cheek and went into his room before

she could come up with any more thoughts to share. His sister had been six when both their parents died of illness, though since they'd been like distant planets to their children, he'd always supposed it hadn't been so much of a loss for her. She'd grown up in the care of an indulgent governess who'd allowed her to do as she liked, but as Eloise was such a good-hearted young lady, it rarely mattered if she was also rather convinced of her own way of doing things.

He put the candle down on his desk and frowned. He was certain he'd left the journal there, and he'd felt easy about doing so because he'd locked the door to his room. With a staff and visitors, privacy was not assured, and now that the journal had come to light, he hadn't wanted anyone poking around in his room.

He opened the desk drawer but wasn't surprised not to find it there as he had left it on the desk. An astonishing suspicion was taking shape in his mind, and as he looked around the room, he noticed that the window was open wider than he'd left it. Taking his candle, he examined the area. A smudgy footprint now decorated the sill.

With a dark grunt, he realized that half a mile away, a blond woman was surely gloating. The minx had climbed the tree outside his window!

Extremely daring. And very, very intriguing. He wondered if she'd made the practical decision to wear pants while climbing, and entertained an image of her, fair chin set in determination as she worked carefully upward through the branches, her legs encased in fabric.

As the spotty moonlight shifted across his fields and lifted the shadows beyond that blanketed

Thistlethwaite, he considered that her trip to his room tonight and the non-appearance of the Woods Fiend might be related. It was obvious that she was determined to thwart Hal's efforts to catch him, and she'd likely warned the man not to come tonight.

Between her interference with his efforts to catch the Woods Fiend the night before and her trip to his room tonight, the gauntlet had been well and truly thrown down. She'd engaged him in battle, and there was no way he was going to let her win, no matter the game afoot.

He had advantages over her. For one thing, she'd obviously had a serious passion for him once—and he knew he wasn't the only one feeling the crackle of attraction between them when they were together.

Oh, who was he kidding? He was a little smitten with her. There was something astringent and pure and unembellished about her that fascinated him, like the notes of a single violin cutting through the babble of conversation at a party.

Well. Once he'd made certain she felt that old magic for him and he'd gotten her to admit it, he'd have the upper hand. Then it would be a matter of *beguiling* to find out what she knew about the Woods Fiend.

When he sat down on his bed to remove his boots, his hand pressed against something wet. He lifted it and blinked at the evidence that a bird had been in his room.

He didn't know if Lily had had anything to do with that as well, but he was more than willing to believe it.

Six

LILY WAS STANDING NEAR THE TOP OF A LITTLE HILL AT the edge of the pasture the next afternoon and discussing sheep shearing with Malcolm, their shepherd, when Buck, who'd been keeping watch over the sheep from under the shade of a tree, jumped up and ran barking over the other side of the hill.

He returned with surprising company: Roxham.

She was startled to see him at Thistlethwaite, and after reading her own words about him in her journal the night before, the sight of him made her insides jump a little. Was he coming to confront her?

He strode toward her on his long legs, of whose muscular firmness she now had personal knowledge. In his beautifully tailored buckskin breeches and gleaming black top boots, he ought to have looked as out of place among the sheep and mud as a decorative Hepplewhite chair taken from a London drawing room and set down in their muddy fields, but he looked at home. His shirt was snowy white, the cravat tied in a snappy knot, and his coat was a distinctive, forget-me-not blue. Ha, a visual joke, as she doubted any woman who'd ever seen him had forgotten him.

He offered a warm greeting to old Malcolm, who looked disreputable and cantankerous with his grizzled beard and knotty hair.

To Lily, he said, "Delia told me you'd be out here."

Malcolm, who in general was interested in little beyond the welfare of animals, nonetheless seemed intrigued by the viscount's presence in their pasture. She sent him away to see to a broken gate before turning to Roxham. Knowing that her journal was now sitting in her desk drawer made her want to gloat, but she resisted the urge.

"To what do I owe the pleasure of your visit?"

Buck was circling around their visitor, who crouched down and ran his hands generously over her dog's fur. He cast a glance up at her.

"As if you didn't know."

"Indeed I can hardly imagine why my lord should favor us with a visit to our pasture."

He left off petting Buck and stood up. "My lord?" he repeated, the corner of his mouth ticking upward and something wicked lighting his eyes. "So formal. 'I am going to write here about Hal…'" he quoted, squinting as if to remember the rest.

She wanted to put her finger right across his lips and stop the flow of her own words from them, but that would pose its own problems. She forced a light tone and tried not to wonder how much he'd read. "Goodness, what does any of that signify now? I was but a child."

"A child. Of sixteen." Those arrogant green

specks in his blue eyes mocked her, said *he'd* never written such things to anyone. "Funny, I've seen 'children' that age married. I'd say you were merely a younger version of the woman you are now. Though the years have, I grant you, been exceedingly kind to you."

It was out of her mouth before she could stop herself: "Is that why you find it more appealing to have a conversation with me now than you did then?"

He absorbed her words. She wanted them back.

At the same time, though, she wanted him to be uncomfortable, and he did look uncomfortable. Briefly.

"I don't remember avoiding your conversation, Lily. I was simply busy."

After he'd taken her journal four years ago, she'd told herself he was only a butterfly of a man, flitting from flower to flower looking for nectar. "Yes, you were," she agreed, though it didn't seem like an entirely accurate appraisal now—there was that shadow she'd seen once or twice now in his eyes, as if he'd seen hard things. And of course he would have, in the war. Still, he seemed to have put it all behind him; he joked and teased as much as he ever had.

"Was there some reason you came today?" she asked.

He crossed his arms and stared down the blade of his nose at her. "What the devil are you up to?"

"I, my lord?"

He raised an eyebrow at "my lord."

She smiled, as if to indicate she had no hard feelings toward him. No feelings of any kind. A lie, but if she had an untidy residual attraction to him, along with a growing awareness that he was a very entertaining man, it was something she would conquer with no one the wiser.

"There was no sign of the Woods Fiend last night, but *you* came to my room and removed something."

"Surely," she said, "you're not suggesting I'm the Woods Fiend?"

"I'm suggesting," he said drily, "that you're in league with him."

"In league. That sounds serious."

He gave her a very haughty look in reply, which drew his golden brows together at bossy angles and made the planes of his face more taut in a perilously interesting way. Her imagination treated her to an image of him in his captain's uniform, dressing down army recruits.

"Don't try to distract me from the issue at hand, which is people sneaking into my room at night. People like you."

"I, my lord? In your bedchamber? How absurd!"

"Lily…" His voice held a note of warning.

"Well," she said, "if something happened to the journal in your possession last night while at the same time nothing happened in the woods, anyone would say that was merely coincidence."

Like reinforcements, Rosemary, who'd been wandering nearby, drew close to him and began to sniff the edge of his forget-me-not coat, while Parsley came at him from the other side; the two were invariably interested in new people. In the way of sheep, the others were not far behind. She hid a smile as he looked down to find himself surrounded.

"The shirt I was wearing the other night," he said

as he laid a hand atop Rosemary's cream-colored head, "still smells of violets."

"Violets?" Though she made her own violet water scent to keep her clothes fresh, she pretended ignorance. "I'm not certain I even knew they had a scent."

"They do. It comes and goes. It's known to be exasperating."

Rosemary stuck out her tongue just then and licked his little finger, which drew his attention even as Parsley leaned in to him. Parsley was prone to leaning on people, and Lily liked the idea that Roxham would leave Thistlethwaite smelling of sheep. Thyme pressed forward to see what was so interesting. Roxham moved his sleeve out of the way of Parsley's questing mouth while still pinning Lily with his eyes.

"Roxham." Her tone said, *darling boy.* "Putting aside the absurd charge of being at fault for retrieving something of my own that had been taken from me, I can assure you I am not in league with an evil spirit."

"Just tell me what is going on in my woods, and with whom you are working."

She swallowed hard at his directness, and his eyes locked on hers, as if willing her to fall apart and confess the truth.

Ha, she was made of sterner stuff, and she held his blue-green gaze with a bland look that offered nothing. Nonetheless, the cost to her was having to absorb the full blast of Lord Perfect's male beauty. Those thick eyelashes that gave his eyes a boyish hint of mischief…

Buck barked sharply just then, scattering the sheep as her brother Rob came over the hill.

"Rob! You're back!"

She was very, very glad for the interruption of his arrival. And glad he was home, too, of course.

"Welcome home," she said, embracing him.

"It's good to be back." He and Roxham exchanged cordial greetings. "It's good to see you after all this time, Hal. Delia said you were out here visiting our sheep, but I thought she was jesting."

His tone was friendly, but Lily could read in his eyes that he thought it odd that Roxham, with plenty of his own sheep, had come for that reason.

"Yes, I'd heard that Lily had some very good ointment used for hooves," Roxham fibbed effortlessly. He *would* be good at fibbing, she thought, overlooking how much skirting of the truth she'd done since he'd returned to Mayfield. "I came to ask after a sample myself, hoping that might induce her to part with it."

Rob cocked his head at her. She smiled. In for a penny, in for a pound, but she couldn't help but feel that she would pay in some way for all the moral lapses in which she was finding herself engaged. "We were just going to the stable to get it."

"I'll join you," Rob said, falling into step with Hal. *Old Duffer.* It was getting harder to remember to call him that in her mind, which kept whispering *Hal.* It was the familiarity, she told herself. He *was* familiar. But it was also the lying on his front the other night that was undermining her. And the mischief sparkling in his blue-green eyes.

They found hoof ointment in the stable— fortunately, they did have some. It was in a large container, and she took it with the intention of putting some in a small jar from the kitchen and sending Hal on his way. But as they approached the manor, Rob obliviously invited their guest to tea. He accepted, shooting her a gloating look.

Ian was already in the sitting room with Delia, and he jumped up when they came in and embraced his sister and shook hands with Hal.

"Why, here we are, just like years ago when you used to come to tea all the time, Hal," Ian said as they sat down. "Except Delia was little and had no conversation, and Lily always used to be scribbling in her journal."

Hal accepted a cup of tea from Delia. "I remember. Although I wouldn't say that Delia had no conversation—she was doubtless preoccupied with more important things than what was being discussed by boring older gentlemen," he said, winking at her. Lily was almost certain she heard her sister sigh in admiration.

The battle of Oporto was discussed—Rob asked Hal for a firsthand account of the victory—but while Hal spoke highly of his men, he didn't linger on the account but steered the conversation to crops and books.

Delia, to Lily's dismay, brought up the woods problem, of which their brothers knew nothing as yet, and said how people thought their sheep were possessed so Hal and Ivorwood were trying to capture the trespasser at night.

Rob was, predictably, not amused. "Good Lord, how ridiculous."

"It is, of course," Hal said, "but I wouldn't want anything to do with my woods harming the Thistlethwaite shawl business."

Rob shot Lily a look. "That's very good of you. I'm sorry you've been put to the trouble. Ian and I will take over now for you since we are the ones most affected."

"Sorry," Hal said, "but I can't allow it. For one thing, it's also causing trouble at Mayfield—some artisans I hired to build a folly have run off in fear of the Fiend. I've wagered John that I'll discover who the trespasser is, and I'm afraid the terms can't be altered. I must be the one to catch him."

"I say, Hal," Ian deposited an enormous spoon of clotted cream on his plate, "speaking of wagers, that was quite a match you won against Dorcot. Read about it in *The Tattler.* You made him look like a schoolboy."

Hal chuckled. "Well, he is only twenty-one or two."

Lily couldn't resist saying, "That *is* a surprise that you did so well, you being so old."

Hal, along with her brothers, looked at her with a puzzled expression. Delia giggled.

"Hal's only two years older than me, Lily," Rob said. "Hardly old."

"Well, *you* do keep in good form, Rob, with all that you do." She let the implication that the viscount was in poor condition hang in the air, though it was preposterous, especially considering how well his blue waistcoat hung from his broad shoulders and hinted at the lithe, battle-tested muscles of his chest and abdomen. She made herself look into her teacup. She could feel herself reverting to the young fool she'd been, and she was getting to the point of being just about unable to stand herself.

"I'll get a jar for the ointment," she said, excusing herself.

When she got back, carrying a small jar filled with the ointment Hal supposedly wanted, Delia and Ian were the only ones left in the room.

"Where did Roxham go?" she asked.

Ian waved his hand airily before plucking what was at least his fifth sandwich off the tea tray. "Rob was going to show him some dazzling new tool that should save the work of four men or some such. I suppose you can just take the ointment out to him."

But at the back of the house she could see through the open door that Rob was talking to one of the servants, with the viscount nowhere in sight. He must have left.

She was tired from her recent late nights—*that* was why her relief that he was gone was mixed with disappointment. Surely otherwise she wouldn't be thinking about those words she'd written in her journal, words about touching him…

Leaving the ointment on a hall table, she decided to go up to her room and lie down. If she were well rested, she'd feel more like herself.

She opened the door to her bedchamber and had walked partway in when she stopped and gasped. Hal was standing by the window, reading her journal. He looked up at her and grinned.

Quickly she shut the door behind her.

"What on earth are you doing in here?" she demanded in a low voice. "What if someone saw you coming in?"

"I was discreet," he said mildly, "and I think it should be obvious what I'm doing in your room. You're hardly in a position to complain, having been in *my* room last night."

"You had something of mine."

He glanced down at the journal and turned a page as casually as if he were flipping through a book of prints. "I notice that either your maid is a fiend for symmetry, or you line up your combs and brushes with a ruler."

He was trying to make her squirm. She very much didn't want him to know how effective he was being. She folded her hands tightly in front of her and pushed down her disappointment that her triumph over him hadn't lasted. "There's nothing wrong with liking order."

He turned another page. Surely he couldn't actually be reading it right now? Surely it would take him time to decipher?

"What about disorder? Doing the wrong thing, the thing you don't think you should do?" His eyes scanned the page before him.

"Why would I want to do something I knew was wrong?"

"Maybe because you were questioning whether it really was wrong? Whether it really is so awful, for instance, to have made a fool of yourself over a man?"

Over him. Yes, it was awful and she wished so much that she hadn't. But she couldn't admit to him how painful the experience had been—it was far, far too private. "I was merely young. It's not a crime to… have dreams."

As she said these vague, easy words she didn't mean, the kind of words with which one might comfort a fussy child who'd failed at some endeavor, something shifted inside her, an assertive rising up of longings she was used to ignoring.

His eyebrow went up skeptically, as if he didn't believe her. "Then you won't mind if I read this? You're not ashamed?"

Oh yes, she was. Terribly ashamed of all those things she'd written. But she was also very, very tired of the shame she felt over that book, over her younger self, over every little misstep she took that she told herself was a mistake. She was sick of the hard inner voice of judgment that was always with her.

How much had he read?

Still not looking up, he said, "I'll ask again, since you avoided answering before: What is going on in my woods and whom are you protecting?"

He was doing it on purpose. Awful, skilled teaser that he was, he knew that the sight of him looking at her journal would be excruciating. He casually turned another page, and she contemplated rushing across the room and simply grabbing the book from him. And discarded it. She'd had years of living with her brothers to get better at keep-away, and a direct assault had never once been successful. Also, he was far taller than she was.

She forced herself to sound surprised. "I?"

He glanced up, his eyes glinting at her. "Oh, would you just confess the details and get it over with, Teagarden?"

Of course she couldn't do that—it was Nate's secret, and a dangerous one, too, for him. No, she'd have to be creative if she were going to get her journal back.

She took a few steps closer to him.

"So... I smell good to you." She made herself

chuckle, which wasn't terribly hard because she felt giddy and off balance. "Or is *good* how you would describe the exasperating scent of violets?"

Was she witless, to be flirting with him like this? And more importantly, was it working?

He finally looked up from the book, which he held open at his chest. "Stop trying to distract me."

Very well, it wasn't working. Or at least, not that he would admit. But now that they were standing closer, she thought his eyes lingered on her face. She gave him her calmest look while inside her heart was whirring. He closed the journal to her vast relief, but he didn't put it down.

"I've remembered," he said, "that there was a family rumor about a treasure buried in those woods. I always thought it was nonsense, but now I'm beginning to wonder. *Is* this all about a treasure buried on my land? And if so, is your accomplice thinking to take it? Because I'm sure we won't have to have a conversation about how wrong that would be."

With each word he said, her heart raced more with worry for Nate. Hal was too suspicious and too clever. She needed to change the subject before he probed any more and tripped her up somehow—and she had to get her journal back.

She moved closer purposefully, hoping to count on the element of surprise. She stopped a few inches from him and, holding his gaze with hers, made a quick grab for the book. But his reflexes were too fast, and in an instant it was high above his head, at the end of one of those endlessly long arms.

He laughed. "Not very original, Lily."

It wasn't, and she did need something original, something he would never expect her to do.

She let her eyes wander to his chest, to the mother-of-pearl buttons on his forget-me-not tailcoat. With a slow, deliberate motion, she put her fingers on the top button.

He was looking down at her, but he didn't stop her or try to move her hand, and she undid the button.

She snuck a glance upward and saw that he hadn't lowered his arm, or maybe he had a *tiny* bit. Her glance took in his look of surprise before she returned to the close examination of his buttons. She was shocked at herself as well, on the one hand. On the other... she thought of all those times she'd allowed herself to fantasize and write and draw when she was younger. She'd already imagined doing something so bold as this to him, and paid for those imaginings in shame. He'd already read at least some of them. What did she have to lose by actually *doing* them?

A whiff of leather hung in the air about him, from his ride over doubtless, and that dry and woodsy scent of his soap that made her think of the heart of the forest. An ought-to-be-illegal scent that certainly wasn't putting her on the path to prudence, because while he watched her, she undid his next button. There were three, and as he was standing still and silent, one arm at his side and the other raised with her journal in his hand, she undid the third button. His tailcoat shifted open.

"What are you doing?" His voice was husky.

"I... hardly know." She gave herself permission to slide the flat of her hand under the opened front of his coat. He wore a dark blue and white striped satin waistcoat, and beneath its smooth cloth and that of his shirt she felt the muscular contours of his chest. He was hard and warm and alive under her hand. She moved upward slowly and felt, with a jolt of wonder, the beating of his heart, a strong thudding against her palm.

She didn't notice the moment when the arm over his head came down to join the other one in pulling her against him, but as soon as she was in the circle of his arms, her senses elevated to a new level of *him*. It felt extremely good. She thought she could stand there in his arms for a long time.

Remarkably, some few of her wits remained unbefuddled, and these alerted her to the hard contours of the book now pressed against her back. But most of her attention was on all the places where her body touched his.

"Lily Teagarden," he said, his voice low and soft. He leaned over to put his mouth to the skin where her shoulder met her neck and dragged his lips against her, and her breath caught. His lips made their way upward along her neck, leaving a moist trail that he teased with the almost unbearably sensual heat of his breath as he hovered over her. "You surprise me."

She was surprised, too. Surprised to find that she was standing in his arms and that suddenly all she wanted to do was surrender. To *him*.

This shocking awareness brought her to her senses, at least enough that she could act. Slowly, incrementally, she let her arm drift behind her hip, where the journal was pressed. She held his attention by pressing her cheek against the side of his face as he worked his maddening mouth up under her ear. Her knees had almost turned to jelly by the time her fingers finally closed over the edge of the book.

With a quick, sharp tug it was in her hand, and she stepped away from him with a wobble. Before he could take it back from her, she pulled the bodice of her gown away from her chest and jammed the book down in front of her breasts.

Seven

SHE'D OUTFOXED HIM.

He'd come to her room in search of the book, feeling justified in doing so as she'd already been in his bedchamber. Once she'd arrived—as he'd hoped she would—he'd thought to tease her with the book, though to what extent he'd not planned.

But now his heart was pounding. This wasn't just playful teasing, it was sexual play, and she was far better at it than he would have thought she'd be. She's a tart, aging virgin, he told himself in an effort to damp down his lust.

She's not that old. Perhaps twenty or twenty-one, though her manner was often older, like that of a spinster schoolmistress. But what she was actually, and especially compared to him, was fresh, and untouched, he'd wager, by any actual *experience*. As pure as a white lily.

Looking at her as she stood there, her bodice absurdly shaped with the journal stuffed down it and her pretty pink mouth curling smugly, he was charmed and vexed in equal measure, and he decided that in battles with Lily from now on, all was fair.

"Well," he said. "That's twice you've used your body against me to gain advantage."

That brought bright color to her cheeks; they reminded him of creamy, pure camellia blossoms. The sight of pink spreading over them, and the awareness that they must be warming, was startlingly erotic.

"I… hmm," she murmured, as if she'd been choked by his blunt words. He chuckled darkly and stepped closer so that he was almost touching her.

"You wish to say that you're not accustomed to using your body to your advantage?"

"Of course not," she said hoarsely.

He leaned in so she could feel the heat of his skin brushing her cheek. Her violet scent teased him. "But perhaps you have *imagined* it?"

"No," she started to say, but he didn't need an answer, and he stopped her mouth with a kiss.

Such a soft mouth. Young, unspoiled lips. A small, delicate tongue that had surely never uttered curses or gossip, or ever shouted in despair. He suddenly wanted to drink her in.

Lily was amazed: Hal's lips were on hers—he was kissing her! She was being kissed!

Her first kiss ever.

A whisper of a kiss, as light as the wings of that butterfly she'd imagined him to be. But a kiss, definitely. Her suddenly girlish heart was beating fit to bursting from her chest with the nearness of him. With the feel of his mouth against hers. So new… a marvel.

His lips lifted and hovered and pressed, barely there, against the bow of her top lip, as though he had all the time in the world. She wanted him to have it, and to spend it on her. His lips brushed ever so lightly against the corner of her mouth. So tender as it was, his touch felt like an affectionate exploration, and she didn't care that affection was unlikely; she wanted only to accept what he was doing and not think about it.

Her bottom lip felt neglected, and he seemed to know this because he dipped his lips lower, as teasing as a whisper whose words she couldn't quite hear. His mouth parted just a little against the fullness of her lip and tugged at her with moist friction. Hot yearning raced through her.

In a distant corner of her mind she acknowledged that he was very skilled. That he knew exactly what to do, that some of what he was doing to her was probably *tactical* in some way, to gain some advantage over her. She didn't care. She didn't care about that, or about the murmuring inner voice that wanted her to know she shouldn't be kissing him.

He ran the tip of his tongue slowly over the fullest part of her mouth, and her lips parted and he nudged them farther apart with his. The warmth and wetness inside his mouth was a revelation, a sensation she could never have imagined, simply because it had to be experienced. She was struck with this: how could you ever *know* what you hadn't experienced? You could yearn to experience it, and the yearning could be an experience in itself, but you couldn't *feel* it. She knew that now, was being taught it in every slow, knowing exploration his mouth made of hers.

His tongue stroked hers softly, and she stroked him back, wanting more, wanting whatever he was going to give her.

She settled her hands above his elbows and ran them up the outsides of his arms, amazed at the hard curves of muscles beneath the fabric. Amazed... she was amazed by him, by the experience of kissing him.

His hands moved to either side of her jaw, holding her steady for his kiss. Hot on her skin, they slid down her neck, their incremental journey making flames of desire lick her. He reached the tops of her shoulders and lingered there, his thumbs stroking the bare skin of her clavicle, exposed just above the high, scooped neck of her gown.

His mouth traveled along her jaw, depositing shivery little kisses on a path to her ear. "Teagarden," he murmured, "you've turned out so beautiful."

The shock of his words was how much her heart thrilled to hear them from him. They were like a strong liquor, and she only wanted more. She clutched the fabric of his sleeves, unbalanced and urgent and thrilled.

Pressed tight against the stiff cover of her journal, her breasts felt fuller as they strained against the book and the taut fabric of her gown. His hands traced the outside curves of her breasts and shaped their contours with his fingertips.

Hal could almost feel the thorny wall Lily kept raised around herself falling away. Here was Lily softened by desire, and the sight, the feel—the sound of her little pants—was nearly unendurably erotic. He rubbed the sides of her breasts, pressed plump by the book in her bodice, a crazy mix of reverence and lust boiling up in him.

A whimper escaped her as his fingers found the edge

of one partially crushed nipple and teased it with a fingernail. He traced the slender curve of her waist and the swell of her hips, their kiss turning wilder. Moving his hands lower, he cupped her sweet bottom, and they both gasped when he pulled her against his stiffened cock.

A little shocked sound hummed from her mouth into his, then sighed into a moan. Her hands slid along his shoulders and touched his neck—small, slim, nimble fingers that knew their way around yarn. Their questing touch on his earlobes—his earlobes, for the love of God—only made him ache more.

Wanting nothing but to pull up her skirts and explore all the dark mysteries she kept hidden, he was more lost to her with each moment. She was like an oyster, craggy and hard with graduated layers of shell, but inside soft and glistening and a feast for the senses. And the pearl that he now dearly wanted to discover…

He had not, thank God, entirely lost his mind, though he intuited she was intoxicated enough with the adventure of her first foray that she might want and allow anything.

He reluctantly moved a hand from her arse, up her straight back, and around to the front, not allowing himself to linger over those maddening slim curves. Smiling a bit against her mouth, he stroked his fingers along the tops of her breasts, and she pressed against them, not realizing that he'd changed his immediate goal, however reluctantly.

Lily, her senses alight as they'd never been in her life, didn't at first realize what Hal was doing. And then, with a cruel stab of disappointment, she understood what he was reaching for.

The awareness that he'd had a different goal the whole time she'd been in his arms was crushing, and she stepped back fast, away from him.

"I should have known." Hurt disappointment gripped at her, but she pushed it away and stoked anger instead—anger at him, yes, but more at herself for indulging her feelings. She crossed her arms hard and the book dug into her chest, and she was glad for the physical discomfort. She never should have let herself want him.

He didn't say anything, just stood there, the open front of his tailcoat reminding her of her idiocy.

"Why?" she said, hating how husky her voice sounded. She swallowed against the lump forming in her throat. "Is it that you just had to tease me again?"

"Actually, that wasn't the kind of teasing I initially had in mind. But come," he said, doing up his buttons, "you're not angry, are you, over a little playfulness?"

She closed her eyes, trying to collect herself, wondering how she'd convinced herself that kissing him was a good idea. She'd slipped up, lost her way, and she needed to atone for that somehow, to silence the part of her that felt so ashamed at how much she'd wanted him.

She forced a coolness into her voice that she didn't feel. This knave of a man had just shown her a new and enchanting side of life, and now she must turn away from it. "I don't know what happened, but this was my fault. I assure you it won't happen again."

He was brushing his hands down his front, smoothing the cloth, returning himself to his usual polished condition—she kept her eyes from the fall of his breeches—and he looked up at her.

"Fault? Assurances? It was only a kiss, Lily. In which we both participated. No one was harmed by it."

But she did feel harmed by it. It had been far more than a kiss, even if essentially nothing had been transgressed, and she felt unbalanced and muddled, and she hated to feel that way. She hugged the journal tighter against herself.

"*Why* do you want my journal? I can't believe it's really so interesting to you."

He shrugged, though something about his eyes made her think he didn't feel as lighthearted as he wished her to believe. "It was just play, each of us taking the journal back."

"That's all you're ever after, isn't it? An amusement for the moment, another folly. Something to kill the boredom of having everything you want or need already."

He just looked at her for several moments. "There's no need to be so harsh."

"Of course there is. I don't—I don't *do* things like this."

"You mean like kissing men in your bedchamber? Is there a set of rules?" he said, then cocked his head. "There is, isn't there? Rules you've made for yourself: Things I Shan't Do, or How I Shall Keep to the Way of Righteousness."

It was so foreign to her, this carefree way of behaving. "Is nothing sacred to you? Or of enough value that you would practice restraint?"

"Certainly there are things that are important to me. But making myself feel bad over kissing a willing woman isn't one of them. Passion is part of life, Lily. Or can't you admit that?"

That word made her uncomfortable. *Passion.* How could he speak it? It was so embarrassing. It was unruly, it was earthy, it spoke of the way she'd let herself go when she was sixteen and writing in this stupid journal pressed to her chest. "Stop using that word."

"Why? Is *passion* too much for you? How about passion for books? Is that allowed? Diana has a passion for gardens. I'll wager you have one for yarn."

"Now you're being ridiculous."

"Well, you felt strongly enough about your shawls to come to Mayfield and ask for help. They're important to you because you make them, with a lot of care and, I'm willing to bet, a passion to get them just so."

"I..." Her voice was dry, a speechless wisp. He'd stolen her words with his twisting talk of passion, with the way he was framing her as a woman she didn't recognize, and the way he was making free with her secret shawl work. "It's not the same."

He laughed. "It's not, and yet, it is. It's about letting yourself go, isn't it? Giving in. Investing yourself entirely."

He was right, she did have a passion, but it wasn't for yarn, however much she enjoyed making those shawls—it was a passion to do something of worth. But how could she admit that to him, a man who might laugh at her dreams? Yet suddenly, she felt so goaded that the words came spilling out of her.

"Do you want to know what I care about? I care about the children of Highcross, the ones whose families can't afford shoes and horses and tutors and even food sometimes. How can I care about my own *pleasure* when people are lacking so much?"

He sucked his teeth, quietly watching her for long moments. She couldn't believe what she'd just said, how bald it sounded—and yet it was also true.

"You're using the money you make from the shawls for somebody else, aren't you?"

She crossed her arms. How had she come to be admitting her most deeply held cares and beliefs, and to such a shallow man? But suddenly she was so tired of the secretiveness, especially over something that she *knew* was good.

"I've been selling the shawls I make to earn money to establish a school for the village girls," she said defiantly. "For girls who would otherwise know nothing of life but caring for other people, doing their sewing and cooking and cleaning. There, are you going to laugh? Will you expose me for being in trade?"

"Of course not," he said quietly. "There is nothing I would mock in what you are doing. It is very good."

Something turned over inside her at the kind, serious way he received her words. A yearning something that made her want to embrace him.

"I would only suggest," he continued, "that amid all the charity you feel for others, you develop some for yourself."

She frowned. "What are you talking about? I have a rich life, everything I need."

He lifted a hand and brushed it against her cheek. "Thou dost protest too much. You are wise about many things, Lily, but in some ways you are very, very young." And he walked past her and quietly through the doorway, leaving her—calm, reasonable Lily—wanting to scream.

What did he know about wisdom, a man who wasted his money on follies and rode horses drunk and read her private journal with no remorse and laughed too much?

She jerked the journal out of her bodice and sat down on her bed, her lips still burning from kissing him and her whole being overcome with fractiousness. She was furiously aware that her room now felt empty as it never had before.

What had happened to her? Somehow he'd left with the upper hand, never mind that the journal was in her possession. And she *missed* being in his arms—in the arms of a man who used his time and considerable funds pursuing pleasure and diversion. And even that—her idea of him—seemed askew now as well.

She was still sitting on her bed when Ian poked his head in her doorway some minutes later. He had the jar of ointment in his hand.

"The oddest thing. I just saw Hal walking off toward the stable, but he forgot this."

"Oh." She forced a smile. Her head felt achy, as if it had been poisoned by too much emotion. The discomfort was no more than she deserved.

"I didn't get the chance to give it to him. He wasn't outside."

Ian looked puzzled. "Can't think what he was doing then."

Oh, she could.

He grinned. "Rob's fairly put out that you asked Hal to investigate the Woods Fiend."

"Well, Hal did agree to investigate, as should have

been done at the outset. So, really, it's just as well I brought it to his attention."

She'd never spoken more ridiculous words, considering the trouble she'd stirred up by speaking to Hal. Nate, for one thing, might have been left to dig in peace and perhaps would have found what he was looking for by now. And she wouldn't be struggling vainly against an overwhelming attraction to Hal.

"Do you think I should send the ointment over to Mayfield?" Ian said.

"I suppose that would be a good idea."

Nate would be eager to get back to digging, and he would still be very much in danger. Maybe more so, now that Hal believed—rightly—that she was in league with the Woods Fiend. If she'd needed proof that Hal didn't want to lose, she'd only to examine how tenacious he'd been about her journal. Nate meant to dig very early tomorrow morning, as they'd planned, and she must be there to watch.

She felt rather less confident about how easy it would be to fool Hal. And not confident at all that she knew what she was doing.

Eight

AT DINNER THAT NIGHT, ROB SAID AS HE CUT INTO HIS meat, "You seem very preoccupied tonight, Lily, and I didn't see you all afternoon. A headache?"

What had happened to her reasonable, ordered life?

"A small one," she replied. "I went for a walk." She pushed her fork into the beef on her plate halfheartedly, not hungry despite the long walk she'd taken in an attempt to clear her head after the incident with Hal. It didn't seem to have had any effect. "It was a nice afternoon."

"I thought it rather buggy," he said. "Did you perhaps meet our local viscount while you were out?"

Her stomach took a wary dip at his words. Did Rob suspect something? "Roxham? Why should I have met him?"

Her brother arched an eyebrow. "Why should he have come to visit you and talk sheep? Perhaps because he is smitten with you?"

"Oh!" said Delia gaily, putting her fork down on her plate with a clatter. "I knew it! I saw him looking at you intently while we were having tea, Lil."

Lily let her eyes drift toward the ceiling in supposed exasperation, but it was equally an effort to appear indifferent. "Such an eagerness to pair me off all of a sudden."

"Of course there's no rush for marriage," Rob said carefully. "But over the last few years you ladies have had little chance for the parties and balls you ought to have enjoyed."

"I don't feel that I've missed anything," Lily said.

"I do!" Delia cried.

"In your case it's understandable, as you never had a Season," Lily said. "I did and am content."

Rob frowned slightly. "I really do think, now that our financial difficulties are behind us, that you both ought to have more opportunities to meet gentlemen."

"I couldn't agree more," Delia said. "As long as they are handsome and eligible."

Ian cocked his head. "But are you sure, brother, that Lord Perfect is the sort of man Lily should be considering? He's always been a bit scandalous, and now he's vowed not to marry until the age of fifty-one, while at the same time enjoying quite a famous popularity among the ladies of the *ton*."

She debated insisting they stop discussing her as if she weren't there, but she could see that Ian was enjoying himself, and she didn't want to display any reaction where Hal was concerned, so she kept quiet.

Rob's square forehead tightened. "I'd forgotten about that not marrying until fifty-one business." Which was entirely believable since Rob had little time for any occupation that didn't involve the running of the estate. Ian, who was far more interested in things like poems and paintings, was the one who took the time to read the paper regularly.

"Surely it's just nonsense?" Rob said.

"I don't know," said Ian. "Now that John has produced heirs for Mayfield, I don't think Hal feels a pressing need for marriage."

"In that case, Lily," Rob said to her, "perhaps you'd better not spend too much time in Hal's company. You wouldn't want to develop a tendre for him."

"Oh for goodness' sake, I'm not going to develop anything for Roxham. He's just the sort of frivolous person to whom I should never wish to attach myself," she said, forcing herself to ignore the conflicted part of her which protested that he made her feel more alive. "And now if we could please have an end to speculating on romantic attachments for me?"

Ian chuckled, and Delia said that she should extremely like to develop a tendre for a handsome man, and Rob said God help them all if she did since she was not in the least sensible, which made everyone laugh.

A storm blew in around midnight, and as the lightning and thunder and winds continued, Lily knew that Nate wouldn't be able to dig in the woods that night, and though she needed the Woods Fiend problem cleared up as soon as possible, she went gratefully to sleep.

She awoke the next morning knowing she'd dreamed of Hal again, which ensured that she started the day vexed.

❧

Hal and Colin had gone out to watch for the Woods Fiend, but it had started pouring rain, and they had to abandon their watch. The next morning it was still raining, keeping everyone inside and making Hal restless.

After breakfast, he tried again to broach the subject of deafness to Prescott, but the estate manager grew shrill and took to his room. Prescott had been a valued servant for decades, and it had always been understood that the viscount would provide a cottage for him at retirement, but he seemed unable to accept that his retirement might be imminent.

Then came a to-do about a portion of the roof in the east wing that was leaking, which Prescott could not attend to because he was sulking in his room. Hal conferred with the housekeeper over the best way to deal with the water and, aware that she had more to do at the moment with Prescott sulking, arranged for the carpenter to see about fixing the problem. After which, Hyacinth wanted everyone to play blind man's bluff.

"Do let's play," she said, swatting him with a posy she'd made for herself from one of the vases of flowers. "I'm bored."

He forced himself to play the genial host, but with Colin keeping to his room because of a sore throat and John playing with his sons, that left Hal alone with the three women. Hyacinth was very happy to be the blind man.

"It's obvious you can see," Eloise accused Hyacinth after Hyacinth ended up blindfolded for a fourth time. "You keep pursuing Hal."

Hyacinth pouted. Hal wondered why he'd never noticed before that Eloise didn't particularly like her, even though Hyacinth only ever wanted a bit of fun. While he was doing his best to keep the peace, he realized that he was missing Lily—reasonable, plain-speaking Lily. She was, though, unlikely to want to see him for the next decade after that scene in her room.

He, on the other hand, had lain awake much of the night remembering how it had felt to have her in his arms. He told himself he had no right to want her as much as he did, and that he'd been deceiving himself into thinking that he could seduce her *just a little bit* so that she'd tell him the identity of the Woods Fiend. He had no business tangling with a gently bred lady.

And though Hyacinth's blindfolded patting left him in no doubt as to what she was offering, he could summon no interest. His own company was starting to infuriate him.

By early afternoon the rain had moved on, and he could stand not another moment in the house. With vague plans about checking on how his Italian folly workers were doing, he escaped and made for the village, where he discovered Giuseppe and Pietro in the The White Dove, drinking ale and playing darts.

He joined them, and by the time a number of pints had been consumed, they'd progressed from darts to a series of unusual wagers, with Hal proposing the one that found them standing at a carefully considered distance from Highcross's small church, which was located just outside the village.

"It has to be done from here," Hal said slowly. The Italians had picked up a decent amount of English, and he knew a little Italian, so they got on with a mixture. "That's the wager."

A burst of too-fast Italian from Giuseppe.

"Well?" Hal said.

Pietro said, "I do it. But if I win and we go back to work on the folly, you will set a guard during we work."

"Agreed," Hal said, wondering where he would get such a person now that Prescott was sulking. Mayfield, being generally uninhabited, didn't have superfluous servants, but surely someone could be found. There must be someone among the locals who wasn't too frightened of the Woods Fiend to stand around and protect a pair of overly anxious builders. He wanted that folly finished... and he liked the idea of how the completed ruin would outrage Lily.

"And I win," Pietro continued, "I get five pounds."

"Right," Hal said.

Pietro grinned. The rock had already been found—it was about the size of an orange—and now Pietro set his sights on his goal: the bell high in the church tower.

"And it has to ring loudly enough for us to hear."

"I am understanding," Pietro said.

He cocked his arm and was just releasing the stone when a female voice rang out.

"What do you think you're doing?"

But it was too late, as it had already been done. The stone, released at the moment that Pietro was startled, shot not toward the church bell, but sailed far below, through the round stained-glass window of St. Luke above the church door.

Horrified silence, then Pietro whispered, "Madre di Dio."

The men turned to face the woman who'd spoken, though Hal already knew who it was.

"Lily."

She was holding a market basket and wearing a simple soft gray gown that fit her neatly; it was the sort of thing a matron might wear. Tidy, presentable, in no way alluring. She dressed as though her femininity were something to hide, but her prim clothes only distracted him with thoughts of the secret curves underneath.

"What on earth are you doing throwing rocks at the church?"

"The rock was intended for the bell, but as you distracted Pietro, he missed. I will, of course, pay for a new window." He could feel the Italians slipping away behind him.

"What a thing for grown men to be doing. And you a viscount and a leader in our community."

"It was a reasonable enough idea until someone startled Pietro," he said. "In any case, it was for a wager, an attempt to get them to come back to work on the folly."

Her neat, pale eyebrows rose as though he'd said something depraved. She was almost too easy to shock. "So you've destroyed the church window in an attempt to get your folly built."

"In a manner of speaking. But come, it was a hideous window anyway. St. Luke looked as though he'd just sucked a lemon."

The corner of her mouth quivered for a moment, but she forced it back into seriousness.

"Shouldn't you go find the vicar and confess what you've done?"

"He's away—someone said so in The Dove. If

you're going home, wait a few minutes for me to leave a note and I'll walk with you."

She frowned slightly. "I don't have time to wait."

"But surely you have more time to yourself now that the shawl business is at a standstill."

"I have other things to do as well," she said. He could see she was trying to edge away from him, but he refused to acknowledge it.

"I'm sure you do. Probably a long, neatly written list."

Mrs. Trelawny, the vicar's housekeeper, appeared just then, coming around the corner of the church with a basket of folded linens. She started to smile at the visitors, but her eyes widened as she caught sight of the broken window.

"Dear heaven, what's happened?" she said.

Hal cleared his throat. "I'm afraid there was a mishap with a rock, Mrs. Trelawny. Entirely my fault. Will you please convey my regrets to the vicar on his return, and tell him that I will replace the window? I would also like to discuss with him a bequest in my brother's name."

Mrs. Trelawny's dismay melted away. "Why, my lord, I'm certain he'll be pleased." She blushed, and Hal smiled at her, confident of the effect it would have. "I mean," she babbled, laughing a little, "not that the window is broken, but I'm sure everyone will understand. Accidents happen. You are very good, my lord."

"He's not," Lily muttered under her breath.

They bid Mrs. Trelawny good day and began walking.

"I wasn't planning to walk with you," she said.

"It's good to do impulsive things. You seemed to be feeling impulsive yesterday."

"I don't want to talk about that. And you ought to be ashamed, breaking church windows and throwing money around and charming matrons. It's all so easy for you, isn't it? You just smile, and people let you get away with anything."

He shrugged. "She's happy, and Vicar will be happy when I've given him a large donation."

"So easy for you. Easy to avoid paying any real price."

He kicked hard at a rock in his path. "You know, Lily, I've been wondering why it was that my brother wasn't the one who interested you. He was such an admirable person and handsome, too. A knight in shining armor. Why didn't you write about him in your journal?"

Lily shifted the basket full of apples on her arm and wished she hadn't lingered talking with Anna Cooper, but they'd needed to fix another meeting time for the girls to come for a lesson.

Hal's question unsettled her. She'd liked his brother very much and respected him, but for some reason she couldn't explain, Hal, with his mischief and his flashing eyes, was the one who had fascinated her.

"Obviously I was too young to know any better."

He laughed. "And now?"

"Now?"

"Meaning yesterday?"

"I told you it was just a mistake. I got carried away."

"It was your first kiss, wasn't it?"

She could feel the blush spreading over her face. "Why are you plaguing me about it?"

"Because I think you would be happier if you let yourself enjoy things now and again."

"Things? If I kissed men in my bedroom frequently, I would be held up as a loose woman."

"I didn't necessarily mean kisses. I'm not suggesting you start kissing other men."

They'd reached the pebble path that led to the gate to Thistlethwaite, and they stopped. She sighed. "That journal was a mistake in my path—it doesn't mean anything. Nor did what happened yesterday. We shall simply have to go on as if it never happened."

There, she thought as she walked up the path, she was glad they'd had that conversation, because now everything was clear and sorted. All done. She wouldn't think about him anymore.

Except for making certain she and Nate outsmarted him while Nate was digging in the Mayfield woods, which he would be doing that very night.

᎑

Hal lay in bed unable to sleep. It was perhaps four o'clock in the morning and he ought to be damned tired after standing around the woods again that night with Colin, who was, he suspected, growing weary of their fruitless watch. Hal was growing weary of it, too, and was enormously annoyed that their trespasser had slipped through his hands that first time and had since been absent. Of course, the Woods Fiend's absence might mean he'd already been scared off, but Hal couldn't feel satisfied since the man hadn't been caught.

And there was the wager. According to its vague terms, he might capture the Woods Fiend any way he liked, the most obvious way now being to get Lily to reveal him, but he'd failed so far at that, and now he didn't even have the journal for leverage.

Though none of these were the main reason he couldn't sleep, which was that he couldn't stop thinking about Lily. He'd wanted to kiss her again today while they were walking to Thistlethwaite, despite everything she was saying to him.

She was so different from other women he knew, with her purposeful ways and her plans and her lack of interest in diversions. And her primness, her strangely fascinating collectedness that made him want to probe what was beneath it. He'd glimpsed a bewitching inner fire when he kissed her.

In many ways she had more courage than any woman he'd ever met—except in this: she wanted to pretend that she didn't want him just as much now as she had four years before. And she would not own that the person she'd been was part of her.

But what did he intend where Lily was concerned? She was a very *good* young lady of good family.

He didn't deserve such goodness.

That's all you're ever after, isn't it? she'd said when he kissed her. *An amusement for the moment. Something to kill the boredom of having everything you want or need already.*

She had a way of cutting to the heart of things.

He found himself thinking of a place he'd visited during the war, a Spanish monastery where he and some of his men had taken shelter for two nights. The monks observed a vow of silence, and he'd at first felt intensely restless in his little monk's cell. But then, as the hours passed, the restlessness that was always with him had started to flow out of him, as if the silence were a sharpness that pared away all the residue of action and pleasure with which his life was filled. Who he was outside the monastery walls mattered not; he was simply a man there.

He had also been relieved to leave after two days.

But lately he'd been thinking he might welcome the bracing experience of confining himself to a monastery for a month. Which was ridiculous, because he could never sit still that long. He'd never been good at order and expectation; it was one of the things his father had most disparaged about him.

It's lucky for us that Everard was the firstborn, his father would say whenever another of Hal's sins had come to light. *If it had been Hal, the whole viscountcy would have come to ruin.* And Hal had been glad, too, that Everard was the firstborn. His brother didn't need to get drunk, or stay up late, or ride his horse too fast, or overspend his allowance.

The sheet had become tangled around his legs and he kicked it off impatiently and pushed aside his thoughts. He might as well get up and get some work done in his library.

As he stood by the window pulling on his shirt, the moon was but a thin crescent. Across the dark land, something caught his eye. A flicker.

Light.

He grabbed his boots.

Taking the stairs by twos, he passed through the doors to the terrace and vaulted over a row of bushes. Running across garden paths and then the open field to the west, he kept his eyes trained on the glimmer in the woods. The sound of an owl hooting softly several times registered as slightly odd, but he didn't realize why until the light in the woods began to jiggle and then went out.

A warning for the Fiend, dammit.

And though he tried to cut the Fiend off by going around the north end of the woods, by the time dawn was breaking Hal had to admit defeat again.

Fuming, he turned for home. As he passed by the rocky thicket that stood off from the woods, something caught his eye, fluttering among the branches of a thorn bush, and he pulled it free: a scrap of fine blue fabric. He held it to his nose.

Violets. Lily.

So he knew, at least, the identity of the Fiend's sentinel.

He put the square of cloth in his pocket, so frustrated—so very *teased*—by her. Turnabout, he admitted reluctantly, being that he was accustomed to being the teaser. She was leading him a merry chase—and one he wouldn't allow to continue.

Rule number one in his strategy book was to completely unsettle the enemy so they lost faith in their plans.

Lily closed her bedchamber door behind her and sagged against it. She'd warned Nate that someone was coming and then fled her hiding place, ripping her dress in the process. But at least she felt confident that he would have gotten home safely. Gray dawn light was spilling into the room as she took off her torn gown and hid it in her wardrobe.

She fell asleep tormented by thoughts of strong shoulders and blue-green eyes, and woke up hours later, feeling rather poisoned, to a vigorous knocking. Delia burst exuberantly into the room.

"Oh! You're still in bed? With the Mayfield ball tomorrow? It's so unlike you to sleep late."

Lily mumbled something about how it wasn't going to take her a day and a half to dress.

"But you don't have a day and a half, because Roxham just sent over an invitation for us to join his house party!" Delia's eyes sparkled far too brightly for so early in the day. "And Rob accepted! Oh, isn't it wonderful?"

Lily sat up. "Wonderful?"

"Yes!" Delia said, missing the note of dismay in her sister's voice. "We're to go after lunch today. Rob says it's a perfect opportunity to reacquaint ourselves with society."

She flopped back on the bed so that her head came to rest next to Lily's on the pillow. "Ivorwood will be there, and I can't wait to meet him after all Eloise has said about him."

Delia propped her head up on her hand. "I wonder who the other guests will be. I imagine everyone will be marvelously elegant. Oh, how merry we will be!"

"Merry," Lily repeated numbly. "You don't suppose Rob would be pleased if I declined?"

"Decline? Why on earth would you want to do that? And when we've had no chance of anything like this for simply years! Anyway, that would look like a tremendous snub, you not coming. And why?"

Delia finally paused to breathe and Lily hid a smile.

"I... thought I might work on a new dye."

"A *dye*? Don't be absurd. You can fool with your dyes any old time." Delia frowned. "You're not going to get moralistic about this, are you, and say it's a waste of money or time or something? That we ought not to associate with aristocrats because they have no souls?"

"Nor do they."

Delia groaned. "Oh, get up, Lil! We have packing to do, and there's no time to lose!" She skipped out of the room.

Lily made herself get up. Hal was up to something, inviting her family to stay, and she had a good idea of what it was: he wanted to keep her under his thumb so she wouldn't be able to help the Woods Fiend.

Bowing to the inevitable, she put out her things for the house party at Mayfield. She also sent a note to Nate at the farm, telling him he should wait to try again in the woods, if indeed his efforts the night before had been unsuccessful. With the extra people who would be roaming the Mayfield property for the next few days, he couldn't afford to be in those woods.

And then, while her siblings were seeing to various other details, she took Buck and headed for the yarn house.

She took the stone path through the garden, where the last of the yellow roses bloomed alongside Michaelmas daisies. The fresh autumn air swept away some of her lethargy. Beyond the edge of the garden, the paving stones sank at odd angles in the lawn, softened by time and moss, and she hopped across them with renewed energy.

At the yarn house she dusted and tidied, then pulled

a chair outside into the shade of the old apple tree and sat with Buck curled at her feet, working the yarn just for the pleasure of it. When had she last done that, with no urgency to make the shawls faster and achieve her goals for the school sooner?

Her life was here, amid the yarn and sheep, dreaming of new ways to use color and patterns, and making plans for the school. She *mustn't* lose this path she'd claimed for herself. She wasn't made for lighthearted romps, and if she allowed herself to be seduced by pleasures she was used to denying herself, who would she be?

Nine

THE TEAGARDENS ARRIVED AT MAYFIELD IN MID-afternoon. While Lily saw to the unpacking of her things in the grand bedchamber she'd been assigned, shouts drifted in her open window, drawing her attention.

Looking out, she saw two gentlemen on horseback racing hell for leather across the open land to the east. They were neck and neck, but approaching a hedgerow as tall as a man, which must force them to go around.

As she watched, one rider—a fair-haired man who could only be Hal—went straight at the impossible obstacle and jumped over, the horse's back legs brushing the top of the brambles. It was a mad, unnecessary thing to do, and she was still standing there incredulously when Delia knocked on the door a few minutes later.

"Hurry up, Lily, we're missing all the fun. Ian and Rob have already gone down to the terrace."

The race was apparently over; she could see the horses coming in at a trot, and she'd no doubt as to who'd won. As if she wanted to go down and listen to Hal's praises being sung. But she could hardly hide in her room.

Eloise saw them as soon as they emerged onto the terrace and came rushing to welcome them. She was wearing a silky, sapphire-blue gown the exact shade of blue her eyes were, and her glossy brown hair had been arranged in an elaborate, pretty style.

"Darlings! Here you are, and just look at your beautiful shawls!"

Lily's shawl was an apple green made from foxglove dye, a bright accent against her cream gown, which had tiny gold embroidered flowers. She hadn't worn the gown since she was sixteen, and it had been tight in the bosom when she'd tried it on, so she'd inserted panels under her arms. Delia's shawl was the soft cream of Rosemary's wool, a pretty complement to her dark yellow morning gown.

Delia thanked her and said they were Thistlethwaite shawls.

A shadow of concern passed over Eloise's pretty features. "I do hope the Woods Fiend will be found soon."

"I'm sure," Delia said, "that with the viscount and the earl on the hunt, it can't be long before the problem is resolved."

"Exactly!" said Eloise. "My brother is nothing if not tenacious."

She shot Lily a look of concern. "Though I don't want him to be tenacious about that journal of yours."

"Actually, it's been returned to me."

"Oh, good," Eloise said, looking very relieved. "I'm so glad he gave it back."

Lily just smiled.

"Can I see it?" Delia said.

"I've always wished I would keep a journal," said Eloise, whose expression suggested she'd like to see it as well. "It must be fascinating to read years later."

"It's not fascinating," Lily said. "Let us say that it was never meant for anyone else's eyes."

"Oh, very well," Delia said, "but I feel deprived."

Eloise linked her arms through each of theirs, and they started walking toward where a cluster of gentlemen stood talking and calling things to the riders, who were approaching the terrace.

"You won't believe this," she said, "since hostesses are forever short on unmarried men, but with all the single men my brother knows, there's almost nothing but gentlemen here for the house party."

Delia's eyes danced. "But this is terribly interesting!"

"It would be," Eloise said, "if some of them had any conversation. But mostly they want to discuss The Thrill of the Hunt. Of course, Ivorwood doesn't participate in such oafish behavior. *He*," she said in a lowered voice, "is all that is divine."

"I can't wait to see him," Delia said.

"He's just a man like any other man, Delia," Lily said.

"Oh Lily," Delia said exasperatedly. "You'd probably want him to do an act of charity before you agreed to talk to him."

As they walked out into the garden, Lily wondered what Delia would think if she ever learned how easy it was for her older sister to be reckless, at least where Hal was concerned. She hated being at the whim of her emotions—it made her feel like a person adrift in a small boat on the open sea. The foolhardy, dreamy girl she'd been years ago *wasn't* who she was now, and even if being in his arms had felt thrilling and each sight of his golden smile made something turn over inside her, she still didn't accept that that passion-drugged, irresponsible person was who she truly was. She didn't *choose* to be that person.

Eloise pointed Ivorwood out to Delia. Now that she had a chance to consider him properly, Lily had to admit that Eloise didn't exaggerate his appeal. He was tall, his build a bit larger than Hal's, and he had glossy black hair and a large, commanding nose.

But it was Hal, whose horse stood at the edge of the terrace, to whom her eyes were drawn. Sitting astride his black charger, his gold hair shining in the sun and a maroon coat gracing his broad shoulders, he looked magnificent, and it was but a small leap to imagine him in his scarlet uniform, ready to lead his troops into battle.

Eloise tugged them toward the group of gentlemen standing near him. Diana and Mrs. Whyte sat at a stone table nearby with small plates of cake, apparently enjoying the entertainment. Mrs. Whyte giggled loudly and called out comments to the men.

Hal caught Lily's eye as she walked toward the edge of the terrace near where his horse stood. The height of the terrace meant that her shoulders were above his knee, and she could easily see the gleam of delighted triumph in his eyes.

"Aren't you going to congratulate me, Lily? I've just bested Donwell here." His racing companion, an auburn-haired man, sat astride a chestnut horse several feet away, smiling ruefully.

"You took an enormous risk jumping that hedgerow," Lily said to Hal. "Most horses couldn't handle it."

"Ah, but Emperor can."

Smug titters echoed around her. Mrs. Whyte called out, "No one has a better seat than Roxham. *Seat*, ha ha!"

There were shouts of *hear, hear,* and more laughter, and Hal gave the pretty widow a jaunty salute.

Rob shot Lily a glance. "Lily," he said, "Roxham knows what he's about."

Emperor took a few small, prancing steps, coming closer to Lily. "It's risky and you know it," she said to Hal. "That's why you did it."

"Are you expressing concern for my well-being, Lily?"

"Not at all," she said and smiled. "I'm merely pointing out that if you maim or kill yourself, it will have an effect on those who depend on you. But perhaps they would prefer John as viscount anyway."

Whoops of masculine laughter greeted this comment, and Lily turned away from him, a little pleased with herself.

From behind her she heard, "For that, Lily, you will have to pay." And the next instant a strong arm encircled her waist and pulled her neatly backward and up as she yelped in surprise. And then she was sitting sidesaddle in front of Hal, with everyone on the patio shouting and laughing in approval.

Through clenched teeth Lily said, "Put me down."

"Not on your life," he said, his arm still snug around her waist. Emperor took off.

Lily shrieked and thrust her arm around Hal and clutched the back of his coat.

"Let me down!"

He only laughed and spurred Emperor into a gallop.

The chilly wind whipped strands of hair across her face and tore at her shawl. She never rode this fast. Turning her face to him, she shouted above the rushing wind, "It's not safe!"

"Nothing could be safer!" he shouted back, giving her waist an extra squeeze.

"Anything would be safer!"

And then they jumped a small bush and she was screaming into the wind, yelling from deep in her chest and not stopping. And as they raced over the land, his arm tightly around her and the powerful animal beneath them and her lungs filling with air for each new scream, she began to feel that she was releasing something—an elemental thing she couldn't name, something that had built up in her with no escape until now.

At some point it occurred to her that, against all reason, she did feel safe. But she kept screaming, to let him know she was mad—and because it felt strangely good.

They were approaching a stand of trees, and he finally slowed the horse.

"You can stop screaming now." His voice was a deep rumble behind her, tinged annoyingly with mirth.

She caught her breath. "You shouldn't have done that. What will people think?" Her arm was still wrapped around him and at some point she'd grabbed a handful of the back of his maroon coat. She ought to let go and move her arm, but his solidity and strength and warmth felt too good, and she wasn't ready.

"They'll think I was cutting a caper as usual. You made a convincing victim. Their ears are probably still recovering. I know mine are."

"Only what you deserve."

"I don't suppose you'll admit that it made you feel more alive."

"Certainly not," she said, though it had. She fought the urge to droop against him and rest her cheek against his chest. This was just the sort of romp in which she shouldn't be engaged, but she was too limp to scold herself for enjoying his nearness.

He glanced at her. "If you look at me like that, I'll have no choice but to kiss you."

"Uh…" She was barely able to think. "No," she said weakly. She made herself let go of his coat now, and she moved her arm to her lap. He still had an arm clamped around her, so it wasn't as if she would fall off.

"You say no a lot. With your words, your eyes, your posture. I can only think it's a constant refrain in your mind."

She frowned.

"And now you're frowning. I wonder, Lily Teagarden, if you have any idea how it feels to have you sitting between my legs. It would make a good beginning to a fantasy."

His wicked words sent a rush of heat through her; she was trying *not* to think about where she was sitting.

They were drawing closer to Mayfield, and she could just pick out the contrast of Delia's cream shawl against her dress. Everyone there appeared to be watching them. It was embarrassing, but it also meant that she wouldn't be tempted to *do* anything she shouldn't. But words were a different realm, and she wanted to pay him back for taking her on this wild ride against her will, even though she'd loved it.

"A fantasy? Like a fairy tale?" she said innocently.

"A sexual fantasy. Like people sometimes write in their journals." He smirked.

Ha. She shifted her seat and pressed a bit closer to the juncture of his thighs, thinking that perhaps this might have some effect on him. She was rewarded with a groan. Never mind that touching him like this was making her blood race.

"Oh, you mean like *my* journal. I'm guessing you didn't get to read the whole thing, or you might have read about something happening on horseback."

He made a choking sound. "*Is* there a scene on horseback?"

So he hadn't finished it. "I really shouldn't say. Possibilities are interesting though, aren't they?"

He pulled her hard against him, and there was no mistaking what pressed against her thigh. Or the pleasure she felt over what her nearness had done to him. But they were getting close to the terrace now—she could see Delia waving, and she waved back and called hello, playing the cheerful victim of a harmless prank. The sound of teeth gnashing drifted over her head.

"You know," he said, "this is just the kind of adventure you would have scolded me for when we were children."

"I'm scolding you now, and you care just as much."

"You used to be such a funny girl. So serious already at thirteen or so—quite the grown woman. I remember being home from university one time, and you happened upon Rob and me plotting some prank to pull in the village." He chuckled. "You told us that you didn't have time for that sort of foolishness anymore."

She remembered the conversation, and—considering the heavy demands on her at home then—how she'd felt that she could no longer be part of the play and fun when her brothers could. Her brothers might have noticed their father's drinking on the occasions when they were home, but everybody behaved as though it were just Papa being convivial. The details of daily life had never been her brothers' affair when Papa was alive.

She pushed the old inappropriate resentment away. Once their father had died, Rob and Ian had come home and taken over and done everything to help the family. How could she fault them for what had happened when they all were younger?

"You were twenty at least, perhaps twenty-two," she said. "Much too old for pranks."

"Some of us are never too old for pranks. And some of us are too ready to grow old."

She had no light reply for that, and she leaned away from him, glad that the terrace was just before them.

They dismounted. As the guests surrounded them, cheerful talk of similar capers led to recitations of Hal's exploits: how he'd swum across the Thames in the middle of the night on a dare, how there was a list of women who loved him scratched into the woodwork of the ladies' retiring room at Almack's in London.

But Lily didn't want to listen or to watch him smiling at pretty Hyacinth Whyte, and she moved closer to Delia and Eloise.

They were talking with Ivorwood and the auburn-haired man, Mr. Donwell. Lily thought the earl seemed to keep himself apart; for someone who was a particular friend of Hal's, he was a man of notably few smiles or words. She supposed a man as handsome and wealthy as Ivorwood had little need to put himself to the trouble of conversing if he didn't wish to.

Mr. Donwell interested her more. He was handsome, his short hair curling around his face in a rough, charming way that had nothing to do with pomade, and his dark brown eyes had a steady, intelligent light. His clothes, though, did not work to his advantage; his brown coat was faded, and dust smudged the knees of his bagging breeches, as if he'd recently been kneeling somewhere dirty.

But his smile was sincere, and he told a brief, drily amusing anecdote about a trip to the Lake District. Lily imagined that, with his unpolished looks, he didn't draw ladies' attention the way someone like Hal or the earl would. It was most unfair, being that he was doubtless more deserving.

She noticed that his eyes were frequently drawn to Eloise, which Eloise, busy adoring Ivorwood, didn't notice at all.

"Ivorwood," Eloise said, "have you seen the folly by the lake yet?"

The earl, who apparently hadn't heard her, turned to address a remark to Delia, and Eloise's smile faded.

Poor Eloise, with her affection for a man who hardly noticed her, even while there were other doubtless more worthy men whom she was overlooking. Lily felt an urge to help open Eloise's eyes.

"Eloise," she said, "the white rose bush behind the bench over there is so lovely—it would make a wonderful backdrop for a poetic scene. I wonder if you would do me the favor of sitting with a gentleman—Mr. Donwell, perhaps? So I might make a sketch."

Eloise looked rightly puzzled by this sudden request, and Mr. Donwell was clearly surprised, but his ready response suggested he was not unhappily surprised.

"I should be delighted to assist, Miss Teagarden. That is, if Miss Waverly consents."

What could Eloise say? She agreed. Lily could feel Delia and Hal looking at her askance, but she ignored them and fixed a time later that afternoon for the sitting.

As conversation turned to the latest fashions in London, about which Hal seemed to know far more than any man she'd ever met, Lily congratulated herself on finding an activity to occupy her mind and keep it away from thoughts of Hal: she'd help Eloise see that the subtle, kind Donwell was a far better suitor than the out-of-reach Earl of Ivorwood.

Ten

IT WAS LATE AFTERNOON WHEN HAL SLIPPED AWAY from Mayfield and made a quick, surreptitious trip to Thistlethwaite. The housekeeper was flustered by such an august personage as the viscount arriving while the family was not at home, but she had no objections to showing him to Miss Teagarden's room, where he'd been sent, he told her, to retrieve a book. He found Lily's journal quickly and was gone with a smile on his face.

Touché, Lily girl, he thought as his horse made its way back to Mayfield. He let the animal walk and allowed himself a few minutes to read.

Which was perhaps a mistake. As he slowly deciphered, each of her words became like a little hammer hitting a pulse within him.

I dream of him touching me, of him pressing his lips to my cheek, the nape of my neck. Of him pulling my gown from the top of my shoulders, down my arms, exposing where my skin is pale and tender. I want so much to know what his lips would feel like.

In my dreams his hands are around my waist, holding

me tight because he doesn't ever want to let me go. I would place my hands flat against his chest and feel the thump of his heart, beating strong and steady and only for me.

Muttering a curse, he closed the book, finding himself uncomfortably astride for the second time that day with an erection. Lily was giving him the worst case of frustrated desire he'd ever endured. Along with the ridiculous idea that if only she would allow him in a little, some of her goodness would rub off on him.

He spurred his horse into a gallop and vaulted over an enormous tree stump and several hedgerows on his way to the stables.

❦

On the terrace at Mayfield, Lily was ready to begin sketching Eloise and Donwell. Eloise sat on the bench with her arms resting on her lap, her graceful white hands a pretty contrast to the silky sapphire fabric of her gown. Her head was tipped up and to the side in a classical pose that Lily had intended to give Eloise ample chance to converse with Donwell.

He was standing at the end of the bench in a slightly bent, attentive posture. His faded brown coat was not right for a pretty sketch, but clothes were a detail of little importance, and Lily easily imagined him into a richer hue as she put her pencil to the paper. The afternoon sunshine lit fiery glints in his curling auburn hair that would have befitted a poet, and she began her sketch with his head.

After a few quiet minutes, Donwell addressed himself to Eloise, much to Lily's delight.

"I would very much like to hear about your trip

to the Continent this year, Miss Waverly." He had a deep, smooth voice and a precise manner of speaking, as if he chose his words carefully.

Eloise was staring across the terrace in her pose, and her eyes were fixed on Ivorwood, who stood just inside the open doors that led into the library. She did not reply.

Donwell waited a moment, then, apparently assuming she hadn't heard him, repeated himself. Eloise still didn't respond, and Lily perceived with a sinking heart that the girl could pay attention to nothing beyond Ivorwood. Apparently Donwell had discerned this as well, because he said nothing further.

But a minute later Eloise seemed to come to her senses, perhaps because he'd used her name. "Did you say something, Mr. Donwell?" she asked.

"I was merely asking after your trip to the Continent. I was there myself in June, to visit a German friend who's made a remarkable new telescope."

"Oh?" Eloise said. "What's different about this new telescope?"

"It's bigger than anyone's ever made before, and it should allow us to see the heavens much more clearly." He paused. "I believe, Miss Waverly, that you once professed an interest in the stars."

Lily wondered, as her pencil described the tip of Eloise's blue satin shoe, how well these two knew each other. If they had some history together, that might make things complicated.

"Hmm..." Eloise said. "Stars." She sounded so vague all of a sudden that Lily glanced up from her work and saw with dismay that Eloise's face had assumed a daft look. And she had no trouble guessing the reason for it—Ivorwood had passed through the doors onto the terrace and was now standing talking with Diana.

"You were saying?" Donwell prompted, but Eloise's only reply was a sigh, and it wasn't long before his eyes followed the direction of hers.

"Your gown is on fire, Miss Waverly," he said in a conversational tone, making Lily blink before she realized that his intention was merely to see if Eloise was paying attention. Several silent moments passed, during which Lily tried to think of something to say as Eloise stared longingly at the earl. But then Ivorwood moved back into the library, and the spell was broken.

"What was that you were saying?" Eloise finally said.

"Merely a remark on your gown," he replied.

"Oh, do you like it?" Her customary charming enthusiasm erased any hint of fishing for compliments. Lily was happy to see that Donwell smiled a little, though the turn of his lips had something knowing about it, and he seemed to consider her question more than such a light topic required.

"It suits you very well, but you already know that, or you wouldn't have chosen it."

Eloise's brow drew together slightly, and Lily couldn't blame her. What kind of conversation was this?

"For shame, Mr. Donwell. Do you mean to suggest I am conceited?"

"Not excessively. You are simply well aware of your many charms."

Eloise's cheeks turned pink, but when she spoke, she managed a playfully scolding tone. "Are you often so severe on ladies, Mr. Donwell? You'll make your-self unpopular with the fairer sex."

"I'm not interested in being popular," he said. "Or in playing games with people."

Lily could only like him better for his seriousness, but Eloise was looking uncharacteristically stiff, her pretty chin tipping higher in the air and spoiling the composition of their pose. Lily tried to catch her gaze, but it was already trained, with a surprisingly hard glint, on Donwell.

"Games?" Eloise said. "Is there some hidden meaning in your words?"

"No."

"Do tell, then, Mr. Donwell," Eloise said, "what you are interested in, if it is not the company of ladies."

"I never said I didn't like the company of ladies. What I dislike is the frequent lack of substance they display."

"Substance!" Eloise said, standing up.

"The pose…" Lily implored without much hope.

"What do you know about substance?" Eloise continued. "You haven't even got a proper coat!"

A wicked tilt tugged at the edges of Donwell's mouth, which made Lily think he didn't truly despair of Eloise's *substance*. "I'm afraid that's all the time I have for posing today," he said mildly. "I hope you've had adequate time to sketch, Miss Teagarden."

While Eloise's dark blue eyes shot sparks, he dipped his head politely and took his leave.

"What an arrogant, horrible man!" Eloise said as soon as he was out of earshot.

"I rather like him," Lily said.

"Like him! How could you? He insulted me!"

"I'm not certain he did, actually," Lily said. "I think perhaps he admires your mind."

Eloise looked taken aback at this, as though her mind were not the sort of thing gentlemen should be admiring, but just then Diana called out, "Anyone for billiards? We're getting up teams, and so far Rob and Ian and Ivorwood are playing."

Lily watched as Eloise fairly sprinted for the doors, calling, "I'm in!"

She sighed, thinking that Eloise's eyes might only truly be opened by time.

"That went well, don't you think?"

She hadn't realized Hal was on the terrace, and she turned around to see him looking smug.

"Where did you come from?"

"I was out riding. And missing your matchmaking fun, apparently."

"What do you mean?"

"Eloise and Donwell, obviously."

How had he guessed?

He laughed, and the sun glinted enchantingly off his white teeth, as if to indicate everything he said was magical. She wanted to growl at him and embrace him all at once. She crossed her arms.

"You were hardly subtle earlier, asking out of the blue if they'd pose for you. It wasn't as if you offered any of the other men the chance to pose with her."

"There was only you and Ivorwood."

"As I am her brother, that ruled me out. And avoiding Ivorwood was the whole point, wasn't it?"

She pressed her lips and watched as Maisy, the stable cat, sauntered over and began making adoring figure eights around his ankles. "It's heartrending the way she wants him to notice her when he won't."

"Is it just heartrending, or is it also familiar?"

She tipped her chin up. "Don't flatter yourself. Anyway, you know very well the earl isn't interested in her."

"No, he isn't. But she's only sixteen. These things happen."

And they scar you forever, Lily thought.

"Sixteen is young," she said, "but soon she'll be making a choice for a husband. Don't you think she deserves a considerate, attentive gentleman who would make her the apple of his eye?"

"And you thought that tractable exemplar would be Gregory Donwell?"

She didn't like the smug glitter of humor in his eyes, and it only made her want to prove him wrong. "Perhaps the posing didn't go well, but that doesn't mean they wouldn't suit."

"And perhaps I don't see Donwell as the ideal escort for my sister."

"Nonsense, he would be perfect for her," she said, aware that she was saying far more than she believed to be true—she hardly knew either of them. But certainly she knew more of human nature and real human connection than a viscount who spent his time playing escort to women he never intended to marry.

"We shall have to agree to disagree, then," he said, "and let true love take its own course."

"But what if it's a foolish course? Eloise has no father or mother to guide her. Your brother and Diana have their own household to preoccupy them. That leaves you."

"She's sixteen and capable—why should she need guidance from me?"

"The choices she makes in these years will affect her entire life."

"I should think you of all people would agree I'm the last person to guide her."

"Perhaps guiding her would inspire you to become a model of propriety. And if you weren't so busy flirting with Mrs. Whyte all the time, you might have thought of a suitable young man for Eloise to notice."

His mouth curled into the kind of grin that had doubtless melted the heart of every last woman he'd ever met. "I'm flattered that you've been paying enough attention to notice with whom I'm flirting. Though for your information, Hyacinth is also very interested in flirting with your brothers and the earl."

"Then I suppose you will have to content yourself with Maisy," she said, leaving him with a puzzled look as she marched back inside through the French doors, more determined than ever to help Eloise see that the world did not revolve around a man who couldn't truly care for her.

Eleven

WHEN LILY AND DELIA ENTERED THE MAYFIELD GALLERY before dinner that evening, their brothers were already there with the other guests milling about the long room, talking and drinking sherry. Enormous portraits of Hal's ancestors lined the red walls, glowing like coins in their gold frames, while stately gilded chairs below stood ready for fashionable occupants. Above a fireplace that could have held a cow, an enormous plaster frieze depicted the goddess Diana hunting.

As Lily and Delia passed the hearth, a footman approached with a tray of sherry. Delia took one. "I wonder if this frieze is new," she said. "The folds of Diana's toga are so crisp."

"I wish I had a toga to cover this bodice," Lily muttered, declining the sherry with a wave. Her pale yellow gown, which she hadn't worn since her Season, had seemed to fit when she'd tried it on briefly, but the neckline was lower than she was used to wearing, and now she was finding that every time she breathed, it pushed her bosom higher. "I shall go upstairs and change."

"Don't be such a schoolmistress type," Delia said. "Gentlemen like softness in a woman."

"What do you know about what men like? You've been shut up at Thistlethwaite your entire life."

"I've read reams of novels. They've taught me all about human nature."

"Heaven help us."

Delia didn't seem to have any qualms about showing her own bosom, which was displayed to advantage in a spring green and white striped gown with a matching green ribbon threaded through a pearl around her neck. She linked her arm with Lily's and pulled her toward the rest of the party.

"Well, Hal," Rob was saying to the others as Lily and Delia drew near, "have you had any success in your hunt for the Fiend of Mayfield Wood, or whatever it is you are calling your ghostly spirit?"

"I call it vexing, as it has escaped me twice."

"I'm sure we'd all love to know who this Woods Fiend is," said Miss Marianne Preston, the pretty daughter of a local bishop. "Though perhaps he's terrifying. Think of how brave your great-uncle was all those years ago, my lord—sacrificing himself trying to rescue that young lady."

How Lily wanted to set things straight, to say that it hadn't been a rescue at all but a lovers' meeting. However, that would only invite displeasure from those who wouldn't want to think of a nobleman attached to a farmer's daughter.

"At least we know our quarry is human," Hal said, reaching into his pocket and pulling out a swatch of familiar fabric, "and that he's working with an accomplice. I found this caught in a bush last night."

Hal's eyes, resting on hers, held a knowing look. She gave him a little smirk.

"Rather odd stuff for men's clothing," Eloise said, peering at the cloth.

"Perhaps it's fifty years old," Lily said. "Like the Fiend."

Something flickered in Hal's eye, seeming to threaten retaliation for her part in helping the Fiend escape him. The thought of him retaliating shouldn't be appealing, but it was.

He waved a hand toward the hearth at the other end of the gallery. "What do you think of our new frieze?" he said. "It was done by the same craftsmen who are working on the folly. Or who were, until they heard about the Woods Fiend."

"Isn't it too bad they're too frightened to finish?" Eloise said.

Miss Preston asked to see the frieze and Rob attentively led her away, followed by the others. Lily knew it would be wiser to go look at it some more, rather than stand there with Hal, but she couldn't seem to make herself leave.

"You don't wish to see the frieze?" Hal asked her.

"I've already seen it."

"And did you like it?"

"It's pretty, certainly. A folly and a frieze. What's next, wallpaper?"

"The family's hardly been here over the last year and the manor needs freshening up. Anyway, *I* like friezes, so what else matters?"

When she didn't reply he said, "Aren't you going to run off then?"

"Run off? Why should I run from you?"

"Because I remind you of things you don't like about yourself. That you are a woman who likes to be kissed, for one thing."

A memory of their horseback ride and how she'd felt both exhilaratingly wild and utterly safe in his arms made her want to listen to him, to be in his arms again and to say yes to everything he'd ask her. But she couldn't. "You are mistaking things again. I'm not like that. Not truly."

He laughed. "You can tell yourself that—it doesn't make it true."

She frowned and looked away from him toward the walls and changed the subject.

"I notice that all the men in that row of paintings are wearing that same ring, except for the last man." The ring was distinctive—made of thick gold, its heavy setting held a large, square ruby.

He gave her a look that said he knew why she'd changed the subject. "That's because the ring was lost some time ago. It always went to the second son. I spent a lot of my childhood on quests to find it."

The group of guests looking at the frieze had moved across the long room, so that Lily and Hal were quite by themselves. But now she was curious; she knew little about his family.

"Were you close to your father?"

He shrugged.

"Didn't you care for him?"

"I didn't know him well enough to care about him. He was very taken up with the viscountcy, and with training Everard to be viscount when his time came."

Her own father had been deeply flawed, but for the first dozen years of her life she'd been held in his love, and that had given her a sense of belonging she knew she'd always have. "You were only a year or two younger than your brother, weren't you?"

"Sixteen months."

"So close in age, yet so different in how you were treated. You must have felt left out of what your father and brother shared. It would only be natural."

He gave her a dry look. "I doubt I thought about it, beyond being grateful that I didn't have to go through the things my brother did—the formal events he was expected to attend, the adults he had to please."

"Perhaps he didn't have the freedom you did, but he had most of the attention."

"Certainly, along with the knowledge that his path in life was entirely determined for him."

"So you were left to do as you pleased and make mischief."

"I had my share of beatings," he said, "but they were never as severe as what Everard got. Everard wasn't allowed to make mistakes."

"And nobody expected as much of you."

"I was lucky then, wasn't I?"

She wondered. Was that lucky, to be so thoroughly branded as second class in your family? Though indeed, he'd always had such a joking, playful manner that no one would have thought him anything but golden, a golden youth now turned into a golden man. Laughing and easy and never much bothered about anything, he teased and pulled tricks and chased thrills. What he'd been good at had been play—and it still was. And yet, she thought about that dangerous swim in the river, and the shadows she'd sometimes seen in his eyes.

"Perhaps," she said. "Perhaps not."

"There are advantages to being left to your own lights," he said. "I used to make up adventures I would've had with the old uncles, the ones I never met. I created an entire society in my mind of all the second sons. We had epic adventures."

He gestured toward the portraits. "A pack of swashbucklers, they were. First Lord of the Admiralty, lost his arm in a naval battle." He pointed to another portrait. "Foreign Secretary, but really a spy for the king who secretly averted war with France."

He obviously needed adventure now as much as he'd craved it when he was young. "You wish you were back in the army, don't you?"

His eyelids lowered. "Feeling sorry for the poor, wealthy viscount?"

"I think you miss the danger of war," she said. "Do you *need* danger?"

Hal didn't like the way Lily was probing him—or how she seemed to see through him.

But she looked so pretty in her pale yellow gown that it fairly made his teeth hurt, no matter that he didn't at all like the conversation they were having. He couldn't seem to stop himself from being fascinated by her.

Her white-blond hair was piled with predictable tidiness on her head, though a few wisps were escaping here and there. With her cheeks pink and her eyes as softly blue as a summer field of periwinkle, she looked fresh and innocent, even if the sight of her creamy bosom was turning his thoughts more wicked every moment. He alone knew the way she might tip her head if a kiss were pressed behind her jaw, an invitation that was all the more a victory from a woman who didn't want to yield.

All day he'd thought about her, and about touching her again. He wanted to trouble the serious light in her eyes, to gain all her attention—and bring her to surrender. The kind of surrender that would also allow him to solve the mystery of what she was doing in his woods. And dammit, he wanted his folly completed.

"Why would I need danger?"

"I don't know, but you seem to crave it. Taunting your colonel outrageously enough to be thrown in jail, racing horses, swimming in dangerous rivers. Maybe exploits make you feel more alive."

"What kind of a man would feel more alive for killing a man?"

"Killing the enemy was what you were trained to do. But it's not without costs, is it?"

He looked away from her. How had they come to be discussing this? Across the room, Eloise laughed musically. He was glad she and John and his family were safe, that none of them had been touched by the war. But, yes, it had done things to him, just as Everard's death had, and he didn't know what to do with those feelings. He damned well didn't want Lily poking at them.

"Save your concern, Lily," he said softly. "I was an indulged young man who had everything he ever wanted."

"Perhaps," she said. "Or perhaps you grew up accustomed to acting outrageous because your older brother outshone you by virtue of his birth, and then through his virtue. Perhaps, because you could never be first in your family, you made being a knave the thing you were best at. Perhaps it was your way of drawing attention where it was rarely bestowed—on you."

She'd provoked something hard in him, and he needed to push back. He crossed his arms and propped a shoulder lazily against the window frame behind him.

"Do you know what I think, Lily? I think you focus on other people's troubles because you don't want to look at your own."

"Me? I don't have troubles," she said, but he had his doubts. He remembered how she'd stiffened in his arms when they were on Emperor and he'd brought up how serious she'd been as a girl.

"What about your father? What happened with him?"

A wary look came into her eyes. "What do you mean?"

"I remember hearing that he took to the bottle after your mother died."

A flush came over her face. "How dare you. My father was a good man who suffered greatly when my mother died."

She was angry with him, but he'd found a chink in her firm, tidy armor, and he needed to explore it, needed her to let him see inside her. "Everybody suffers sometimes," he said. "But it's hard to respect people who wallow."

She sucked in a breath, and he knew he'd come

up against something. "I hardly think a man like you could have appreciated someone like my father."

He ignored the harshness of her words. "I liked your father very much when I was young. But I remember seeing you at the wine merchant one day when you were little more than a girl, discussing a bill. And now that I think about it, I see why you were there."

"You know nothing about my family, and I'll thank you not to say another word," she said in a hard voice that should have made him stop. But this felt important.

"It only takes adding up the details to guess what happened. Your brothers would have been away at school, and your sister very young. With a father drowning in drink, that left you to be the responsible one in the household, didn't it? And you would have been all of twelve or so, far too young for so much to be asked of you."

Her eyes snapped at him, and she turned to go, but he reached out and grabbed her arm. Suddenly he saw so much about her. "Ian and Rob and Delia don't have any idea, do they, of how much you took on back then? How much you did for them?"

"You're inferring far too much!" she said, even though it was obvious he'd guessed the truth.

"I doubt it. Life in the army showed me just about everything men are capable of, including a colonel who was so constantly drunk that a captain was secretly running his regiment. I suspect you were the family captain for a number of years. It certainly accounts for why you are so bossy."

"My father was a good and loving man," she said in a rough, forceful voice.

"But that doesn't mean he didn't shirk his responsibilities."

"I won't listen to another word!" She tugged her arm from his grasp.

"Go then," he said. "But think about this: maybe you are such a sharp judge of yourself and everyone else because you are angry."

Lily rushed away from Hal, aware that she was furious. She forced herself to slow down so she could use the length of the room to calm her breathing. What was wrong with her? She never got upset, and she despised emotion.

But how dare he accuse her of being judgmental when he so uncaringly did everything he wanted? How dare he speak of her father as if he understood anything about her and her family?

And what was worst, she thought as her shoulders slumped, how could a man like Hal guess so many private things about her?

She reached the group of guests just as dinner was announced, and she forced herself to stop thinking about what she and Hal had said to each other. As they all left the gallery, she prayed she wouldn't have to sit near him.

She was, luckily, placed at the opposite end of the long table. Eloise sat on her left, and Donwell was across from them. Lily made herself try a little to get them to speak to each other, but they both seemed adept at evading her efforts and spoke instead to others, and the dinner passed without any connection between them. The meal felt glum and endless, though certain of the gentlemen kept guffawing loudly.

Ian was sitting to her right, but for once her brother's lighthearted conversation didn't engage her.

"You are rather dull tonight," he said after the main meal had been cleared and they addressed themselves to dishes of sliced pears. "I hope you are not ill?"

"Not in the least."

He lowered his voice. "You and Hal seemed to be having an intense conversation in the gallery."

Warmth stole up her neck. Their conversation had felt so intimate—more so, even, than the kiss they'd shared in her room. "We were merely discussing family history."

"Is that so?" He sounded skeptical.

"We talked about some old ring belonging to his uncles that went missing years ago."

As she said these words, it dawned on her that what Nate was looking for in the woods might be the ring. It had apparently disappeared some time ago. But it seemed so very unlikely that such a costly heirloom would be given away by anyone in the family that she decided it couldn't be what he was looking for.

"Yes, I remember something about that. Hal used to want to look for it when we were children. He had a real fascination for it."

She had an image then of Hal as a boy, his face set in the serious way of children with some mission to accomplish, next in line behind a beloved brother who would always be more important than he was, and it tugged at her heart though she didn't want it to. She wondered if his childhood had anything to do with how very adept he'd become at charming people.

Ian gave her a shrewd look. "Are you certain there is nothing between you and Hal?"

"Ian…" she said with a note of warning in her voice.

"Good, good," he said with a relieved grin. Though she couldn't imagine why he thought this was so very good, she didn't linger on the thought because she was watching Donwell brush the crumbs off his coat sleeves—they seemed to be scattered up to his elbow—and wondering how she could get Eloise to linger and talk with him.

But Eloise was already standing up and trailing after the earl, and as she watched her go, Lily couldn't avoid Hal's gaze.

"Will you join the card party, Lily?" he asked as she passed near where he stood by the door.

"No, thank you," she said. "I do not care for cards."

"Of course you don't," he said, and she'd never wanted anything so much as she wanted right then to wipe the smirk off his face. The sound of his wicked laughter as she walked past him made her gnash her teeth.

Twelve

AFTER BREAKFAST THE NEXT MORNING, ELOISE DID NOT want to linger in the breakfast room—Ivorwood had just left, on his way to finish some correspondence in his chamber, he'd said, and that meant an opportunity for her to walk with him to his room. But Lily had stood when she stood, and now she seemed intent on engaging her in conversation.

The only other people left in the breakfast room were Hal, who was talking to the butler at the far end of the table, and Donwell, apparently examining the likeness of a goat in a painting on the other side of the room. After the irritating way he'd behaved while Lily was sketching them, she had little wish to spend any time in his presence. She thought she'd felt him looking at her a few times across the dinner table the night before, and she hoped he wasn't lurking about with the desire to speak with her.

Lily had apparently just asked her a question while she was calculating the likelihood of catching up to Ivorwood, and what they might talk about if she did. Still waters were said to run deep, and the earl was so reserved and handsome and mysterious that she just knew he was thinking fascinating things.

"I'm sorry?" Eloise said.

"I was saying that I haven't been to the conservatory yet. Might you have a moment to show it to me this morning?"

Repressing a sigh, Eloise smiled. "Of course. Shall we go right now?"

"Yes. I wonder if anyone else would like to join us?" Lily said, turning as if to include Donwell in the invitation. He didn't turn around.

"Oh, I don't think that's a good idea," Eloise muttered. After the disastrous posing episode, she'd spent more time than she'd cared to thinking about Donwell. In particular, she'd remembered a conversation she'd had with him at a house party just before she'd left for the Continent.

Though she'd been in company with Donwell any number of times—he was a good friend of Hal's—she'd never paid much attention to him before then. But he'd happened on her sitting in the garden, and they'd begun to talk about nature. He was very interested in the night sky, and as he warmed to his subject, he'd become as impassioned as a poet. Though it was oddly intense, there had been something charming about his enthusiasm, and when he'd proposed that she bring a maid and come out to see the stars with him that night, she'd thought it sounded rather lovely. She'd even thought she might bring her paints and try to capture the heavens at night.

Then Ivorwood had arrived at the house party, and Donwell and his invitation had been as easily forgotten as five minutes spent brushing her hair. Perhaps not well done of her, but she didn't like to think about it.

Hal thought Donwell was brilliant, which was a good thing for him, since Donwell had few social graces and only a small, apparently crumbling estate in Ireland. She supposed he deserved her compassion, but she didn't feel inclined to give it to him now.

Lily gave her a furtive look. "He seems like such an interesting man. Did you know that he's discovered a meteor or some such in the heavens?"

But Donwell was now moving toward the door. "Ladies, do please excuse me," he said pleasantly, as though he hadn't heard anything about the conservatory, or said outrageous things to her on the terrace. They stepped aside and let him pass through the door.

"I'm sorry," Lily said, looking pained. "I thought you two might enjoy each other's company. It was terribly interfering of me, only Mr. Donwell seems like just the sort of man I might have liked when I was your age."

Eloise frowned. How could Lily not notice that Donwell wasn't quite the thing? "I'm sure you meant well, but we don't suit."

"But he seems so engaging."

"Perhaps it's only me he doesn't like."

"I'm certain that's not the case," Lily said.

But Eloise just shrugged. "Did you really want to see the conservatory?"

"I really do," Lily said.

As they were passing through the doorway, Hal called out, "Oh Lily."

"Yes?" Lily said in an oddly impatient voice.

"It's good to know when to surrender."

Eloise thought that an odd thing for her brother to say to Lily, but then, she'd noticed that he was different around Lily, and she wondered if he fancied her. She didn't seem like his sort of woman.

Strangely, it almost sounded as though Lily growled as they passed through the doorway.

The hour of the ball had finally come, and Lily and Delia were descending the grand staircase in the company of their brothers, who were very handsome in their black tailcoats and buckled dancing shoes. Delia's gown looked marvelous on her, a pale cherry blossom silk with tiny white rosebuds at the bodice.

Lily's gown of silvery white satin trimmed in silver cord whispered softly against her legs and kissed the tops of her silver slippers, which still had a faint scuff mark from four years before. A strand of silver cord meandered through her hair, which was piled neatly on top of her head with a few soft curls escaping.

The broken hum of stringed instruments being tuned drifted up the stairs. The foyer was alive with the sound of arrivals and merry voices and the soft tapping of dancing shoes on polished floors.

"How wondrous," said Delia in awed tones as they entered the ballroom. Two enormous crystal chandeliers scattered gems of light over murmuring groups of richly dressed guests. "What a glow."

Ian chuckled. "Glow is expensive."

"So let's enjoy it!" Delia tugged them all near the dance floor as the orchestra struck up a tune. Rob led

Marianne Preston out, the white-haired vicar invited Delia, and Ian went to claim Eloise's hand. Donwell was standing with another group some yards off, determinedly not looking at Eloise, Lily thought.

Across the room, Hal was talking with a group of people from Town, including Mrs. Whyte, who looked stunning in a bronze satin gown. Lily couldn't help but notice he was giving the widow the same wicked half smile that made her own heart beat faster. She hated seeing him share it with someone else and hated that she cared at all. Though she wanted to look away, she made herself watch as a reminder that this was who he was, a handsome charmer.

She wasn't alone for long, because at the end of the first dance Rob appeared at her side and presented Mr. Thomas Noone, who invited her to dance. Mr. Noone was followed by Mr. Bendick, a widower with six children.

While she danced, she reluctantly found herself noticing Hal's succession of partners: the vicar's doddering mother; Christabel Cox, who'd just turned fifteen and had the spots to prove it; and Mrs. Ramsay, an impoverished widow. No doubt he was beguiling them all.

Lily next found herself being danced feebly about by Sir John Chatham, who stared mutely over her head the entire time. All of her dancing partners had been introduced by one or the other of her brothers, and each had seemed eager to meet her. A veritable crop of willing suitors, but none of them gave her anywhere near the same feeling as... *as what*? she demanded of herself.

But she knew what the *what* was, and it had to do with the way a certain very *imperfect* gentleman made her feel. Which made her annoyed with herself, and she was already beginning to fume by the time Mr. Noone asked her for a second dance. She declined kindly, but she *was* cross. Her brothers' intention to marry her off couldn't have been plainer: she was an aging lady in need of social charity. In need of marrying as soon as possible.

Was that how everyone saw her? Because that wasn't how she saw herself.

She was only twenty! Why were they treating her like a spinster in her last good years?

Her shoulders slumped a little. Maybe because that was how she acted.

And she was so tired of the inner voice that was always judging her actions and thoughts. Her conscience wanted her to feel ashamed of her journal, of her attraction to Hal, of the time she spent on frivolous things that could have been used productively, of the tinge of anger that she felt toward a beloved father who wasn't even alive. It wanted her to be ashamed of the way her body reacted to Hal, and it didn't want her to admit that she wanted the things she did.

She watched the dancers and wished, strangely, that she were someone else. Someone like Eloise, who was so carefree, so willing to say and do just what she liked.

Free. Eloise was free, Delia was free, Mrs. Whyte was very free. But Lily always felt as though she were in an invisible cage she couldn't escape—an internal cage whose bars became evident whenever she did the sorts of things that someone like Eloise did. No matter what she did, she would always be tormented by the restraints of her own shame and judgment. And that made her angry.

She closed her eyes and clenched her teeth and forced herself to relax. She would go and sit alone on the terrace and look at the stars and claim the peace that solitude brought.

"Might I have the pleasure of this dance, Lily?"

She opened her eyes, and there was Hal. She took in the ironic tilt of his mouth, the chiseled line of his jaw, and the way his black evening coat skimmed the tall, masculine frame underneath. Trouble in superfine.

She let his question hang, and he tilted his head. "Are you angry with me over our conversation yesterday? Or perhaps you are weighing whether I have some ulterior motive."

That startled a laugh out of her, just when she was feeling so horrible. He was so *charming*. He was also, in ways she could not predict, dangerous to her, but she was certainly not afraid of him. And as he had already declared his intention to remain a bachelor until he was doddering, he was, in a way, safe, because no one could suppose he wanted to marry her.

Dancing with him would be thumbing her nose at everything that told her she shouldn't, but peevish as she felt, the idea pleased her. Also, Hal was simply more entertaining than anyone else she knew. And suddenly, she felt so in need of that.

"Don't you always?" she said, setting her hand on his arm. She thought of his talent for strategy and wondered if he really was up to something. She would relish a battle of wits just now, if it came to it.

They moved into place among the other dancers, and the dance began.

"I suppose you're not going to admit that was part of your dress which was left on my bushes early yesterday morning," he said in a low voice.

She tipped her head in a gesture of bemused innocence. Really, it was shameful, all the avoiding of truth she'd resorted to in the last week, but she couldn't make herself care. "Why ever should I have been out by your woods yesterday morning, my lord?"

"Because you are trying to muddy my efforts to capture the Woods Fiend."

The steps of the dance drew them apart then close, and he leaned in to her ear, his breath coming to her in a way that made her close her eyes for a moment just for the pleasure of absorbing it.

"You know," he murmured, "I have the swatch of fabric in my pocket. We could settle right now whether it's familiar."

A little thrill ran around inside her. Probably her good sense fleeing.

"I think not."

"I will not be bested in the matter of the Woods Fiend, Lily."

Her only reply was a little smile. The steps of the dance separated them again, and she was at the same time dreading the moment that would bring them together again and anticipating it. She knew herself to be alive to his every word and movement.

Dear God, she'd been truly hooked by him again.

No. No! The effect he had on her was simply the effect that a very handsome and charming rogue had on a woman. Elderly ladies and happily married women found him irresistible; likely toddler misses and baby girls did, too. Female cats, certainly. But she was made of sterner stuff, and she could resist him if she wanted to.

To reassure herself, she looked at Ivorwood, who was dancing nearby, and tested herself against him, willed herself to feel for him something of what she felt for Hal. But just like all the other men she'd danced with that evening, Ivorwood had no effect on her.

"Finding something especially interesting about the earl, are you?" Hal said as they drew together again.

"He's an interesting man." *Old Duffer, Old Duffer*, she chanted silently as the scent of Hal came to her again, seemed to *infiltrate* her. How could plain old clean smell so intoxicating? But the nice soap smell held other faint notes, liquor-like whiffs of manly scents that could only be Essence of Hal.

It was no use calling him Old Duffer in her mind, not when she could feel the leashed strength of his forearm under her hand, see the sturdy angle of his jaw and that masterful glint in his eyes. There was nothing aged or feeble or in any way repellent about him to discourage her. No, he was smart and kind and good with children and animals.

She wanted him. And maybe it would be better to simply accept that and stop fighting it. Fighting it was taking up a lot of energy. Delia was right: he was like a demigod, and weren't mortals helpless before them?

Apart, together, the dance drew them. A tease, when every part of her was so attuned to the moment when her hand would be in his again.

"And how are your sheep, Lily?" he murmured as they rejoined. "I hope they are able to sleep well at night with the Fiend about."

"They are quite well, thank you."

"I see why you like animals; they don't contradict you."

The dance came to an end just then, and the dancers applauded the musicians. Hal offered Lily his arm to escort her back to where she had been. As they walked she tried not to think of what his bare arm would be like.

She couldn't afford to spend any more time with him. She felt warm, and not just from the exertion of dancing, and she needed to get away from him before she did something foolish.

He's just a man like any other, she repeated to herself. If only she could find a way to make him seem less enchanting, more human, dull even.

"If you will excuse me?" She started to lift her hand from his arm, but he pressed his own on top of hers, holding her there.

"Wouldn't you like some lemonade, Lily? I for one am quite parched."

"Oh. No. I… that is…" She tried to pull her hand from under where it rested on his, a small struggle as he pressed his hand with seeming obliviousness on hers. "I want to take the evening air."

"Then I shall join you."

"Surely you wish to continue dancing? There are so many lovely ladies here tonight."

"But I want to go outside with *you*."

His words made her heart beat faster even as she knew he was only toying with her and that she must discourage him, however much she didn't want to. But before she could think further he was leading her through the terrace doors, away from the light and music.

She found herself standing alone with him on the far side of the terrace under a softly shining moon. And suddenly a whimsical part of herself was insisting that maybe there was a way to cure herself once and for all of her fascination with Lord Perfect.

Hal watched Lily's face, wondering if she was aware of how beautiful she looked. A torch stood to the side of them at a distance, put there to supplement the moonlight. The edge of its glow fell against her white-blond hair and limned it with silver that seemed to shine out from within, like a personal incandescence. Her gown was a soft white silk satin, richly lustrous and trimmed in silver cord that traced along the tops of her breasts and made a sort of belt that reminded him there was a slim waist underneath, and a soft-in-the-right-places body. She looked like something ethereal, a moon nymph, perhaps. Or, more likely, one of the goddess Diana's band of warrior maidens.

She also looked—the thought made him smile—calculating, like someone choosing moves on a chess-board. Doubtless plotting something.

"Tell me, Lily," he said in a soft voice. "What ever happened to the carefree girl who wrote in that journal?"

Her eyes lifted upward toward the dark sky, which was anointed with a profusion of tiny stars, like salt shaken on dark velvet.

"You *would* want to talk about the journal. It's all about you."

He chuckled. "Though I will admit to finding the picture painted of myself through your young eyes fascinating, I'm much more interested in that dreamy girl who had such a grand imagination. Do you use that imagination anymore?"

She seemed to consider his words seriously, but then she did generally take things seriously, to a fault. "I suppose I use it to think of yarn colors."

"Probably the most unromantic words ever uttered on a moonlit terrace."

"I'm not trying to say romantic things."

"I know. Tell me, Lily, why are your brothers so industriously lining up dance partners for you when, lovely as you are, you need only smile and the gentlemen will come running? You don't want to be courted—but why?"

She kept her hands folded in front of her, a vision of composed femininity that he itched to ruffle.

"I like my life just the way it is, and that's something over which I would have little control were I to marry."

"The shawl business and your plans for the school."

"Yes."

"Then do you mean to be a spinster?"

"Perhaps I simply haven't thought about marriage particularly. Perhaps I was merely busy and forgot about it."

He laughed. "You are either a bold liar or the most unusual woman I've ever met."

His words fell into a silence on the terrace as she made no response. She was looking at him intently, her eyes serious and focused, but her brow was furrowed as if she were struggling with some thought. He found his eyes drawn to the pretty, pert bow at the center of her mouth, which was currently pressed against her bottom lip.

She cleared her throat delicately. "Would you kiss me, please, Hal?" she said.

What?

The steady look she was giving him told him that he'd not misheard her. But what the devil was she up to?

"You would like me to kiss you?"

"Yes. I was thinking about… the things I've said no to in recent years. And, well, you're right."

"I'm right?" This was new.

"Yes. I'd like to experiment a little. Like we did in my chamber," she said in the straightforward tone of one ordering a coat from a tailor.

He'd never been asked for a kiss before. Asked with eyes, yes, and hands. But never bluntly, in words. Somehow, it seemed like the very way Lily would want to be kissed. With *her* deciding, her issuing the invitation and being in control.

"Hmm," he said, "I would say the kiss in your chamber was an exploratory kiss. But what about other kinds, like scorching kisses? Or long kisses? Or desperate kisses?"

Her eyes widened a bit. "Yes," she whispered.

Thirteen

HAL HAD THOUGHT TO ADDLE LILY A LITTLE OUT ON the terrace, tease her into acquiescing a bit—and here she was, asking for it. Was she up to something? He didn't care. He wanted her, and he didn't care how she came to him.

He leaned closer. "So... scorching," he murmured. "And what if I want to touch you, Lily? Would that be part of your plan?"

She blinked, as if beginning to realize that what happened might not be under her control.

"Touch me?" Her voice was hushed, a little strained, and her eyes were dazed.

He leaned closer still, until he was only a few inches from her tilted-up face, his mouth just opposite hers. "Yes," he said, something turning over inside him. "I want to touch you."

"I don't know," she whispered weakly. She lifted her mouth a little closer, expectantly, and the beginnings of trust he read in her eyes tugged at him.

"Give me your hand," he said, and she slipped her hand into his. He led them down the short flight of

steps that met the lawn, and pulled her out of the circle
of torchlight and around to the far side of a thick old
cherry tree.

He guided her back against the tree. Her expression was obscured now in the shadows, with only the
moonlight and the glow of the manor behind them to
counter the vast darkness of the fields before them, but
he could see the intent light in her eyes. So like Lily,
to bring focus to whatever she did.

He planted a hand on either side of her head, steadied
himself, and moved forward to kiss her. Scorchingly…

He paused, lifted a hand to tuck a loose strand of
hair behind her ear. A very pretty, endearing little
apricot of an ear.

"I doubt your brothers would approve of what
we're about to do. Being that they're evidently intent
on you marrying someone soon."

He thought he heard the sound of teeth grinding.
"I'll be twenty-one next month, Hal. I can and do
make up my own mind."

"Yes, you do," he said. And kissed her.

Oh *my*, Lily thought as he took possession of her
mouth. His tongue licked cleverly along the line
where her lips met, inveigling his way inside, and she
opened to him. Pleasure trickled through her as his hot
mouth came against her.

She realized then, with the partial awareness that
a drugged person might have, that he'd been making
love to her with his words and his eyes ever since
they'd come onto the terrace. He couldn't be sincere,
though she'd felt a wave of tenderness for him when
he'd stopped himself to be certain she wanted to do

this. But she didn't care about sincerity or reason or moderation now. Her only sense was of wanting him to kiss her more.

His mouth moved on hers in hot, greedy exploration, and she sighed, her body softening against him. The ridge of his erection pressed against her, a shock... and a pleasure. This hardened part of him was intruding against the propriety that was meant to surround maidens—and she wanted him right where he was. She pushed her hands through his surprisingly silky hair and over the warm skin of his scalp, feeling she was gaining secret knowledge of his hidden places.

Dear God, she should stop right now, cut off the wildness surging inside her, but for once she wasn't going to listen to the voice of censure. She ached for him, and all she cared about was where his hands would go next. Would he touch the skin bared by her scooped neckline?

He broke their kiss to drag his moist lips along her jaw and down her neck, his breath huffing against her, her own seeming as loud as a horse off the gallop. She shoved her hands up the back of his coat and spread them upward over the shifting muscles beneath his shirt. An unladylike moan escaped her, and she didn't care—he felt that good. Strong, tall, hard, male. So different from her and the very thing she'd been craving without knowing it.

"Can you feel what you've done to me, Lily?" His voice husky and deep at the base of her throat, he crushed his hips against her, making her feel his hardness more.

"Yes," she whispered.

"I love it when you say yes. It's a new language to you, isn't it? The language of not-denying."

"Yes... yes..." Her words melted into a hum of pleasure. Sweet, hot yearning pooled damply between her thighs.

He grunted against her neck and tugged at the shoulder of her gown, inched it down on one side with slow intention. She shuddered as he bared her breast to the cool night air, and while he kissed her collarbone and made a leisurely exploration of the base of her neck, she admitted to herself that there were volumes of wicked things she wanted him to do to her. She arched her back, willing him to find all the places where she needed him.

His mouth traveled lower but just a bit, and lingered. If only he would kiss her breast, but he was teasing her with his endless, maddening, exquisite dallying. With his hands on either side of her, she was imprisoned, held there for his plundering, dizzy with desire.

But not entirely helpless. She fumbled at the front of his breeches and yanked his shirt upward, desperate to feel the skin and muscles she'd touched through his shirt, to have her hands on the body about which she'd wondered with varying degrees of desire for four years. There was no saying she didn't want him desperately now.

The fabric came loose—he groaned as though a torture had deepened, the sound of him *suffering* because of her touch making her feel as if liquid was pouring through her, soaking her—and she worked her hands upward, sliding them against the flat, hard muscles of his abdomen. *Ohhh*. The heat and tautness and aliveness of his flesh lit her hands. She was hot, throbbing with heat all over.

His hand—warm, large, the skin a little rough and creating exquisite friction—skimmed over the rounded, bare edge of her shoulder and down her arm as if he meant to leave no chance for the night air to cool her.

"I'm willing to bet," he said, his husky voice sliding inside her, "that you've never had a man's hand here before."

"No," she whispered, slumping against him, enfeebled with desire.

"Or here." He worked his hand slowly sideways, across the top of her breast, and spread it over her fullness to cup her.

Scorching… *oh*. And melting… Her legs quivering, she slid a little down his body.

"Steady on," he tugged her up, husky laughter in his voice.

His head dipped and he kissed the upper swell of her breast. Yes. So good. His mouth moved lower in kiss-steps, and she'd never wanted anything so much as what he was going to do, what he surely must do, what she so needed him to do.

Kiss… kiss… kiss… His taunting lips moved, maddeningly, with seeming ambivalence toward the tip of her breast, while his hand pulled the other side of her dress down. Now she was bare from the waist, offered totally to him, her whole being anticipation.

He paused in his kissing and pulled his head back, and she wanted to cry out from frustration. He was panting, his eyes glittering hard in the moonlight.

"Tell me what you want."

She shook her head. She could never speak such words.

He read her silence. "You don't want to say?" He leaned over and dragged his moist lips slowly down her breast, drawing a shudder from her. And stopping short again.

She kept silent. Stood there frozen in movement but burning inside, her senses alive and wanting. The ache between her legs hummed urgently.

He lifted his hand and pinched her nipple.

She moaned. The bite of pain was exquisite, and it only made the wanting deepen.

He dragged his moist lips across her breast again, drawing closer to the dark rouge circle of skin.

"Still nothing to say?" His breath rushed hot against her puckered skin. *Ohhh.* She couldn't take much more of his teasing. Hal, always teasing. A master at teasing. Had she known on some level he would be accomplished at *every* kind of teasing? Had she guessed that there was a kind of teasing that was exquisite torture?

Her only reply was to push her hands down his front, past the waist of his breeches. He sucked in a breath. Her fingertips touched crisp hairs. Dangerous territory. Forbidden and fascinating. With a single, daring fingertip, she stroked the silky, hot tip of his erection.

With a groan he moved his head and finally closed his mouth over her nipple. Desire bloomed in a mad rush between her legs.

His hips began a rhythm that met something within her—the something that had lain dormant, unknown because untasted: the need to join herself physically to a man. She'd felt inklings of it with him, but never the full-bore insistent desire, and now it was alive in her. Now she *wanted*—and knew *what* she wanted. She pushed her hands past his hips, to the firm, high swell of his buttocks, and pulled him against her.

He grunted. Ground his teeth. "Ah, Lily, you know what you want, don't you?"

"I—" A breathy whisper. "Maybe."

He exhaled, the barest hint of a chuckle that was saved from smugness by its being shaky.

Leaning lower, he tugged up her skirts, and the night air sighed against her leg as one side of her gown opened a space for him. His hand brushed the outside of her thigh, teased the bare skin under her bottom, and then moved around to her front. Her mind was on nothing but his hand and what he would do with it. He slipped it between her legs.

She moaned.

"We shouldn't…" she whispered with the last vestiges of sense.

"Shh." He stroked her there, his fingertip silky and knowing, and she forgot why they shouldn't do this. Such earthy heaven, such yearning, such a thing that she would never have allowed herself to want. Hal exploring her most secret place… a sensation she never could have dreamed of, because how could such incredible pleasure be imagined without tasting it first?

He pressed slow, sweet kisses against her cheek, her neck, her breasts, all the while using a single fingertip to make her dizzier, weaker with desire, desperate for some sort of release. She wanted to move against him, press herself to his hand, but the ghost of who she was restrained her.

"Let yourself go," he whispered in that husky voice.

She didn't know specifically what he meant by letting herself go, what that would entail. And yet, she also did. It was an allowing that he meant. Letting the exquisite sensations overtake her, letting *passion* rule her. She'd never wanted anyone or anything to over-take her—and now, suddenly, she did. She wanted *him* to do it.

Yet some unconscious, long-restrained part of her resisted.

"Lily," he said softly, "you were made for this."

The note of tenderness in his words undid her, and that was it. She gave herself over to passion, pressed against his hand, and let him carry her up and over this summit he'd been climbing with her.

Sweetness welled up within her. Then a rush of peace, a kind of joyful nothingness.

He held her in his arms, her face cradled against his chest. Bliss.

She gradually became aware of his erection straining hard against her and thought of how he had just... pleasured her. Expertly.

He'd known exactly what she wanted. Probably he knew what all women wanted. But he had been tender also. Generous. It had all felt genuine.

She thought how he was left now, with himself still—obviously—wanting.

Affection for him had stirred deeply in her tonight. Forcing herself to regard him as a wastrel had helped keep her from liking him, but there was so much more to him than what she had allowed. He was smart and kind and witty and knowing and sensual. And tender. It was the tenderness that was undoing all her resolutions, that was making her want—against everything she'd ever thought about herself or him—a deep connection with him. Friendship, yes, but something much more.

And maybe this was what she'd been afraid of: that once she'd opened the door to her heart even a crack, something would rush in and she'd lose all control over herself.

Her gown was still pooled at her waist, and she pulled it up over her shoulders and adjusted it back into place while he tucked in his shirt and straightened his coat. She looked up at him. His eyes shined down at her, shot through with starlight, and she thought she read softness there, along with desire. His smile was rueful, an admission that they'd shared something in which he'd been left behind.

"Do you know what pillow talk is, Lily?"

She blushed. Funny that words would make her blush when actions hadn't. "I can guess."

He laughed softly, leaned in a little to brush his chin against the side of her cheek. "It's when a man and a woman have come to understand each other a little more, and they are then a little more open to hearing each other. And so," he said with, always, that hint of laughter in his voice, that underlying bent to tease, "I think it must be a very good moment for you to tell me what it is you are up to with this Woods Fiend business."

She was, it turned out, as much of a fool as she'd

been afraid she might become. She'd been right. What they'd just done had meant nothing to him. It had been a moment of playful fun in the service of something he wanted, when to her it had felt like her eyes opening.

The slamming, harsh voice of remorse filled her head. Scolded her. Demanded she despise herself and her weakness.

But. She felt a little changed now. The night felt different, the moonlight, too. She felt spangled, glittering... as though she were alive now to secret layers of things she hadn't known about before. And she didn't want to go back to the way she'd been. She'd just tasted some of what men and women could do for each other, and it had been a wonder.

So this was something of an answer to the shame that wanted to reproach her: how could something which had brought her that peace she'd just known, that joyful emptiness, and yes, that pleasure, be shameful? With his tenderness and his expertise, Hal had shown her that there was a beauty to her body and what it could do. There was something a little sacred in what had just happened that made her feel in awe. Also a bit afraid.

But now she knew that for him there'd been an ulterior motive. She hated that—and yet, was this so different from when she'd begun unbuttoning his waistcoat so she could get her book from him?

The difference, of course, was that now something deeper in her had been touched, while for him this was all just amusement.

She forced herself to look him in the eyes. Pushed

away from his chest and pulled her dignity around her like a cloak.

"I wish to go back inside now."

Even as she said these words she wanted him to say *No*, to say *Don't go, you've got it all wrong*. To say that the kiss had been special, that *she* was special. That, like her, he'd never experienced anything similar to those moments when they were touching, caught up in a spell they'd woven together. But that couldn't be true for him, could it? It wasn't new for him. And, so light of spirit as he was, it would not be precious to him the way it had been to her.

It came down to this: she could not be casual about what they had just done, and he could.

He gazed down at her, the air that stood between them cool now when everything had been so hot moments ago. His lips compressed into a line. "So you won't be beguiled."

He wasn't even going to deny he'd done what he had to entice her into giving him the information he wanted. She made herself remember that *she'd* asked *him* to kiss her. That she was the one who'd initiated all of this. It helped her stir up the pride that had gone soft while she was resting in his arms.

"I won't. But…"

"Yes?"

She made herself smile a little. Forced a far lighter tone than she felt. "Thank you for the… kiss."

And without waiting for him to reply or say or do another thing that might tempt her, she turned away and made for the light and sound of the ballroom.

Inside, the dancers were still swirling to the music,

and no one seemed to have taken note that she and Hal had disappeared. She stood watching without really seeing as blurs of cream and black and rose fabric danced past her eyes, and faces damp with perspiration smiled and laughed. It all washed over her.

The world had shifted, and yet everyone else was still just chattering and moving about.

She knew that he'd not yet reentered the ballroom, so that their absences might not be connected by anyone who had noticed.

Delia was talking to Ian, and Lily joined them, though contributing to their conversation, which seemed to be about the merits of the fiddle over the cello, was beyond her, and she stood and smiled feebly and nodded in what she hoped were the right places.

She felt it the moment Hal came through the terrace doors. Slanting her eyes, she watched as, with nary a hesitation, he directed himself to a group of lovely ladies whose fashionable clothes announced they'd come from Town, and invited one of them onto the dance floor.

Just as easy as you please. She watched him glide into the motions of the dance as if nothing had happened to him outside. As if his breezy heart hadn't been touched at all.

And that was how different they were. True, she had approached that kiss with a certain calculation. She'd wanted to make herself see that he was only human, to teach the part of herself that persisted in being fascinated by him that he was no god.

She must declare her plan a success. He now felt more human to her—more real, now that she'd touched his skin and hairs and muscles, and more funny, considerate, and generous than she would have thought. But in the process she'd also discovered that *she* was far more human. Far more vulnerable than she wanted to be. Passionate. Yearning. And all too ready to feel deeply. Even to do something out of control.

He wasn't heartless. He was, she now freely admitted, not even shallow. His heart was simply impervious, as if it was made of some bouncy substance that repelled penetration.

And though he doesn't allow anyone into his heart, she thought with a deep tug in her belly, *he can't resist trying to work his way into everyone else's.*

Fourteen

GREGORY DONWELL STOOD IN THE FOYER OUTSIDE THE ballroom and watched Eloise leave the ladies' retiring room. He knew she'd left the ball, just as he'd known when she arrived, because he always knew when she was near. A room with her in it was changed.

But to Eloise, he hardly registered. Some of that was to do with her infatuation with Ivorwood, but not all. She was a beautiful, aristocratic young woman who'd just had her coming-out Season, and he was an impecunious man of obscure origins.

She was coming closer—he stood in her path to the ballroom, between a loud gaggle of matrons and a group of tittering young ladies—and now she perceived his presence. Her eyes flicked over his black coat, her brows lifting slightly, and he realized that he'd forgotten to brush off after playing with a white dog that had been in the garden earlier. And perhaps the coat was rather old, having been his father's, but he'd used up a good portion of his ready funds on his voyage to the northern climes.

He crossed his arms and leaned against the column to the side of him, effectively blocking her.

"Miss Waverly."

"Mr. Donwell." She made as if to move past him, but he didn't budge. "If I might pass," she said coolly, "you will not be afflicted with my lack of substance."

"You have plenty of substance," he said. "It just doesn't interest you as much as dresses and gossip."

Her sapphire eyes snapped at him. "Truly, you are the most arrogant man I have ever met. For you to stand there in ancient, filthy clothes and talk to me in this way is the height of idiocy."

He grinned. "It is, isn't it?"

He was so very pleased by her look of surprise and her bark of laughter.

"Donwell, you are an utter knave, after teasing me so horribly. Whatever are you up to?"

She was willing to forgive him; it was one of the things he liked best about her, this ability to hold things lightly.

"I hardly know," he said, which was far too true. She was entirely opposite everything he knew, great leaping strides different. But she fascinated him, and the whole passage north he'd thought of her, so that when he'd finally glimpsed the aurora borealis, his first thought had been that now he'd seen something as splendid as Eloise Waverly.

He was on the verge of telling her something of this—just a hint, an introductory suggestion that he admired her—when the sound of a small sneeze came from behind one of the columns.

They looked at each other in surprise, then moved closer and peeked around the column.

"Freddy Waverly," she said at the sight of her

nephew, "what on earth are you doing down here, and at this hour?"

The boy was in his nightgown, and his rumpled hair told of time spent in bed, but his eyes were bright.

"Who could sleep with all this noise?" he said. "Besides, I wanted to see what a ball looked like."

"And now that you have, what do you think?"

"It's just a lot of dressed-up people talking and twirling around. Nobody's even laughing."

"Sometimes there's a bit of laughter," Donwell said.

Freddy looked skeptical.

Eloise held out her hand. "Come, Freddy, I'll take you back to bed. It's almost midnight, and if Nanny finds you gone, she'll be frantic."

Please don't leave yet, Donwell thought.

"Nanny's snoring in the chair, and I don't want to go back," Freddy said with a tight, mulish look.

"I thought it was too boring for you down here," his aunt said.

Freddy crossed his arms, the very picture of a haughty miniature aristocrat, save for the faint quivering of his chin. "I'm not tired."

Eloise crouched down and said gently, "Are there perhaps monsters under your bed?"

"'Course not!" He tipped his chin in the air bravely but snuck a sideways glance at his aunt. "But I suppose *you* believe in the Woods Fiend, even though it's just a grotesque old legend."

"Grotesque, is it?" A smile teased her lips. "Come, I'll read you a book."

"Not yet. Please," Freddy said.

"Freddy," Donwell said, "would you like to come

up to the roof with me to look for Orion? He'll be especially bright tonight. A small adventure, and then to bed."

"Yes!" Freddy said, brightening immediately. "And Eloise can come, too."

Donwell shot her a look, not daring to hope. "Eloise will doubtless prefer dancing."

"Nonsense," she said. "I am very partial to the roofs of buildings, and I have a great yearning to see Orion. Besides, my dancing card is empty for the next set."

"I can hardly credit it," Donwell said.

She stuck her nose in the air, mirth tugging at the corners of her pretty pink mouth and making her glossy brown curls dance. "I always take a break every five dances."

As much as he wanted her to come with him, he knew this wasn't entirely proper. "Perhaps you ought not to come," he said over Freddy's head, "since there's no suitable chaperone."

She waved her hand. "No one will know, and it will only be a few minutes. Besides," she said in a low voice, "a five-year-old is the perfect chaperone—they never leave you alone."

Freddy took hold of each of their hands. "Let's take the servants' staircase," he said, tugging them down the hallway. "It's fantastical."

❦

Hal watched over his partner's shoulder as Lily stood talking with her sister and some of the ladies and gentlemen who'd come from Town. His dancing partner, Lady Isobel Danfield, looked charming in her red gown with a saucy feather curling over her head. He liked Isobel, who could usually make him laugh. But at the moment he was wishing she would stop trying to have a conversation with him so he could think.

He'd been far more affected by what he and Lily had just done than he would have expected, and it was working upon him. She'd been sweetly, unconsciously erotic, and what had flared up between them outside had left him feeling as if he'd been drizzled in something hotly luxurious. Her violet scent clung to him; perhaps that was contributing to the feeling that she was still filling his senses even though she was across the room with her back to him. His heart was still beating fast, and he couldn't stop thinking about how she'd felt in his arms.

He took stock of his campaign: things had gone well in some respects, if he could describe seducing Lily in the garden in such cool terms. But obviously his plan to beguile her into giving up the secret of the woods trespasser had been a failure. She thought that had been his main interest in kissing her. Far from it.

He decided, as he watched her talk with her sister, that it was her white-blond hair that made her unique among a room full of other women. Or… maybe he needed to acknowledge that she might stick out more for him than she would for other men, that while they would simply see her as an ethereal beauty, he wanted to *know* her, to know what she was thinking. Any man would count her desirable, but for him it went beyond that.

He was more than a little enchanted.

What was he going to do about it?

He watched Rob approach her in company with the village doctor, Fforde. Eloise, who only needed to hear tell of a handsome gentleman for her to wish to make his acquaintance, had insisted Fforde be invited to the ball. According to Eloise—whom he supposed to be in the retiring room, as he didn't see her—all the local ladies thought Fforde was a dream. If you like that sort of thing, Hal thought as the doctor bowed to Lily, all shiny black hair and neat eyebrows.

The quadrille that Hal and Isobel were dancing came to an end, and he led her over to her friends. The orchestra took up the opening strains of a waltz, and he decided that this would be his best chance for a private word with Lily. She wasn't happy with him, but he could start with offering to return her book, which she still didn't know he had.

But when he turned toward where she'd been standing, there was Fforde leading her out onto the floor for the dance.

Hal gnashed his teeth.

Fforde seemed to be a serious, scholarly man. Lily would probably think him a dream, too, though she'd never use that term; no, an educated man who helped the suffering would be irresistibly *worthy*.

"You're not dancing, Hal?" Ian said, coming to stand next to him.

"Not this one. But your sister is, I see, enjoying herself." And she did look quite enthused; doubtless she'd told herself that a little dancing, like a little kissing, was necessary in life. She was so driven

to seriousness, with her plans for what she meant
to contribute to life, the world, and doubtless the
universe as well. She ought to be a perfect bore, but
instead she was a heady mystery.

"It's good to see, actually," Ian said. "She's not
much for fun."

"Do you really think so?"

Ian looked surprised. "Why, yes. She's happiest
when she's reading with the children of the tenants or
visiting the sick. I suppose thinking about our sheep is
what she does for fun."

"Sheep," Hal said. "I imagine it's suited all of you
to believe that. And now you and Rob mean to make
up for lost time by pairing her off with any man in
possession of two legs and adequate funds."

A flush swept over Ian's cheeks. "What the devil
are you getting at?"

Hal shrugged. "Merely the observations of a friend
of the family."

"Rather sharp observations. You're suggesting
we've pushed her into a role as spinster. But you're
wrong—she's always liked being responsible, probably
because it lets her tell everybody else what to do. You
might even say the family has indulged her, letting her
do as she liked."

Ian meant her secret involvement in the yarn business, an undertaking Lily obviously cherished. Hal
knew she wouldn't welcome his interference, yet he
was angered by the thought of her throwing herself
away on a dull marriage to one of the local worthies.

Ian cast a shrewd glance over him. "Why all the
interest in Lily's affairs, Hal? It's not as if she's your

sort. You'd be bored with her endless charity work, and I don't think she cares a fig what she looks like."

Hal gave him a careless look. "I haven't got plans where your sister is concerned." Which was the truth in that he didn't know what to do about his violent attraction to her. "But should anybody really be concerned only with virtue?"

Ian shrugged. "I suppose there's no changing who we are."

They both watched her twirl past on the arm of the manly doctor, whose intent expression indicated he was making some point. Her gossamer moonlight skirts floated gracefully about her, and Hal thought her hair still held some of the starlight that had been caught in it earlier.

His jaw tensed as they twirled by again, her blue eyes sparkling and her mouth curled up in a congenial smile the likes of which she'd never once shared with him. He knew Ian was probably right, but he was not accustomed to accepting what he didn't like.

Lily and Dr. Fforde completed the last steps of the waltz, and he bowed to her and led her over to the table where lemonade and sandwiches were set out. The doctor was handsome and well mannered and reasonable, and she couldn't help thinking that if she'd danced with him earlier in the evening, she might not have spent that mad time outside with Hal.

But she couldn't say that she wished she hadn't gone into the garden with him, because it wouldn't be true. It was just the price to be paid that she minded, that tugging inside when she caught sight of him among the dancers. There he was, listening and chatting and flirting and smiling his breezy Lord Perfect smile, the one that made whomever he was talking with think he found them unique and fascinating.

Well, she liked Dr. Fforde. And he was the village doctor, a man who valued virtue and charity and, from what she knew from the occasions when Rob had invited him for dinner at Thistlethwaite, moderation and sobriety as well. An estimable man.

"Miss Teagarden, allow me to say how grateful I am for all you did to help the Thomas family through the fever. Your care and the baskets of food made a great difference."

"You are too kind, really. It was only a little help."

He shook his head. "No, you are too modest. It's evident you are a fine nurse, and teacher too, from what I hear. A steadfast help to those in need." He hesitated. "I wonder, Miss Teagarden, if you have ever considered turning your charitable impulses toward another avenue, something that would benefit a wider section of humanity?"

"That sounds intriguing, sir. What did you have in mind?"

"I'm speaking of something large—in fact, of the fever hospital I've committed to helping establish in the north of the country. Of the work that will be done there among those who have very little."

A flush of excitement came over her at his words, and an image filled her mind of hundreds of sick people in need of care—the kind of care she would so dearly love to provide.

"I can think of nothing more valuable," she said. "When do you begin this work?"

"Construction has already begun; we are still raising the funds to help complete it. My partners and I hope that the hospital may be open for patients by late spring."

What a fine, beautiful idea.

"You spoke of my helping you," she said. "How do you envision that might happen?" She pressed her lips together, thinking of how little, really, were the funds she might be able to offer in support of such a grand scheme. And she must not compromise her plans for the village girls' school.

He looked at her steadily for a moment, seeming to weigh his thoughts. "If you'll forgive my speaking so frankly, I believe the good work you've done in Highcross is but the beginning of what you might do."

She'd felt that, too! Longed for something grand of worth to do—it was why she'd begun saving for the school. But what exactly did he mean? How was she to help this work? To help—him? Was it possible... could it be that Dr. Fforde was suggesting something along the lines of a romantic alliance to her?

An unwelcome voice from behind her interrupted her thoughts.

"Talking of work, are you?" Hal said. "When there is dancing to be done?"

Dr. Fforde chuckled.

She didn't want to turn around and acknowledge Hal. She didn't want to see him, and she certainly didn't want to talk to him. But to ignore him would cause a scene. And her pride would not let him see how their encounter had shaken her.

She faced him, forcing mildness into her voice. "I think I've danced my last, my lord."

He gave her a look that said he was perfectly aware she would dance not a single other dance that night if it had to be with him. "Surely not. The night is young."

"It's almost one in the morning."

"I'm afraid, Miss Teagarden, that is early by Town hours," Dr. Fforde said ruefully.

Hal's jaw tightened, as though he was grinding his teeth. "Surely Lily doesn't need Town customs explained."

She laughed. "I know it's early to some, but I am a country mouse, and I shall have to retire shortly."

"My dear Miss Teagarden," the doctor said warmly, "there is nothing in the least mouse-like about you. But I wish you a good evening, and look forward to the pleasure of your company—and a continuation of our discussion—when next we meet." He bowed, taking his leave.

"Gads, what a windbag," said Hal as he watched Fforde move away. "And his eyes twinkle too much."

Lily sighed. "He is a very agreeable man in every way that I can perceive. Why should you think him a windbag?"

"Perhaps you find him appealing because he is handsome, and anything sounds good, at least initially, coming out of the mouths of pretty people."

"Well, you ought to know about that, being excessively handsome."

"And I have it in your own hand to prove it," he said.

"No, you don't—" she started to say, but the wicked glint in his eyes stopped her.

"Don't I?" he said. His eyebrow quivered with mirth; of course it did. He was bored, and he wanted to tease her.

"How on earth did you have time?" she said.

"Is that a grudging note of amazement?"

She scowled. "It's just general grudging, where you're concerned."

"I slipped out yesterday before dinner."

"You simply rode over to Thistlethwaite and waltzed into my home and took it?"

"Exactly."

She wanted, idiotically, to stamp her foot. "Really, Hal. How could you?"

"All's fair in love and war, as they say. And there is the little matter of the Woods Fiend. You tell me what's going on there, I'll give you back the journal."

She considered his words. Then she shrugged. "Keep it, then, if you like it so much."

That took the wind out of his sails.

He frowned. "You're going to just surrender it?"

It was entirely worth whatever humiliation that book might still hold to watch his disappointment.

"Yes."

His eyes narrowed. "You haven't somehow taken it back again?"

"I haven't. You've won."

He didn't look happy about that at all. But then, she was refusing to play his game. He crossed his arms. "Why did you ask me to kiss you tonight?"

She wished she'd already left the ball instead of

remaining, after what had happened on the terrace. But that would have felt like running away. Besides, talking with Dr. Fforde had left her a little soothed, and hopeful, too. She would be a fool, though, to continue to stand there talking to Hal.

She cocked her head at him and let that be her only response.

"Good night, my lord," she said and turned to go.

He took hold of her forearm. Firmly. She looked down at his hand, counting on the presence of those in their general vicinity to make him release her, though no one was paying them any attention.

"Ever unruffled and in control," he said softly, still restraining her.

"Let me go."

"I want to talk to you."

"I don't want to talk to *you*."

He tugged her closer and said in a low voice, "You like me."

She made a scoffing sound.

"You do, or what we did tonight wouldn't have been so pleasurable for you. You *enjoyed* it."

She would *not* blush. She had done those things on the terrace with him—she must be brave enough to acknowledge them. "Well, I already thanked you. And now you wish to suggest I owe you more than that?"

"No, I wish to suggest that we like each other. *I* like *you*."

His words, uttered with what seemed very like sincerity, sent a shiver down her spine and touched something in her that had apparently been waiting her whole life to hear them. She was suddenly terrified of what that yearning part of her might make her say in response.

She discounted the almost vulnerable look in his eyes. Surely he'd employed that very look countless times with other women before her. It didn't feel good, thinking of him that way, but she made herself face reality: he was a charmer born and bred, and not to be trusted.

"No you don't. You merely like what we did. Which clearly you undertook as a way to win your wager by getting information about the Woods Fiend."

"That was only a small part of why I did it. A very small part. The rest was genuine attraction."

"Stop. Please stop. I don't want to hear it. And will you *please* let go of my arm?"

He let her go.

"Lily, it was marvelous out there with you. But it was marvelous because I like you."

"I don't need—I don't want—" But she couldn't seem to speak what she needed, and perhaps that was because it went against her nature to be harsh to someone who'd just said something kind to her, even though this was Hal. He was trying for some reason to tangle her in all this attraction further, just when she needed to firmly do away with, lock up, and otherwise eliminate that lustful tendency in herself that had been making itself known ever since he came back to Mayfield.

"There can't be any more between us, Hal. Surely you see that?"

"No, I don't. Stay—talk, at least. Talking's harmless,

and I can tell you about how I've been looking for that ring you saw in the paintings, the one that belonged to the second sons."

Was this supposed to be some way to keep her attention? "It's not magic, you know. It's just a ring."

He frowned. He wanted to joke and jolly her along—that was his way. She let the silence stretch out a bit before saying, "The valor and the adventure you dreamed of as a boy—what doubtless drew you to the military—that could be part of your work as a viscount. There's nothing stopping you from doing important work now."

Something tightened around his mouth, a hardness she could imagine he'd used with his troops. "I'm not a wastrel, Lily. I run several large estates, and my employees are fond of me."

"But you don't *care* about that work, do you? You haven't really invested yourself in it. You're just existing, taking pleasure, doing the minimum that needs to be done. You haven't made it your *passion*, to use your own word."

"I have no idea what you're talking about," he said tightly.

"This: you've been dealt a significant hand, and with it comes the opportunity to do valuable work. To peer deeply into the workings of your estates, to put your heart into its present and its future, to better the lives of your tenants and servants, to do something for the larger world. But you don't want to be that invested because you're too busy being the playful second son."

"This is all because I haven't been back to Mayfield in so long."

"No, it's because you have much to give, and you're holding it back, spending your energies in diversion."

"I'm not like you, Lily," he said in a voice gone chilly. "I'm not driven to save the world."

"Every person has the chance to do great things in his or her own sphere. You've simply been granted a larger sphere than most people. But you don't, oddly, have enough respect for the work of a viscount to see it through."

"That's ridiculous."

"Is it? You had little love for the viscount your father, who clearly valued your brother over you. Why would you want to give yourself over to a position you were never meant to fill?"

His eyes flashed at her, and she supposed she'd said too much, but she didn't believe she'd said anything he didn't need to hear.

"Remarkably condescending of you," he said in a hard voice she barely recognized. "But then, what should I expect from a woman who so clearly wants to be a saint?"

"I don't think of myself that way," she said, the bluntness of his words shocking her. "I know I have many flaws."

"And you can't ever let yourself forget them, can you? All those mistakes, those times you give in to your animal urges—those missteps are the very things that keep you always striving and depriving yourself. You want to run that school you're planning for, but in a few more years, alone with your hard opinions and your judgmental ways and your need to refuse what you don't find useful, you risk becoming just that kind of sharp, cold woman children fear and dislike."

His words made her feel ill, and she told herself that was only because of how the evening had started— with her brothers foisting partners on her—and that Hal wasn't someone whose idea of the truth should matter to her. But she still felt wounded.

She lifted her chin. "A perfect ending to a ridiculous night. I think we've said quite enough to each other."

And she turned away from him and left the ball.

Fifteen

"You seem to know your way around Mayfield's nooks and crannies quite well for a visitor," Eloise said as Donwell led the way up the narrow staircase to the west tower. She knew going to the roof with Donwell and only Freddy was a little wicked, but doing forbidden things gave her a thrill, and she hardly ever had the chance.

The tower was in the oldest part of Mayfield. Somewhat hidden by the grander, more recent portions of the hall, it had an antiquated charm that Eloise had always liked. Walking at the rear of the party, she held the skirts of her gold satin gown well up and away from the dust and cobwebs festooning the stairs and walls.

"I've been to the roof a few times so far," Donwell said. "It's one of the best places at Mayfield."

"What a peculiar guest you are, making free with people's roofs."

He just laughed. He had a nice laugh.

"I think it's a terrific idea, going up to the roof, sir. You needn't listen to Eloise," her traitorous nephew said. "She's only a girl."

"I had noted that fact," Donwell said in a serious voice that made the corner of Eloise's mouth slide back. Who ever would have guessed that she might find Donwell's company entertaining? Especially after all those things he'd said about her "substance."

But Lily was right, she'd realized—she'd come to see that he was interested in her as a person, and she liked that. He didn't pile compliments on her or strut about arrogantly pleased with himself, as so many gentlemen did. He was plain—not his face, which while not handsome was interesting, but his manner, which was unadorned by flourishes and flirting.

So much of her life was about beauty, and gestures meant to attract, and expectations—and being with Donwell was not like that at all. She supposed some of his unprepossessing appearance might have to do with the fact that he had very little money, and he didn't seem even remotely interested in that usual competition among gentlemen over horses and clothes.

It was refreshing and different to have this new kind of a connection with a man (well, Hal and John liked her, but that didn't count because they had to), and as she followed behind him, she smiled. For some reason, she sensed that they might become good friends. She'd never had a friend who was a man, and she liked the idea. He might even be able to help her understand men better.

He'd reached the top of the stairs, and he pushed against the small old door to the outside. It gave with a heavy whine, sending a rush of clear, cold autumn air into the mustiness of the stairway.

Freddy surged forward, making Eloise gasp, but

Donwell caught him with one arm before he could get very far.

"Easy there. Roof visiting requires great maturity and deliberation."

"What's deliv-ation?"

Eloise smiled; Freddy collected big words.

"It means taking your time."

"Oh. All right." Freddy dropped his head back and gazed upward. The night was clear and dark and quite brisk, and the stars shone hard and true. "Tell me the word again, please."

"Deliberation," Donwell said a bit slowly, and Freddy repeated it.

Eloise was only partly listening to their conversation because the view of the heavens from the roof of the tower had taken her breath away. It felt as if they were *in* the sky, right inside the incredible, mystical darkness. Just over her head floated the cloudy white swath of the Milky Way, speckled with bright stars. Her heart felt suddenly full.

"I'd almost forgotten about the stars," she said. "There they are every night, you need only come out and look up, and yet I never do."

"I'm never allowed," Freddy said.

Eloise turned toward Donwell, who was little more than a tall, dark shape. "I see what I missed a few months ago, when you invited me to stargaze and I didn't come. I'm sorry that I forgot."

"That's all right. Perhaps tonight is a better night for stars."

Freddy moved between them. "Which one is Orion, please, sir?"

Donwell crouched down behind him and stretched his arm out across the boy's shoulders. "There, see the three stars together that make his belt? He's a hunter—you'll see his club if you go up from his belt, and over. And his shield, there."

"I see it!"

Eloise wanted to see as well—she'd never been very good at making out constellations—and she gathered her skirts in her arms and crouched down behind Donwell and tried to follow the line of his arm.

"Can you see it, Eloise?" he asked without turning. A breeze sighed over the battlements at the edge of the tower and swirled around them, its coolness bringing out goose bumps along her bare arms and tugging at her coiffure. It really was too cold to be out in just her ball gown, but she didn't care.

"The sky feels so much closer from here," she said in a hushed voice.

"Doesn't it?" he said.

She leaned closer to the back of his shoulder, which had a welcome aura of warmth, and searched beyond his outstretched arm.

"Oh! I see his belt—there he is." It really was thrilling. Next to her cheek, Donwell's hair ruffled in the breeze.

"Is Orion always there?" Freddy asked.

"Well, the stars are always there, but Orion is best seen in the fall and winter."

"He looks ready for battle."

"He does," Donwell agreed, and Eloise saw his purpose in bringing Freddy to the roof. "I like to think of him as watching over things here on Earth."

Freddy was quiet a moment. "Tell me about all the other stars, please," he said over a yawn.

She thought Donwell must be smiling. "That would take rather too much time for one night."

He stood spryly up and held a hand toward her, which she accepted, and he tugged her upright, so that suddenly she was standing just before him. She didn't think she'd ever stood so close to a man, but this was Donwell, her new friend, and it felt comfortable. What if it had been Ivorwood? How amazing that would have been. But she was glad to be here with Donwell. It was nice.

"Tomorrow, then, please?" Freddy said. "Can we come up again?"

"Perhaps," Donwell said, but his head was turned toward her. "You would have to ask your parents."

"I'm sure they wouldn't mind," she said. "Perhaps I would come as well." And they could invite the others, too, she thought. Like Ivorwood.

"Perfect," he said, and though it was dark, she could feel him looking at her, and she smiled. A new friend was a wonderful thing.

Freddy slipped his hand into hers. "I want to go to bed now, please," he said.

They made their way quietly down to the servants' stairs, and Freddy dashed off to his room.

Donwell and Eloise were still in the stairwell, standing by a sconce, but they couldn't linger there.

"Will you return to the ball?" he asked.

"Yes. Won't you?"

"I think not. But… thank you for coming up to the roof."

Donwell was smiling, and Eloise thought that it quite changed his face, which was usually serious. He had nice crinkles at the corners of his eyes. Actually, he might be a quite presentable man if he only took a little trouble.

She reached out and briskly brushed a few stray white hairs off the front of his coat, as easily as she would have done for her brothers, but Donwell seemed to stiffen when she touched him, and she pulled her hand back, aware that she'd been forward. Still, they were friends now, and she could offer him some advice.

"Your coat has a remarkably weird look," she said with a smile. "The collar is wrong, and it's fashionable to have buttons in the front, you know. Why, it must be a good twenty years old."

Donwell swallowed hard, still recovering from the feel of her hand brushing his chest. It had been a very familiar thing to do, and he *was* familiar to her, being a frequent visitor with her brother. And now she was giving him advice about his clothes. He was excited by her noticing his personal appearance and making recommendations—it felt intimate. Yet he could not read her meaning. Was she giving him encouragement? Was this something she might say to a lover?

"Thirty," he said. "It was my father's."

"You might consider buying something from this decade. It's remarkable what a good coat can do for a man. Why, it would make you look like a man of substance."

"Touché," he said. "I shall consider it."

"I rather think you will forget it while you

are staring out telescopes or crawling around after animals," she said. She put her hand on the door that led out to the corridor, and his heart skipped a beat. "Good night then," she said. "See you tomorrow."

"Wait," he murmured, far too late, because she'd already gone through the doorway.

Why didn't Lily mind now that he had her journal?

Hal was still racking his brain over why she'd given up on it as he followed the heartiest of his houseguests up the stairs late that night with a candelabrum in his hand. Ivorwood turned into his chamber first, with calls of good night to all. Eloise lingered to whisper a soft good night back as the earl's door closed, then continued on with the other guests. The glitter and sound of the ball had given way to darkness and the drudgery of the familiar, and it would be light soon.

Lily, who'd retired hours ago, would doubtless arise early and accomplish something productive—write letters, organize a charity, create a poultry cooperative. And she would, apparently, be untroubled by thoughts of her journal's whereabouts. But why? He passed her room, where she was likely sleeping the sleep of someone who'd not had too many glasses of punch.

He wished he hadn't spoken so harshly to her. He'd said more than he meant to, had somehow been driven to it. Yet it would take something strong to get past that wall of virtue she'd erected around herself. And she hadn't crumpled, but drawn herself up straighter.

And told him he lacked passion for the viscountcy.

She was right.

She was right, dammit, that he connected the viscountcy to his uncaring father, and that he'd come, however poor this was of him, to resent it because it had never been meant for him. Because he *had* been defined by the viscountcy: it was the yardstick against which he'd been found wanting from the moment he was born. It was the most important role in the family, and it belonged to the brother he loved. There was nothing to be done about this, but some urge in him—competition, contrariness—hated to be put in second place. And it had meant that who he was had never been of value, except that he was the spare.

So how was he supposed to develop a passion for being a viscount?

Ridiculous, she'd called the night. A feint, surely? She hadn't felt ridiculous when she was surrendering to desire in his arms.

Alone now, he passed beyond the guest quarters and into the family wing. As soon as he was inside his bedchamber, he pulled his cravat loose and sat down at his desk with Lily's journal. After that incredibly erotic scene behind the cherry tree, he hadn't been able to think of anything but her all night, and this was the closest he could get to her just now.

He hesitated with his hands on the girlish fabric cover of the book, admitting fully to himself that in reading this he was invading her privacy. He'd given himself permission to read it before, discounting what that might mean to her, but now he could think only of her, of what she would want.

But she had told him to keep it, as good as giving him permission to read it. He opened the book.

I dreamed last night that we all walked out to the daffodil glade in the woods. I say dream, but it was a fantasy, really, a waking dream I urged into being. There was Hal, Eloise, Ian, Rob, and myself, and some shadowy ladies and gentlemen, in that way of people in dreams and fantasies who are there but you can't really see them.

The day was sun-kissed and beautiful, and we entered the woods. Everyone was suddenly dappled with the golden sunlight that slipped through the canopy of leaves, a lazy scene of warmth and soft light and beauty.

The others continued on to see the daffodils, but Hal drew me away so that we were separated from them. I could feel how he wanted me.

Well, Hal thought. Very good. Despite the excessive nature talk, the plot thickens. He read on eagerly.

He took my hand and we wandered deeper, until we came to a place he seemed to know, a shady clearing carpeted in thick, soft moss and clusters of violets and lilies of the valley. He leaned in to kiss my neck, then my lips. I touched his face, moved my hands to his shoulders, and felt their muscled strength.

He turned the page quickly, as if the words might give him the release for which his real embrace with Lily had left him yearning. The next page held fewer words and he read on avidly.

He kissed my cheek and told me he found me beautiful, that there was no one like me in the world. That he'd noticed me with a gradual dawning in recent months, and that now he couldn't think about anything but me.

Hal found himself getting impatient with the young Lily. Enough talk, girl—get to the action.

And then he held me against him, and the moonlight shone down on us so heartbreakingly beautiful, and he kissed me again, and we lay down together and he held me. And we knew as surely as we knew the sun would rise every day that we'd always be together, and that our hearts would always be one. It was perfect.

Yes? Yes? And? There was plenty of blank space left on the page for more of the fantasy, but nothing else was written, as if that were the end of the scene, which, how could it be? The best parts were missing. He turned the page but there were no more words, just the unfinished sketch of him from the terrace. Obviously he'd taken the book at that point.

This fantasy of being in the woods alone with him—it was a good fantasy, she'd had the right idea. But where were the details, the sensual descriptions she'd lavished on his appearance and their imagined kisses earlier on? The woods fantasy should have been the satisfaction of all the lust she'd built up for him. But it was chaste. Unfinished. *Unsatisfying.*

He felt cheated. Deeply vexed right down to his

cock, which had had about as much teasing as it could take in the matter of Lily Teagarden. What was wrong with that girl? At sixteen, if he'd embarked on such a fantasy, he would never have stopped at kissing. Not when everything within him was urging him toward the stiff and hot meeting the wet and snug.

And then it came to him, the reason she hadn't cared if he finished the book. He slumped back in his chair and tugged his shirt loose to gap wide, pressing his lips in vexation with Lily bleeding Teagarden.

Tonight she'd already gone far, far further with him than those fantasy kisses from the journal. The tentative touching and kissing she'd imagined in its pages had been the most detailed—and doubtless the most embarrassing—part of the book for her. She could imagine a kiss back then; she might even have seen one. But her sixteen-year-old self had no real idea of what the sex act would be like.

And now that she'd had a taste of the actual experience of passion—and he was fairly certain that kiss in her bedchamber had been her first sensual contact with a man, never mind what they'd done that night—she'd known how dull the rest of her journal would be to him. She was probably lying in her bed right now, laughing at him.

He sucked his teeth, then burst out laughing. What a minx she was, no matter that she meant to be serious and worthy.

Closing the colorful cover of the journal, he put it in his desk drawer. Despite his frustrated lust, he had a charitable feeling toward it. As a girl Lily had thought so much of him that simply being with him was enough—they hadn't, in her mind, needed to even do anything besides hold each other. It was funny, but it was also sweet and innocent. There was no mistaking the deep trust she'd imagined between the lovers.

He'd never trusted anyone like that, or wanted to. He wasn't even certain he knew how to do so. But he knew suddenly that he wanted to try.

What would it take for her to trust him now, as a living, breathing man?

He undressed and moved toward the bed, passing the window on his way, which was when he saw the tiny glow of a light in the woods. He quickly reached for his boots, but before he'd pulled the second one on, the light had disappeared.

Damn it all.

Sixteen

LILY AROSE EARLY THE NEXT MORNING, WELL BEFORE the rest of the sleeping guests with the exception of Rob, whom she encountered in the breakfast room. She supposed being country people, the Teagardens were more used to farmers' hours than those who lived in town.

He whistled cheerfully under his breath as he loaded his plate with kippers and steak in substantial quantities. She helped herself to toast and a boiled egg and sat down at the table.

"Well, Lily," he said, tucking in, "I think you must have enjoyed yourself last night. I don't think I saw you alone once."

"That was perhaps due mostly to your efforts, dear brother."

"Nonsense, those gentlemen wouldn't have been eager to dance with you were you not so lovely and charming."

"Be that as it may," she said, tapping her egg with the edge of her spoon, "I did have a pleasant evening." She repressed a surge of hysterical laughter at the absurdity of referring to what had happened the night before with such a mild term as *pleasant*. She'd practically rutted with Hal.

Don't be dramatic, she told herself sternly. *It was a little education you were in need of.* Whatever it was, *pleasant* was a poor description for it.

Scorching, yes. It had also been enchanting, though she never would have thought such an innocent word could be used for something so earthy, so… animalistic?… as what she and Hal had done. He'd made her think about things she was better off not thinking about, like bodies.

She was glad he'd said those hard words to her. Knowing he couldn't respect the person she was made it easier to push thoughts of him aside. She must focus on significant things, like the school, and Dr. Fforde's fever hospital.

Rob slid a glance at her. "Matthew Fforde told me before he left that seeing you was the best part of his evening."

A warm blush of embarrassment mingled with shame spread up the back of her neck as she wondered what the doctor would think of her if he knew what she'd been doing outside with Hal. Doubtless he would not then have been expressing an interest in her.

Still, she liked Dr. Fforde and liked very much his talk of the important work he was going to do in the north. He seemed like a very good man. Perhaps the very sort of man who might induce her to consider marriage.

For something had shifted inside her last night, and she was thinking now that perhaps she really ought to consider marriage. For one thing, she felt suddenly afraid that she couldn't trust herself where passion was concerned. She'd allowed, no, encouraged Hal to do all that he'd done last night—what might she do on another occasion with another handsome, seductive man?

A little voice whispered that Hal was different from other men as far as she was concerned, that she wouldn't be susceptible to other men, that he was singular, special. She didn't want to hear it.

"I enjoyed spending time with Dr. Fforde."

Rob grinned. "Good, because I think we'll be seeing even more of him."

And that, thought Lily as she dipped the corner of her toast in her egg, sounded like a very good and reasonable thing.

❧

Hal was awake earlier than he wanted to be considering his late night, but he'd been thinking about that ancestral ring and all the places it might be, and he felt compelled to find it. He'd already been looking for it in the unused rooms of the house (supposing that in the rooms which were cleaned regularly, it would already have been found), and now he'd come to the attic.

Methodically, he opened all the trunks of clothes and rifled through them, squeezing the fabrics in case the ring had been forgotten in a pocket. He opened every drawer and inspected every shelf and sifted through boxes of papers, among which he found a series of letters between his parents, in only one of which was he or John or Eloise mentioned:

> *Hal carries along unremarkably as usual. John and Eloise continue in the care of Nanny.*

Unremarkably, goddammit.

The rest of the letter had to do with the brilliance of Everard's ideas related to economies the estate could make.

Lily would probably have wanted to say something compassionate on the subject of inadequate parental love, and he could only be thankful she wasn't there.

Except he wasn't thankful; he was sorry they'd quarreled, and he wished he knew how to talk to her without ending up in a dispute. It was only that she frustrated him so much, with the way she kept herself distant from him when they so clearly lit each other up.

The ring was not to be found in the attic, which was not really surprising. Though he was strangely disappointed. In fact, the only things of interest he found were an ancient quintain for practicing jousting and several equally ancient battered lances.

He left the attic and went to the stables, and took Emperor out for a punishingly fast ride. By the time he got back people were stirring from their chambers, and he rounded up several of the gentlemen to try out the jousting equipment.

∽≥

Lily, Eloise, and Delia sat companionably embroidering in a second-floor sitting room early that afternoon. However, Delia and Eloise were so engaged in their review of all the gowns that had been worn to the ball, Lily noticed with a private smile, that they weren't getting much done.

A distant thumping sound came in through the open window, followed by shouts, and Delia hopped up and looked out.

"Gad, what on earth are they doing?" she said.

"Who?" Eloise said, going to look as well. "Why, I think they're jousting! Well, practicing, it looks like, with that mannequin."

"How medieval!" Delia said. "Is this a family custom?"

Eloise laughed. "No, it must be something Hal dreamed up. I think that old thing was in the attic, at least it was years ago. It must be full of dust and bugs."

"Ugh," Delia said.

"Yes, look!" Eloise laughed. "Now they've broken it."

Lily finally could not resist looking herself, and she squeezed in at the window. Several gentlemen and a pair of horses stood about on the greensward near a pole that had the remains of a quintain sticking to it.

"Look," Eloise said, "Donwell's putting on a chain mail or some such, and Hal too. How funny they look, walking—it must weigh a ton."

"Oh," Delia said as Donwell and Hal awkwardly approached the horses from which they'd demolished the quintain. "Are they really going to joust?" she said as, with some effort, the men mounted. "I wonder if this is a good idea."

"Of course it isn't," Lily said, reluctant admiration at what appeared to be sheer, antic folly making her lips quiver. "That's why they're doing it." Another of Hal's diversions. She hoped they didn't maim themselves, but they were grown men. She supposed he'd already forgotten all that had happened between them the night before. It had been just one more entertainment.

"They really are going to do it," Eloise said in a horrified voice.

Lily turned away, unable to watch.

"Oh heavens!" Eloise said. "Oh dear!"

Heavy, ringing thumps.

"Ah," Delia said. "Well, that's it then." The sounds of masculine guffaws came through the window.

"Is anyone hurt?" Lily asked, trying to keep the depth of her concern out of her voice.

"I don't think so," Delia said. "The lances crumbled when they made contact with the armor." The men were shouting now with laughter; apparently they'd never been so diverted.

Lily let out a huge sigh of relief as she walked away from the window, silently cursing Hal for making her care so much. "Well, that's two fools saved from themselves."

"Oh, Lily, it's not wrong to be silly sometimes," Delia said.

"No," she said with a sad wistfulness, "I suppose it isn't." And for the first time, she wished just a little bit that she were able to be silly.

❧

Lily was standing by a small stone table in the garden late that afternoon, going through a pile of books on Greek history someone had abandoned there and pondering bringing them inside so they wouldn't be ruined by the elements. At the far end of the garden,

Freddy and Louie were running about under the watchful eye of their nanny. No one else was about, most of the adults having retired to their rooms for a rest before dinner. She was glad, because she didn't at all wish to speak with anyone. And yet she'd not felt restful in her room, where there was nothing to distract her from memories of the night before.

She didn't, unfortunately, feel any less restless in the garden. As she absentmindedly paged through a discussion of the Peloponnesian War, a shadow fell across the book.

"Lily," Hal said.

She looked up, determined to be unaffected by him even if something inside her was turning over like a lock with a key in its chambers. He was wearing a vivid green coat and tan breeches with gleaming top boots, all his attire cut to fit his beautiful form splendidly. His golden hair was windblown, though this only made him look charmingly careless. She would not entertain thoughts about how it had felt to have his hair brushing against her collarbone and his lips on her skin.

They'd said everything last night—as much as could be expressed—and she knew deeply how foolish it was to entertain any idea that they could really mean something to each other.

"Back from the wars?" she said in her best uncaring tone.

"It was only a skirmish."

She made no reply, and the silence stretched out between them.

"Lily," he said in a surprisingly urgent tone,

"forgive me. I said too much last night. I said more than I meant."

"Oh? Which part was that?" she examined a drawing of ancient weapons. "When you were telling me you liked me? Or when you said I was in danger of becoming a witchy spinster who'd scare children?"

"That part, obviously."

She didn't believe him. In truth, his words still stung. She didn't want to be a hard, sharp woman; she wanted to be kind and caring. But the truth was, she wasn't good at being warm and relaxed and open, and this was a fault.

He said her name, drawing her attention, and she looked at him. His blue-green eyes were dark and missing their customary sparkle. He raked a hand through his hair; he almost looked anguished. Which was ridiculous, since he'd clearly been full of merriment while jousting.

"I *do* like you," he continued. "Very much."

She left his words hanging there because she didn't know what to do with them. She didn't trust them.

"Am I forgiven then?"

"Of course. We spoke harshly to each other. It's best forgotten."

His hand started toward where hers was on the table, but he checked himself. Several moments passed, which she was determined not to fill.

"Perhaps you'll be interested to know," he said equably, "that I saw a light in the woods last night when I returned to my room. It went out immediately, or I would have given chase. Though doubtless the presence of the Woods Fiend is not news to you."

"Of course it's news to me," she said, which was

true, as she didn't know Nate's plans. Remorse pricked her as she realized that since she'd arrived at Mayfield she'd practically forgotten about his need to find his buried treasure as soon as possible. Apparently—as had been well demonstrated—the presence of Hal chased all sensible thought from her head. But now she knew that Nate had disregarded her advice to stay away from the Mayfield woods for the moment.

"Come," Hal said, "do you deny feeding him information about my efforts to stalk him?"

Though she'd done nothing to encourage Nate's efforts last night, Hal was in general correct. She conjured up a vacuous look that she hoped would discourage further questions.

"Cat got your tongue? Or perhaps you'd rather communicate in writing. You seem to be more free in the written word."

"I'm delighted you enjoy my writing. You've certainly had enough time with my journal."

"Ha. Yes, I have. Though, you know," he said in an oddly regretful tone, "I'm sorry I didn't appreciate its charms when I was younger."

"I rather doubt the book holds so many charms for you now."

"There you would be wrong." He smiled finally, and she thought that it ought to be illegal, him smiling and making those slashes form in the taut planes of his cheeks.

She knew a spurt of compassion for herself right then; with his charm and his mischief and his male beauty, he was like a shiny thing amid the everydayness of life—who, in fact, would not find him dazzling?

"Don't you ever look bad?" she asked. "Pasty skin, a spot, a sign of softness in the middle?" She sighed. "Really, my only consolation is that you are getting old."

"Old?" He laughed. "I'm not even thirty." He leaned his hip against the edge of the table, the master at ease among his fine possessions. In the distance beyond his shoulder lay the half-built folly. "I'm going to interpret these little thoughts of yours as compliments, an affirmation that I can still hold a candle to the younger man who inspired you."

"You do realize, don't you, that I was merely young and dazzled by male beauty?" True and not true, but she didn't owe it to him to confess that her feelings had been deeper than she was admitting—or that they had a new hold on her. Last night had shown her, if she needed reminding, how easy and blithe he could be about intimacy. And how much she could not.

"Maybe," he said, his eyes dropping down as his fingers toyed with one of the books, a slim, brown volume whose exquisite cover had been softened into floppiness by years and use. "And maybe you wrote things down without realizing you were setting them down. Not about me, but about yourself and your own essential qualities."

She lifted her eyes toward the sky, where streaky clouds hung overhead like bars. A chilly breeze teased the edge of her sage-green walking dress and carried a reminder that the roses of summer would not last much longer.

"If you found anything interesting in that journal, it was merely that you liked reading sensual things." She shrugged. "I was young and dreamy."

"And now you are too old for dreams? Too old, at almost twenty-one, to care for beauty and pleasure and anything else you've decided doesn't have a moral value?"

"Well, I certainly wouldn't build a folly when there's so much important work to be done in the world. People are starving and hurt and sorrowing, and you're spending a small fortune on something with no earthly use."

"I *like* the idea that it has no use, that it only exists to conjure a smile, a laugh, some pleasure. Beauty has purpose. I would even say it puts us in touch with the divine."

Her brows drew together. How dared he—of all people—come to be claiming a true interest in the divine?

"In any case," he continued, "the folly is providing employment for two people, or it would be if you'd surrender the identity of the Woods Fiend. So really, who's the one stopping people from having what they need? Or do you not believe their work valuable?"

It seemed he never would see her way of looking at things. He took what she said, worked it over, and presented it back to her in such a way that she didn't recognize herself. "No. Of course honest work is valuable. And art and beauty. Just—in moderation."

"Where's the moderation, then, in your own beauty? Because it overflows profligately—the moonlight hair, the blue-lilac eyes, the shape of your hands, the creamy skin of your shoulders. None of it is necessary, and yet it's there. You are just as beautiful as I am handsome, Lily. It's one of your gifts, and yet you refuse to enjoy it, to truly accept it."

His words had a physical effect on her, stirring a heavy flutter in her chest like a bird beating its wings. "I—this is absurd. The issue is not appearances, it's the calculated *charm*."

"You're against charm?"

"I'm against insincerity. The way you have of making women enchanted with you just because you can."

He laughed, extended an arm against the table and leaned closer to her, a hint of eagerness playing about his mouth. The smooth, clean-shaven plane of his cheek made her envision the everyday domesticity of his valet at work over him with a razor, but she blinked her eyes and sent the image away.

"Are you saying that you're enchanted, Lily? Just a bit?"

She wanted to scoff, but considering what had passed between them the night before—and the fact that she *was* more than a little enchanted—that would come across but weakly. She moved back from him, ostensibly to stack the pile of books.

"I meant all the women you've left in your wake as you've made your way from one house party or ball or country to the next. Though I almost think you can't help yourself, that it's a compulsion, or even a reflex, that impels you to charm people. Women."

He crossed his arms, the arrogant nobleman in his domain. She wanted, perversely, to ruffle up his hair, or unbutton his coat and button it again with the buttons in the wrong holes.

"You love to reform a sinner, don't you, Lily?"

"I'm hardly in a position to do that, am I?"

He waved his hand. "Don't take yourself so seriously. You know, I do genuinely like women. It's not an act."

"Not that you're aware of, certainly. You like them, as playthings and entertainments. But what about who they are as people? Their hopes and wounds and needs? What about Eloise, who has no parents and is going along with little guidance, now, when her future will hinge on the man she marries?"

"And you would be so much better at helping her pick, simply because your guiding principle is 'no handsome aristocrats.'"

"It's not a bad principle."

"Eloise will be fine—she has a good head on her shoulders, and I won't give permission for her to wed any fools. Why don't you admit what this is really about: you're disgusted with yourself for what we did together yesterday." His words were strong, but his tone was gentle. "Lily-who-should-have-tea-in-the-garden-and-never-think-about-the-bedchamber."

She looked down at the Thucydides volume on top of the stack she'd arranged, though she wasn't really seeing it. It was foolish to stand here with him having this outrageous conversation, but she needed to make sure he understood. "I consider it simply an educational experience."

His bark of laughter made her look up. "So this was, what, a new window into the ways of men? An experience you've had now, and not to be repeated, to be filed under the category of things you can't learn about men from your brothers."

That startled a disgusted laugh out of her, just when

she shouldn't be laughing with him at all. "Ugh, what a thought."

"You know, Lily, you're clever and beautiful and absolutely wonderful company. But you won't *let yourself go*."

She didn't like the way his words made her feel, as if she were sanctimonious, when what she wanted—what she'd always wanted—was to be a good person. He'd succeeded in riling her again, but she reached for calm.

"There, do you see why we don't actually have anything to say to one another? You want to let yourself go, as you say, for every passing whim, and I don't. It's not what I choose for myself. The things each of us cares about couldn't be more different. There's simply nothing more to say."

She moved past him, toward where the boys and Nanny were, aware that she wanted the security their presence would provide without wanting to admit of what it was that she was afraid.

Hal watched Lily go, those upright shoulders stiff as usual, the pale blond, dignified back of her head an austere rebuttal to all the ways he'd tried to make her see. She wanted him to understand that she wouldn't accept him, no matter how much she might be attracted to him.

He was at sea. Intuition had deserted him, or facility—whatever it was that had allowed him to charm women had decamped, leaving him awkward. What was wrong with him?

He thought of the brilliant smiles she'd given Fforde the night before. Fforde, with his blasted fever hospital. He knew a stab of self-disgust that it had never occurred to him to use some of his now-considerable funds for an undertaking like the hospital. His family had never gone in for that sort of thing because the viscountcy had always only been about the family. His father's guiding words had been, "*Every step, every choice must enhance the viscountcy.*"

His father's emphasis on family had always seemed idiotic to Hal, when it was so evident that most of the *people* in his family meant so little to him. But then, his father had wanted a dynasty, not a family.

He *could* fund a significant project like Fforde's; in fact, he very much liked the idea of establishing a far better way of caring for ill and wounded soldiers. He had the means now to do something for men like the ones who'd served with him. He'd take it up with his man of affairs.

Lily would respect an undertaking like that.

But he didn't want her to want him because he could pay for good works.

He felt a strong, sudden urge to forgo wine at meals and talk only to men and spend hours in prayer in his room, simply because she wouldn't expect it of him.

They were all urges he'd easily mastered by lunchtime.

At which meal he had the uncomfortable sense that his sister was paying rather a lot of attention to Donwell, who seemed smitten with her, and also to Ivorwood, who was ever-oblivious. Something about that situation did not bode well, and Hal supposed he ought to provide Eloise with some brotherly guidance.

But the idea of his giving romantic advice to anyone seemed like the purest hypocrisy. Perhaps Diana could help.

Seventeen

An unusual housekeeping situation came to Eloise's attention as she walked away from lunch in the company of Donwell. Mrs. Pratt, the housekeeper, had apparently been waiting to speak with him, and she waylaid him in the hallway.

"If you please, sir, there's been a small accident in your room."

"An accident?" Eloise said before Donwell could reply. "What sort of accident?"

Mrs. Pratt flicked a rather hard glance at Donwell. "His vermin have escaped."

"His *what*?"

"Only some harmless beetles," he said. "And what do you mean they escaped?"

"They are the size of mice, sir," Mrs. Pratt said with remarkable evenness, "and the maids are terrified of them. Sally accidentally knocked into the box when she was tidying your chamber, and the creatures came out, frightening her to death."

"Foolish of her. They're harmless."

"So you say, but I can't blame her. She ran shrieking

out of the room, and who knows where they've gone. Nor do we know how to collect them—"

"Please do no such thing," Donwell said sternly, starting up the stairs two at a time. "You might injure them."

Eloise ran after him.

"Donwell," she laughed, "what have you done?"

They reached the corridor, which was carpeted in a Turkey rug, and he said, "We must step carefully—they may have escaped from my room."

With anticipatory glee, she imagined Mrs. Whyte coming upon a creature in her room, but hardly had she gone five steps when one of the flowers in the carpet pattern moved. She shrieked.

"There," she gasped, pointing to an enormous beetle with a large pincer scuttling toward the bottom of a guest bedroom door. Donwell dropped to all fours and crawled toward it.

"Dear God," she breathed, "it looks evil."

"Nonsense, it's the gentlest creature," he said. "Only don't make any sudden motions, as he may fly if startled."

She kept very still while he put a hand in front of the beetle.

"Dare I ask how many you brought?"

"Only two," he said, coaxing the beetle onto his hand. It seemed to accept him, and she thought he even petted it before he stood up. "They were a gift from a friend who was recently in Brazil."

The beetle really was the size of a mouse, dark and shiny. It was revolting, and yet, perched on the palm of Donwell's hand, it didn't look menacing. "And so you brought it to a house party."

He glanced up from his creature with a puzzled look. "Well, I couldn't leave them in my rooms in London—who would feed them?"

"Who indeed?"

They walked to his room, the door to which was closed, and he had her open it while he stepped carefully inside. Leaving the door wide for propriety's sake, she followed him, and he put the beetle in a box that stood near the window. They discovered the other creature feasting on a soft log among a stack by the hearth.

"There," he said, tenderly collecting it and putting it in the box with the other one, "if only Sally hadn't made such a fuss and scared him off, he would have been there with the female, eating the wood. It's what they like."

"Naturally."

He glanced up from the box. His cravat, which had not been neatly tied to begin with, had come loose when he was crawling around. He was wearing the same faded, horrible brown coat again—Eloise suspected he didn't have much else to wear—but it had begun to amuse her, and she grinned. He frowned a bit.

"What's funny?"

"You. I rather think you're not ready for polite society." She tipped her head to the side. "I could help you, you know. Be more the thing."

Something tightened around his mouth. "No, thank you. I'm not in need of a mother."

She'd offended him. "Well, of course not. You're older than I am." Though in terms of what was required of gentlemen, she thought, he was more like a boy. Unschooled, unaware—whatever it was, he wasn't masterful like Ivorwood or her brother.

"Eloise," he said, but then he paused. His brows drew together, and an intent quality in his eyes made her think he was going to say something serious, but she didn't want to hear serious things from Donwell.

"Come, tell me what else you've brought," she said, glancing around the room. "A snake? Fish? A small tiger?"

He looked peevish. "Nothing else."

But a box on top of the wardrobe had caught her eye, and she was reaching for it when he said, "That's only a rat."

She pulled her hand back. "A *rat*?"

"I didn't bring it, I found it here."

"Oh, Donwell," she said when she could catch her breath from laughing, "you *do* make me laugh. How amusing you are!"

Although Donwell loved to hear Eloise laugh, having her laugh *at* him like this was far from a pleasure.

"Did you still want to walk in the garden?" he asked. She'd mentioned doing so at lunch, and though he had to suppose she'd mostly said it to attract Ivorwood's attention, last night and this morning she'd been equally attentive to him, and he wasn't about to squander what chances he had.

"No time now—I'm to meet Delia in a little while and it will take me an hour to change."

"A waste of time," he said softly, meaning that she already looked exquisite. But he couldn't seem to say that part; he felt he'd sound obsequious, or insincere.

She sighed. "You *would* think so," she said, walking toward the door.

"I'll see you tonight, then?" he said.

"Right," she called over her shoulder on her way out.

It was a larger party that went to the roof for stargazing that night, and at a more suitable hour for a five-year-old. When Freddy had asked his mother about going to the roof with Donwell and Eloise, Diana had insisted, not surprisingly, that it wasn't appropriate for a lady and a gentleman to be alone with only a five-year-old for a chaperone. Eloise had advised Freddy not to mention that such a thing had already happened. And anyway, now the issue was resolved, because she'd invited Ivorwood, Hal, Ian, Lily, Delia, and even annoying Mrs. Whyte to join her and Donwell and Freddy.

As the group made their way to the tower in the interval between dinner and cards, Eloise savored the excitement of Ivorwood's presence ahead of her. Though the house party was not large, she still hadn't had as many chances as she'd have liked to spend time with him, and they'd hardly talked at all. Being on the roof together would be so much more intimate—hadn't it felt so when she was up there with Donwell? Surely it would be the perfect time for something—even just a little something—to happen between them. She'd settle for a conversation of more than one sentence, or even his coat sleeve brushing against her arm.

Once on the roof, everyone exclaimed over the

sky. The night was cold and clear, and Eloise found it all beautiful again, and listened a bit as Donwell pointed out constellations to Freddy. But most of her attention was claimed by the sight of Ivorwood talking to Delia a few yards away, by a torch near the battlements. Their heads were bent close—what could they be discussing so intently? She felt horribly left out.

She hadn't noticed that Donwell had stopped talking about the sky until she realized he was standing next to her. It was too dark where they stood to see much beyond the flash of moonlight in his eyes.

"I liked it better when it was just us with a five-year-old chaperone," he said.

A husky note in his voice plucked a skittish chord in her, and she forced lightness into her voice, the same tone she'd have used with any gentleman. "Oh, a scandalous thing to say, Mr. Donwell."

He made no reply, and they stood for a few moments in silence. She wondered what he wanted.

"You're watching Ivorwood," he said.

"No, I'm not," she said, irritated.

"He's a very reserved man," Donwell observed. "I think what he is for you is a blank slate on which to compose your fancies."

She felt as if she'd been smacked—not pain, but the shock of his words, and the sense she didn't want to acknowledge that there was something in them. "I can't imagine what makes you speak to me this way."

He was quiet, and she thought that probably they were done speaking to each other, and that was certainly for the best because now she felt horribly peevish. But then he did speak.

"It's because I fancy you, of course. And that makes me hate to watch you looking at him."

A shiver ran through her at the masculine directness of his words. How had he said such a thing—Donwell, who made her laugh and hardly knew a cravat from a stocking?

"I don't know what you're talking about," she said, barely knowing what words she spoke. What was she supposed to say? She didn't fancy him, she fancied Ivorwood—handsome, mysterious Ivorwood. Her embarrassment sent her on the attack.

"And you're wrong. He's not like that at all."

"What's he like then?"

"He's a deep river—I mean, this is ridiculous! I don't have to justify myself to you."

"No, you don't." He was silent a moment. "I only wonder whether you're ready to experience some-thing real, or if you're too afraid to step away from girlish fantasy."

Afraid? She wasn't afraid—she was bold. But she didn't want to talk about things like this with Donwell, and she was just about to tell him so when he turned away and made his way toward where Hal was crouched down, talking with Freddy. Eloise felt cross and strangely hot and stirred up, and deserted by Donwell, who'd left before she had set him straight.

By the battlements, Delia laughed musically at something Ivorwood had said, and jealousy pricked Eloise. Ivorwood never practiced witticisms on her. *Why* didn't he? She'd always been sure he was reserved with her because that was his way, because he was a very careful gentleman, and she valued that. Yet there he was, still talking to Delia.

She imagined Donwell with a scornful expression she couldn't see, and anger prodded her. Something *must* happen between her and Ivorwood tonight. This was her best chance to enable things between them.

She moved closer to Ivorwood and Delia and joined their conversation, which was about the planets. Eloise couldn't have cared a fig for planets just then; her mind was spinning, trying to find a ruse.

Delia, thank heaven, made it easy for her by going off to ask Ian something, which Eloise suspected was merely an effort to keep him from talking too long to flirtatious old Hyacinth. That left Eloise with Ivorwood. She surreptitiously removed one of her ear bobs and slipped it into her pocket, savoring how bold she was about to be.

"Ivorwood, I wonder if you would help me. I seem to have dropped my pearl ear bob, and I think it fell somewhere on the tower staircase. But I'm rather afraid of the stairs, with all the cobwebs and bugs."

"I'd be happy to look for it, Eloise. But shouldn't we ask everyone to help, and multiply the effort?"

"I think not, because that would also be more feet, and someone might step on it."

"Then I shall go alone."

The heavy door to the stairs was close by, and it had been left partially ajar. The others were all standing together at the far side of the roof, facing away and up at the sky, and when Ivorwood passed through the doorway, Eloise waited a moment, then slipped in behind him.

"Eloise?"

There was a lantern hanging on a hook in the wall a few feet away, and in its murky light she saw the surprise on his face. He was two steps down from her.

She descended one step.

"I thought you didn't like it in here," he said.

"I don't. But I like *you*."

There! She'd said it.

He seemed to be contemplating her words, his shadowed face a study in strength and manliness and sheer handsomeness, though was that a leery light in his eyes? But he was everything that was good and desirable and honorable. And that meant he was too constrained by his gentleman's breeding to take action.

"Eloise," he began, "you are a lovely, gracious young woman—"

Oh, hurrah! He did love her a bit. Donwell was wrong, he didn't understand at all. Not waiting for the earl to finish lest she lose her nerve, she leaned closer.

"Wait," he began, but this was her chance for her first kiss ever, and with the man of her dreams, and she couldn't let gentlemanly scruples stand in their way. Quickly she leaned closer and pressed her lips to his. Everything in her thrilled for the culmination of this moment she'd yearned for, even if she'd always imagined he'd be the one doing the kissing.

It was not quite as she'd thought it would be, which confused her. He smelled good, and his lips were soft, though prickly at the edges with the beginnings of whiskers. But why wasn't he kissing her back?

He seemed to be leaning away.

"Don't be silly, Hyacinth," came Donwell's voice

just then from the doorway behind her, causing Eloise to spring backward and fall against the steps.

"Of course Eloise isn't in the stairwell with Ivorwood."

Eloise's eyes flicked upward, and there was Donwell just above her, looking down at her sprawled on the steps.

How much had he seen?

"I'm sure they're both in there," came Hyacinth's eager voice from a slight distance, making Eloise's stomach drop.

"I don't think," Ivorwood began, but Donwell jerked his chin toward the bottom of the stairs.

"Ivorwood's left already," Donwell said, staring at both of them.

"I'm certain I heard something in there," Hyacinth probed, her voice coming closer.

"If Miss Waverly would consent," Ivorwood began in a grim voice, "to be my—"

"No, don't!" Eloise broke in, horrified at what she'd done so impulsively. "I'm so sorry. Just go—now!"

With a dark look, Ivorwood disappeared down into the shadows of the lower staircase just as Hyacinth appeared in the doorway.

"Oh. It's only Miss Waverly," she said with a note of disappointment, as if she'd been done out of something. And she had—an extremely juicy piece of gossip.

"I was looking for my ear bob," Eloise said in a tiny voice, getting to her feet.

Ian, Delia, Hal, Lily, and Freddy appeared in the doorway as well. "Shall we go down to the card party now?" Ian said.

"Yes," Donwell said. "I believe Ivorwood was called away."

Dear God, what a fool she'd been. She'd almost unthinkingly forced Ivorwood into the position of having to marry her whether he wanted to or not. And it was *not*, she knew that now.

She squeezed her brimming eyes shut and dashed at the tears spilling out with the back of her hand. She was bitter and disappointed and hurt, and the only thing she wanted in that moment was her bedchamber.

Not waiting for the others, she fled down the stairs.

"Eloise?" Delia called.

"I think she has a headache," came Donwell's reply. And in that moment, she hated him.

⁂

Lily had been avoiding Hal ever since their conversation in the garden—she'd kept to her room for much of the afternoon and spent most of her time on the roof talking to Freddy and Ian. She could feel Hal's eyes on her frequently, but he did not come near, for which she'd been grateful. When she was with him, she said and did far too much.

But she'd seen the earl go into the stairway, and now with the distress in Eloise's voice and the rushing footsteps disappearing down the darkened stairs, she guessed something had happened. Hal was behind her, the last one of the roof party, and she turned and said quietly to him, "Eloise is upset. You should go to her."

"Me?" They slowed their steps while the others continued down the stairs in front of them.

"I think something may have happened between her and Ivorwood," she whispered.

"Surely not. Ivorwood is a thorough gentleman."

"Perhaps it wasn't something he did. Maybe words passed between them that upset her."

"Even supposing that's the case, surely it would be something for her to discuss with a female friend."

"No, you're the perfect person."

"Don't be absurd—we never talk about things like this."

"She's upset, possibly over a man. Who better than you to provide her a perspective into a group of people she may not understand?"

"Her sister-in-law? You?"

"Go find her."

And remarkably, he went.

Standing outside Eloise's door, Hal thought he must be the last person who should be there. Putting aside his lack of experience or desire for discussing girlish feelings, he had been miserably aware all day of a weight in his chest that was his need for Lily. She was avoiding him, which he hated. In the garden that morning she'd let him know that she didn't want to like him, but he couldn't seem to accept this. She felt something deep for him, he was almost certain, even if it couldn't have been half so intense as what he felt for her.

If he'd believed that she truly didn't care for him—if he'd felt his presence left her cold—he would, he thought, have been better able to turn away from her. But she did want him.

He couldn't think about a blessed thing but Lily, so how was he supposed to talk any kind of sense to Eloise?

He knocked quietly on her bedchamber door.

No reply.

"It's Hal, child. Let me in."

"I'm not a child," came the muffled reply.

He smiled a little and turned the knob.

She was sitting on her bed with her knees drawn up, her head resting on them. Her face was splotchy.

"So," he said, coming to sit at the edge of the bed, "is something amiss?"

"I don't want to talk about it," she said in a husky voice that tugged at his heart. Sixteen was so young. It was not lost on him that Lily had been this age when she'd come to care for him, and he gathered she'd suffered acutely. He'd never suffered over a woman in his life. Until now.

"I see." He gave her foot a jovial pat. "Well, that's it then. We'll see you downstairs for cards shortly?" He made as if to stand.

"Wait," she said piteously.

He sat back down.

She gave a huge sigh, as if the world were a place that would never be right. "I don't understand gentlemen."

He forced himself not to smile. "Why don't you tell me what happened?"

Her eyes dropped to the coverlet, where her index finger prodded a loose thread. "You won't like it."

"I'm sure it can't be anything that awful."

"What if it is? You have to promise you won't be angry."

That sounded a bit ominous, especially considering

how she'd been flirting with Ivorwood and Donwell at the breakfast table. Still, he could hardly play the moralist. "I promise."

"I kissed Ivorwood. In the roof stairway."

"You did *what*?"

"You said you wouldn't get angry."

"I'm not angry," he said carefully, refusing to entertain an image of her pressed up against Ivorwood. "But what exactly do you mean?"

"I told him I'd dropped my ear bob on the stairs, and he said he'd look for it, and I followed him and kissed him. He was as surprised as you are," she said miserably, her voice going thicker, "and not happy about it. It wasn't his fault—he didn't know I was going to do it."

"And how did he respond?"

"He didn't like it—or me. Ohhh," she moaned, hiding her head in her hands. "I shall never be able to look at him again. I shall have to leave Mayfield immediately—I can't see him." She looked up. "Or could you send him away? And Donwell too?"

Hal's eyes widened. "Donwell? What's he got to do with this?"

"He saw us. Saw Ivorwood trying to put me off."

Ah. He asked as casually as possible, "Did anyone else see?"

"No, just Donwell. And he rather arranged it so that Ivorwood could escape and I wouldn't be compromised."

Well, that was a relief. And he knew he could trust Donwell never to speak of this.

But he was struck with how right Lily had been,

that harm might easily have come tonight of Eloise's misguided affections. Her *unguided* actions. She and Ivorwood might have been forced to wed, something nobody had wanted. Well, he hoped at least that hadn't been Eloise's plan. And all this time he'd been so busy with his own affairs, his own diversions, that he'd made it easy for himself to take no notice.

She pulled at the loose thread on the counterpane and it unraveled several inches, which she twisted around her fingers and broke off. "How Donwell must be laughing."

"I'm sure he's not. Why should he laugh?"

"Because he told me Ivorwood was wrong for me, and he was right." She sobbed a little. "And now I hate him."

"Ivorwood?"

"No! Donwell."

What a soup. "Eloise, what on earth is going on?"

"I don't *know*, can't you see? I don't know anything at all."

He thought of how he'd been content enough until he came to Mayfield and met Lily again. "I'm somewhat familiar with the sensation. Perhaps... perhaps it's even something we are meant to experience."

"Ugh, I hate it. And now Donwell will know he was right. And Ivorwood will think I'm a lovesick ninny."

This thing with Donwell seemed to be bothering her almost more than the kiss Ivorwood hadn't wanted. But he could put at least one of her concerns to bed.

"Ivorwood won't think you're a ninny. You're not the first young lady to be so overcome in his presence." She moaned in shame. "I'll have a word with him on your behalf."

She lifted her head off her knees, her eyes brightening a little. "Would you? And would you tell him I'm sorry? And that it was a mistake that won't be repeated?"

"Certainly," he said, envisioning an awkward conversation. He felt awkward himself, seeing this inside view of a smitten female after having been on the receiving end of so many tendres. He had the uncomfortable feeling that Lily had a point about his careless flirting. Not that he felt himself to be in need of any more uncomfortable feelings.

"What about Donwell?" he said. "Do you want me to speak to him as well?"

"Good God, no!"

❧

In the drawing room, Lily sat with a book in a window seat and watched for Eloise to come to the card party. She was worried about her, and she couldn't shake the thought that she herself was somehow at fault for what had happened, because it seemed to involve Donwell and Ivorwood. Was there some sort of love triangle? Though that seemed unlikely, in that Ivorwood appeared almost studiously not to pay particular attention to Eloise. And perhaps that was intentional; perhaps he understood that she fancied him. In which case, Ivorwood's lack of notice was a deliberate way to spare Eloise's feelings, and Lily had to respect him for that, when all along she'd been judging him.

She was also looking out for Dr. Fforde's arrival, because she was counting on his steadying presence to keep her thoughts turned from Hal. But Diana, sitting out a game of piquet, stopped with her at the window seat and said that the doctor would not come after all because he'd been called to a patient.

Hal appeared in the corridor and beckoned to Lily from outside the doorway, and she guessed he had news of Eloise that must be kept quiet. She made for the door, pausing on the way to tell Diana she needed something from her bedchamber.

Once in the hallway, they moved down the corridor, at the outside edge of the light provided by the sconces on the wall. No one else was about.

"How is Eloise?" Lily whispered.

"Well enough," he said. "She rather declared herself to Ivorwood—sixteen, and she's kissing a man of almost thirty!"

"Goodness! Rather impulsive of her."

"Yes, and don't say 'I told you so,' and 'this is what comes of flirting.' I do see the irony in my speaking to a heartbroken young lady—though I find it hard to believe I've ever actually done more than dented an occasional heart."

Lily chose not to respond to that. "What did Ivorwood do?"

"Behaved nobly. But they were almost discovered by Hyacinth—she suspected something—but Donwell bought him time to disappear. She would have been compromised otherwise, because Hyacinth is a tremendous gossip."

"Do you even *like* Hyacinth Whyte?"

He sighed. "I hadn't much thought about it before. In any case, Eloise seemed wrought up about what Donwell would think, as if he were her worst enemy or something like."

"I'm sorry this happened," Lily said seriously. "My matchmaking efforts... I shouldn't have interfered."

His features softened. "Come, Lily, you had good intentions. And you were right—I should have done more to guide her, especially where gentlemen are concerned."

"I was right?" He looked so kind that it tugged her heart, especially now, when he had every right to blame her.

"Eloise is good-hearted," he said, "but perhaps a little spoiled. Definitely too exuberant at times, and maybe a little scandalous. I should have paid attention to what she was doing and guided her. I'm afraid I'm not a good model for her."

"That's not *entirely* true," she said. She laughed a little, feeling suddenly that she needed to lighten the moment because the intent look in his eyes was making prickles of excitement break out along the back of her neck. "You can be very kind. Old ladies love you."

"I'm more interested in someone nearer my age." He smiled, but the tentative tilt of his mouth looked oddly vulnerable. He made as if to say something but stopped himself. She felt close to him—from their shared concern over Eloise, but also from an awareness that they *knew* each other.

Abruptly he took her by the elbow, saying, "Come here," and tugged her farther down the hallway, away from the light.

"Why?"

But his only answer was to open a door and pull her briskly inside. He shut the door behind them, and they were in darkness.

Eighteen

"WHAT ON EARTH ARE YOU ABOUT?" SHE SAID IN AN urgent whisper. She was standing in a lightless room alone with a man, in a house full of people. It smelled strongly—if nicely—of lavender; a linen closet?

"I needed to be alone with you."

"Are you out of your mind? What if someone comes in here?"

Her words were greeted with a heavy pause, and she thought she heard the sound of a diabolical chuckle. If only she could see him. She felt behind her for the door, her hands coming against folded cloth, the edge of a shelf.

He set his hands on her waist and pulled her closer. She couldn't imagine how he knew where she was; it was so dark she couldn't see him at all.

"What are you doing?"

"I just told you: I needed to be alone with you."

His words sank in. *Need*. He wanted her, just as she wanted him. Her breath gave a hitch. Whatever frailty had found its way into her expression, at least he couldn't see it.

With another tug, he had her against his body. His arms clamped around her waist and shoulders as he crushed her to him. He felt so good against her—a profoundly welcome return of his body against hers, and what could she do, kidnapped as she was? Her grateful arms went around him, and she told herself it didn't count because they couldn't see.

Her face was pressed against his chest, and she breathed in his fabulous scent like air she'd been lacking. His head brushed against hers, lowering, and she lifted her face and received his kiss.

And then it was madness.

They thrashed against each other, tugging, sliding hands, grabbing. She ran her hands greedily over his shoulders; he cupped her breasts and groaned. He buried his face against the top of her bodice, the rasp of his incipient whiskers teasing the tender skin of her bosom and making her nipples harden. Rubbing the swollen tips through her gown, he drew soft moans from her.

Their energy pushed them around, and they stumbled against the shelves. He urged her backward to rest against a wall and, lifting her as she clutched him, pushed between her legs and ground against her. His erection pressed hard into the apex of her thighs and his hips rocked into her, into the heat pulsing between her legs.

"Oh God, Lily." He almost sounded in pain.

Panting, she gripped his backside—everything on him flexed, rocklike—and she tugged him to her harder, moved against him in a way that felt natural and so incredibly good.

He was moving in a rhythm they both needed, and

she was meeting his thrusts. But then, abruptly, he stiffened, and with a deep groan slumped against her. A moment later he muttered a curse.

The closet was now remarkably quiet, save for the sound of panting that was returning to normal breathing. Her feet returned to the floor. Still a little dizzy with desire, she understood what had happened, and a little laugh escaped her.

"What are you laughing at?" he demanded softly, making some sort of adjustment in his breeches. He nuzzled her neck where his head rested.

"If I understand rightly..." she began, but his hand started working at her dress, gathering it upward, and her thoughts were growing hazy.

"You sound like a lawyer," he whispered. He sucked lightly on her neck and she closed her eyes as his bare hand met the back of her bare thigh. She trembled, aching for him.

"Something happened to you just now," she said in a voice gone husky.

His hand inched toward the beating heart of her.

"An unplanned event the likes of which has not happened to me since I was a youth," he murmured. "Though not surprising, given the unremitting provocation." His clever, arrogant fingers slipped among the slick folds between her legs. "Your turn," he said with a wicked chuckle.

And there was that little slice of heaven again. She bit her lip to keep quiet as he stroked, sending her over the mountaintop.

He held her while she floated in the bliss, and it felt wonderful.

But far too soon she had to leave it behind. She knew she could only stay with him for a few moments because they would be missed. Every moment longer in the closet meant taking the chance of discovery.

"Hal," she began, not knowing what to say. She tried to lean away from him, but he kept her against him.

"I want to court you," he said. "We mean something to each other, and we are incredibly good together. We could have a future. Let me court you, Lily."

Her heart jumped at his words. She heard the sincerity in them. She tipped her head up and wished she could see his face and read his eyes, but it was too dark, and that was probably for the best.

She didn't want to think about how much, actually, she wanted him to care about her, truly care about her. It was madness, and flying in the face of everything she wanted for her life.

But she allowed herself right then to imagine what it would be like for him to court her openly with the goal of marriage. He could become someone special to her, she thought as a certain glow hovering inside her started to spill over. It was a glow that had everything to do with Hal and the way he made her feel—not just his touch but his presence. And really, he already *was* special to her; he already made her heart sing. In a hundred ways that she needed to deny.

She let herself imagine being married to him: sitting across the breakfast table, riding to Town, discussing the servants, sitting together after dinner.

The glow receded. She couldn't imagine it; she couldn't imagine him being truly satisfied by the mundane kinds of things she thought were important—the birth of a new lamb, or the church jumble sale, or, most significantly, helping those in need. It wasn't that she thought him uncaring, but these were unremarkable things—how would he not be bored by them, he who needed merriment and adventure and parties?

And most of all, she couldn't imagine him caring as deeply and everlastingly for her as she knew herself to be capable of caring for the man to whom she gave her heart. How could she give it to a man who might let it drift through his fingers when the next fresh thing came along?

She leaned away, stepping back a little, and he loosened his hold. "You do me a great honor, Hal, but whatever this has been between us... we *must* call it finished."

A pause. "Where is your spirit of adventure, Lily?"

"I don't want adventure, don't you see? Anyway, I'm only a novelty because I'm different from your usual woman."

"You are, very much."

"Exactly. I'm not a woman who's willing to giggle and flirt and offer herself to you."

"Like Mrs. Whyte, you mean?"

"Yes, like Mrs. Whyte," she said, not wanting at all to say another woman's name right now, but forcing herself, "if that's what you two are to each other. I don't wish to know."

"We are not anything to each other. And I've never felt one whit of interest in her as compared to what I feel for you." A pause. "You can't trust me, can you? *I* trust *you*."

Trust between them? Deep, real trust? No. She didn't know why was he talking about trust, but it made it easier to speak plainly even as a foolish part of her wanted to lean into him again. "We don't like the same things," she said. "I like quiet and reflection, you like society and adventure."

"And why does that mean that I can't also value charity and usefulness and sacrifice? Will not my time in the army speak for me?"

She didn't want to weigh his time in the army with the balance of him; she told herself that it had been undertaken because of how fine he would look in a uniform and how he might be admired for valor. A truly unkind, unworthy thought, but she held onto it.

"You like to talk about fashion," she said.

"Not overly. Women like to, and I am willing to indulge them."

"Only so you can entrance them. Aren't you more than a little satisfied about that tally at White's, of the women who admit you've broken their hearts?"

"It's just in fun. No one is making them do that."

"You are! It's what you do—you make people want you. Don't you see that what you love best is just that—making people want you? That it's almost a competition for you, and that you're willing to do whatever it takes to succeed?"

A lump was forming in her throat, emotion pressing against her, wanting to hold sway over her and lead her down all kinds of paths. She forced it aside and reached her hand for the knob behind her. "We have to put all this behind us. We… dabbled, that's all. Nothing more."

"We didn't begin to dabble," he said in a dark voice that made her glad she couldn't see his face. "You have no idea."

"I have to go." She pushed the door open and left.

❧

As Lily walked out the next morning toward the carriages that had been ordered for those who wished to go to church, she wished rather desperately that it were time to leave Mayfield entirely. She liked it far too much here; she accused herself of developing a taste for this grand mansion and all its attendant luxury, of exchanging her values for the pursuit of pleasure... and most serious of all, of becoming besotted with Hal.

She'd given in to temptation the night before in the linen closet, and it had felt so good even while it was all wrong. What was worse, she couldn't even summon enough anger to berate herself properly. She felt askew—even her hair was untidy. She'd sent the maid away, wanting to be alone, and stabbed pins in her coiffure all anyhow.

As she stepped into the carriage with Delia and Rob, she told herself that she could certainly manage two more days at Mayfield without disgracing herself. Just forty-eight hours.

The first thing she would do when she got back to Thistlethwaite would be to contact Nate to find out if there had been any results from his digging, and to concentrate on helping him so the Fiend could go away and she could get back to the shawl work.

Just as the carriage was about to pull away from

the drive, Hal appeared and squeezed in among them with a jaunty grin. Rob discreetly lifted an eyebrow at Lily, as if to say that this must have something to do with her. She frowned at him and looked out over the fields.

In church, despite Lily's intention to sit next to Delia, Hal arranged it so that he was next to her. It was a tight fit in the pew, and as soon as she sat down she found herself pressed against the warm solidness of his leg and arm. When she dropped her hymnal, he bent down to retrieve it and returned it with a smile.

"Why are you here?" she demanded under her breath when the congregation stood to sing "Now Thank We All Our God."

"The same reason you are, I should think," he murmured as the music swelled.

"You just want to vex me," she said.

"That's not what I want at all," he said seriously, and joined in the first line of the hymn. She was standing in church, gnashing her teeth. The music rose stirringly around her, and she stumbled over the words, trying not to notice how good Hal's deep voice sounded.

After the service, coming out of the cool dark of the church and into the late-morning sunlight, Lily saw Nate walking behind his mother and hurried to catch up to him when his mother stopped to talk to someone.

"Your light was seen the other night," she told him in a low, urgent voice.

"Well, nobody came after me—but I haven't found anything either." He shook his head, his expression gloomy. "And time's running out."

"But you *must* wait to dig again, at least until the day after tomorrow, when I'll be back at Thistlethwaite and can be your lookout." She kept an eye on Hal, who was in conversation with a delighted Vicar. He periodically looked over the top of Vicar's head at her.

"I'll be careful," Nate said.

"But you need me to watch for you!"

"Lily, stop worrying. You've already done enough."

"Nate—" she began, but he'd already turned away. She watched him pass through the stone gate with his mother, deeply concerned for him, and for what might befall the Becketts if he were discovered.

Hal was making his way toward her.

"Another of your suitors, Lily?"

"An old family friend. He wants to buy a shawl for his mother." What an accomplished liar she'd become. Only the top of her list of sins. "The Becketts, at least, are not afraid of possessed sheep."

"He wished to discuss shawls with you?"

"As I said."

"Right." Suspicion darkened his eyes. "I wonder," he began, but just then Eloise came up and linked her arm through his. Lily was glad to see that, aside from a faint puffiness around her eyes, Eloise seemed collected.

"Do let's get back to Mayfield, brother," Eloise said. "All the ladies will need time to change before the picnic."

He could make no reasonable objection, and the party returned to their carriages, leaving him no further chance to quiz Lily. She could only hope he'd forget any suspicions he might have about Nate.

The afternoon came on hot and lacking in breeze, and Lily thought its heaviness rather matched her mood. She knew she should be glad that she'd be leaving Mayfield soon, but the thought of going back to the way things had been before Hal came left her unhappy, and the awareness that she felt that way made her disgusted with herself. She wanted to beg off the picnic, but she couldn't make herself do it.

The party set off walking in the early afternoon, the servants going ahead with a cart full of food and blankets. Though pretty, the path to the lake didn't provide much shade from the late resurgence of summer heat.

Lily walked with Delia and Eloise, who had their heads together and were giggling. At one point Delia squealed and tugged Lily close to them.

"Lily!" she said in a heavy whisper. "You'll never guess what Eloise has just told me about. I wager you've never even heard of them."

"And what is that?" Lily said, supposing she was to be told of a new sort of shoe. She felt rather grouchy; several paces behind them, Mrs. Whyte was strolling with Hal and tittering musically.

"French letters," Delia said in a whisper that was so quiet she was almost mouthing the words.

"I'm sorry, but are you saying letters from French people? What's remarkable about that?"

"Shh!" Eloise said, giggling. "French letters. They are meant for the marriage act."

Lily blinked. "I... don't know what you mean."

Delia smiled, looking very pleased with herself, as if she'd ever heard of these French letters before now. "They are like tubes that go over the man's..."

"That will do," Lily said with her cheeks burning. "I believe I understand."

"They're to prevent disease and conception," Eloise whispered. "Men use them with their mistresses."

"How on earth do you know about them?"

Eloise grinned. "I listened at the door when the men were having their port."

"Heavens," Lily said. "I don't know that you two should even know about such things. For goodness' sake, don't speak of them to anyone else."

Which only made them giggle more.

And yet, Lily thought as they walked, what if more women—not just mistresses—knew about these French letters? Her mind began to entertain shocking, rebellious thoughts that would never have occurred to her two weeks ago.

Dr. Fforde and Ian, who'd been at the front of the party, dropped back so that Lily caught up to them. She was glad—quite happy—to see good, kind, serene Dr. Fforde.

"Lily," Ian said, "did you know that Fforde is going to start a fever hospital in the north?"

"Yes. Highcross's doctor is a man of grand aspirations," she said warmly.

As she listened to the doctor explain the details of his planned work, she wished fervently that she had something good and serious to occupy her right then—not in the future as the school was, if it ever came to be, because surely then there would be no space left for her to be vulnerable to thoughts and dreams of Hal. She hated that nothing could make her entirely forget he was behind her.

"This is all most admirable, Fforde," Ian said. "But you are not leaving Highcross very soon, I hope?"

"Not for some months yet."

"Good, good," Ian said, casting a significant glance Lily's way. "You must allow our family to contribute in some way. Perhaps your work would benefit from additional funds?"

Fforde smiled. "That would be most appreciated. In fact, I had thought that perhaps Miss Teagarden—"

He was interrupted by Hal drawing even with them, having apparently shed Mrs. Whyte, who was now in company with Eloise and Delia. The widow looked somewhat sour about the mouth at the change in her companions, though not for long as she called out to Ian to join them. Mrs. Whyte was not so charming a person if you weren't a handsome, wealthy man, Lily thought, and she faulted Hal for associating with her.

"I say, Fforde," Hal said, "what will happen to you if you catch one of the fevers at this hospital of yours?"

Dr. Fforde inclined his head. "That would be unfortunate, though not so different from the usual risks of the medical profession."

Lily could feel Hal's eyes on her. "It's very brave of Dr. Fforde to want to help people," she said, "and to further the course of science. He *could* sit home and be comfortable, but he chooses to act."

Hal looked irritated.

Dr. Fforde chuckled. "There's much to be said for the comforts of home, Miss Teagarden. Lord Roxham surely must have appreciated them after the time he spent in the army fighting the Corsican."

"Fighting is hardly the same as curing," she said.

"Indeed, it is more like making the troubles of humanity worse."

A heavy silence greeted her words.

"So you would have preferred that Napoleon take over the Continent?" Hal said.

"No," she said with a rush of shame at how bad-tempered and ungenerous her comment had been. Both men were looking at her strangely. What on earth had made her say such an appalling thing? "Of course not. I have the highest respect for the men who've sacrificed for our country. It's just that I should have preferred that war not be necessary at all."

"So should I have," Hal said. "I lost many good men. But though peace and perfection in human relations are a worthy goal, there are times when one must go to war."

She bit her lower lip unhappily. Bother it all but she was so jumbled up she didn't know what she was saying. "I—yes, of course. I agree that's true. But... we were talking about comfort and the pleasures of home and, well," she looked almost pleadingly at Dr. Fforde, "you would not put pleasure first, sir, would you? I think we ought not to seek our own comfort and happiness, but instead to spend our lives in living for others."

"A worthy sentiment, Miss Teagarden," the doctor said. "I believe we ought to welcome hardship if it means that we will do some true good."

Hal gnashed his teeth as he listened to Fforde. He supposed that any moment Lily's eyes would simply change into little glimmering stars as she dreamed of the moral beauty of a life of hardship and deprivation.

"It's no crime to fully enjoy all that we've been given," he said. "Indeed, one might even say we are wrong to refuse to do so."

"Spoken by someone who's been given everything," Lily said.

Fforde's eyebrows rose at her sharpness, though Hal suspected the doctor only liked her better for it. She was trying to push him away. And why was he even having this conversation with her? Why, when he knew exactly what she would say? Though her heedless quest for virtue made him want to grab her and kiss her until she could no longer deny what she needed. He should have forced some kind of understanding with her last night before she left the closet, but she'd slipped away so quickly.

Delia swept by them and insisted Fforde come and settle a dispute about the best way to cure a headache. Which left Hal and Lily at the end of the snake of people wending their way toward the lake perhaps a third of a mile distant, where the servants could be seen arranging the picnic blankets and provisions.

They walked along without speaking for several minutes. Hal knew he should abandon the argument they'd been having, but he couldn't let it go.

"It's not just the poor who need help in life. Even wealthy people are sometimes terribly unhappy and in need of compassion, Lily."

"Wealthy people can find ways to relieve themselves."

"Can they? Can money cure a soul-deep sorrow?"

"I don't care about the wealthy!" she burst out. "They can help themselves."

"Ah," he said. "So we are not all equal."

Her pale eyebrows drew together, and her pretty lips pressed into a hard line. "Of course there are people with troubles everywhere," she said without much conviction. "But what Dr. Fforde proposes to do is extraordinary."

"And what would happen to the school for girls you were going to establish if you left Highcross?"

She didn't reply at first. "If I were ever to leave here," she said finally, "I would hope to have something in place for the girls first."

"I can give you the money for the school. I'd like to, actually, regardless of what happens. But I suppose you want to struggle to earn it all yourself."

She absorbed his words. "No, that would be selfish of me. If you will pay for a school for the girls of Highcross, then I thank you. Truly, that would be wonderful."

"But you might not be here to run it."

"Anything is possible."

She looked away from him. Her ivory frock was striped with thin red lines, and the regular straightness of the design seemed a perfect complement for a woman who probably disliked softly flowered gowns.

Another silence fell between them. Ahead of them the others were all deep in convivial conversation—there were delightedly scandalized shouts of *He didn't!* and *Yes, he did!*, and Hal's nephews ran hither and yon, requiring much herding from the adults, so that Lily and Hal had been for the moment forgotten.

He kicked the shining tip of his top boot at a chunky stone in his path, sending it ahead of him.

"So," he said, apparently unable to stop himself,

"Fforde is the kind of man you wish to marry. *Will* you marry him?"

"Usually gentlemen ask for themselves," she said tartly. Their pace began to accelerate—it was Lily driving it, face forward, marching faster. He refused to increase his speed, though, thereby keeping her somewhat in check through the rein of inbred good manners.

"You know what I mean. He likes you. He's *like* you. With him you could have your tidy, calm life and save the world at the same time."

Her brown half-boots crushed the dirt faster.

He felt he should be able to read her eyes, to see if she was hiding something behind her restraint, but he couldn't. He knew women, knew their desires, their attachments, their hopes, their secret wishes. He'd always *understood* women, and he'd had any number of them declare they were in love with him. But he'd never once said the same thing back, because it had never once before been true.

"Fforde isn't right for you," he said. "You would be as exciting together as a plate of cheeses."

"I like cheese! And Dr. Fforde is a kind and decent man."

"Well, he seems to have a keen interest in plants—I heard him discussing them at length with Diana. So you'd have *that* to talk about. And medicine. Warm topics all, to be sure."

He wanted to punch the good doctor, except the man was too blasted decent.

Ahead of them the rest of the party stopped in front of Mayfield's original folly, which was a small version of a Roman temple. Delia could be heard expressing a desire to go in, and the party began moving inside, Freddy and Louie leading the way. Hal and Lily, both with their arms crossed, stopped where they were, beside a profusion of peach trees with a few stray, overripe fruits still hanging. He counted it as a small victory that at least she would stay and fight with him.

"It's normal and human to want a companion who would also be a friend," she said. "Someone you can trust and care for."

"You make a husband sound like a faithful hound."

"And you will keep misunderstanding and refusing to see." Her slim, blond eyebrows slanted in hard angles. "Or perhaps," she continued, "it's that you're incapable of seeing."

"Because I am unmarried at my advanced age, I therefore am unable to be a good husband?"

She threw up her hands. "A wife would never be enough for you."

He gave her a hard look. "I hope you're not suggesting I would be unfaithful to any woman I married."

That brought her up short.

"Ah," he said, unable to keep the anger out his voice. "You are."

"You need distraction and amusement."

Heat crackled along his neck. "And you like your own company too much. It's as though you think people will take something from you if you let yourself be close to them."

"That's ridiculous. What would I be afraid of people taking from me? I haven't got anything but sheep."

"Your time. You have all those goals, and you don't want anyone interfering with them. But what about the people you help? Do you even allow your-self to care for them, or are they just an opportunity to do good?"

She drew in a sharp breath. "Of course I care about them. Why else would I be helping them?"

"Maybe you need their weakness to feel good about yourself."

"That's a terrible thing to say."

"Is it? I think it says more about how you've closed yourself off to your own needs. You're so used to being in charge, to doing the responsible thing and looking out for others, that you've hardened yourself against wanting anything for yourself."

A flash of anger darkened her eyes to violet. "I already have everything I want."

Hal had no chance to reply, because just then Rob shouted for them to hurry up. Apparently the others had finished exploring the temple folly.

He couldn't help but notice the look of relief that came over Lily's face as she rushed toward the others without another word to him. He let her go ahead of him, watching her trim figure move forward in that purposeful way she had, and thought how much he needed her.

Nineteen

BECAUSE IT WAS SO HOT, PEOPLE INEVITABLY WANDERED into the cooling water of the lake. Hal's nephews went first, three-year-old Louie rushing in while his mother was looking the other way. His squeals of delight as he splashed in his clothes made it impossible for Freddy to be kept from joining him. And then because someone had to keep an eye on them—or at least, that was what he said—Hal took off his boots and waded in.

With the viscount as example, Ian, John, Rob, Donwell, and Ivorwood were soon splashing about in the water as playfully as dogs, and far more than their feet got wet. The little boys thought it hilarious. Diana stood on the shore shaking her head but smiling, Mrs. Whyte appeared unable to take her eyes from the view of the men's well-splashed shirts while announcing that country manners were certainly different, and Eloise and Delia seemed unable to stop giggling as they watched Ivorwood try to drown first Hal and then Ian. Lily noticed that Eloise and Donwell seemed adept at avoiding each other.

Lily arranged herself on a blanket and was joined

by Dr. Fforde. In answer to her questions, he began telling her about his studies at university. His voice was softly deep and pleasant, and it soothed some of the anger her conversation with Hal had stirred up.

"You are not, I think, as interested in fractures of the tibia as you had suggested," the doctor was saying, a smile playing about his lips.

"Oh," she said, "well." She pulled her mind away from Hal's words and smiled back at Dr. Fforde. "I think I might be, another time. I do find medical things interesting. I'm afraid it was only that my mind was wandering."

"And would you care, my dear Miss Teagarden, to share the subject on which your mind was dwelling?" The friendly light in his eyes told her that almost anything she said would interest him, a flattering sensation to be sure.

"Oh, nothing of consequence, truly."

His hand was near hers on the blanket, and he looked down at both their hands, his gaze telling her that he would like to take hold of her hand, but he did not. He was not domineering.

He looked up at her again. "Miss Teagarden, I should be very honored if you would call me Matthew. And… may I call you Lily?"

"Certainly. Why, you've been to Thistlethwaite countless times, and goodness knows you are very good friends with Rob."

"But I should very much like to be far more to you than a friend of your brother's."

She could not mistake his meaning. He was talking about courting her.

A shadow fell over them, and she looked up to see Hal, in his shirtsleeves and with bare ankles and feet and much splashed with water, standing and dripping at the edge of their blanket.

"Fforde, I've come to invite you for a partial swim. It's the very thing on this hot day. And you, too, Lily, if you'd like to get your feet wet."

"No thank you," she said without looking up.

Matthew Fforde frowned slightly and took out his watch. "Most vexing," he muttered. He cleared his throat. "An interesting offer, Roxham, which I shall have to decline just now as I see that the afternoon has advanced further than I'd realized while in the extremely pleasant company of Miss Teagarden. But I had promised Mrs. Eldwin that I would look in on her today. She is suffering from a bad sprain."

He stood up and took his leave. She watched as his well-proportioned form disappeared down the path to the manor and hoped Hal would leave if she ignored him.

He sat down next to her on the blanket.

She twitched her skirts closer, away from the soaked cuffs of his pants and his wet feet. There were golden hairs on the middles of his toes, and the skin of his feet was very fair and shining with lake water.

"Shouldn't you be in search of a towel? And shoes?"

He stretched out his long legs, the light fabric of his breeches darkened with water and clinging to his legs in places, and propped himself up on his bent elbows. He'd turned back the wet cuffs of his sleeves, and the white fabric of his shirt stuck to him in odd places where large splashes had hit, offering glimpses of the muscular curve of his upper arm and the flat firmness of his abdomen.

He ignored her question and gazed up at the sky as if he were entirely peaceful, as if their fighting had been nothing out of the ordinary. She begrudgingly admitted to herself that she liked him better for seeing that she was his equal in battle, even if he'd accused her of needing people to need her, and closing herself off to caring as deeply for them as she could. Maybe it stung because there was some truth in it.

Several minutes passed, during which she refused to perform the gracious role assigned to women and engage him in conversation. But finally she couldn't stand his contented silence anymore and said, "What, exactly, are you doing?"

"Sitting down. I was tired of standing."

"That's not what I mean, obviously." Ian was watching them as he talked with Mrs. Whyte, and he smirked at her. "People will notice that you're paying special attention to me. You'll start gossip about yourself, sitting next to a lady in your wet clothes. Your feet are *bare*."

He let his head drop back between his shoulders and closed his eyes. "I *am* rather in disarray, though I'm hardly the only gentleman here who is, so any gossips will have to complain about Ivorwood and the others as well."

"You do realize that with all your promises not to marry until you're fifty-one, you've only made people want to catch you out."

"I never promised anyone I wouldn't marry until I was fifty-one. It was merely a prediction. Anyway, I don't care if people think I'm paying special attention to you."

He turned his shining golden head to her, turned that stunningly handsome face on her, and for once she saw it as simply a face, just an accident of nature that he'd been born with, an arrangement of features that might just as well have not been harmonious. It wasn't as if people could order up their looks before they were born, or earn them by work or virtue.

She knew this, and yet she'd blamed him for being so beautiful. Well, blamed him for profiting from his beauty. She thought now that perhaps his appearance had been a sort of tool that he'd used in his life to help him win the kind of affection and attention that had been missing from a childhood with a brother who was always held up as superior.

She was better off not feeling compassionate toward him.

Hal watched Lily as she sat next to him on the blanket, her arms wrapped around her bent legs, everything about her saying she would be closed off to him.

She sighed. "You're doing it again. Trying to charm me."

He'd never known a woman to be so against charm. How did you get on with a woman if you weren't charming her in some way?

Charm was circuitous; Lily prized directness.

Perhaps that was his answer.

"Come to me tonight."

She blinked, absorbing his words. "I beg your pardon?"

"You heard me. Come to me tonight. Come see

what it is you'll be giving up if you marry a dry stick like Fforde."

"He's not a dry stick!"

"Well, *I'm* not. I'm someone who has your contentment very much in mind. We've—as you say—dabbled a bit. But I want to make love to you. Properly, slowly, privately."

She looked surprised by his words. But not horrified. Her eyes flicked beyond him, probably to see if anyone nearby could hear them, but everyone else was still by the water.

"Why should you want to do such a thing with a hard woman like me?"

"Because I want to uncover the fragile flower of your softness and encourage it to bloom."

"The fragile flower of my softness? What nonsense," she said, still not looking at him, but a husky note in her voice gave him hope. He let the silence stretch out.

"How can you just ask me this?" she said.

"Because you make your own decisions. So I should think you would do so about something like this. That you would choose to see what might be between us."

He *knew* what she wanted, but whether she would allow herself to have it was another thing.

She finally looked at him. "I shall choose to pretend we never had this conversation."

He hoped she was braver than that. He *believed* she was. He stood up. "I'll be in my chamber at one o'clock tonight, awake and waiting."

❧

Eloise was standing next to Diana and ostensibly enjoying her nephews' antics while secretly watching Donwell out of the corner of her eye. He was standing in the lake at some distance from the other men, his breeches rolled up to his knees, and bent over looking at something in the water. Probably following the path of some minnows, or maybe an exotic water snake no one had ever seen before—creatures seemed to find him.

They hadn't spoken to each other since she'd fled down the stairs after kissing Ivorwood. She'd felt so horribly jumbled up and sick with emotion that night, but talking to Hal had helped. She'd never before thought of talking to her brother about men, but now she thought he might be good at advising her, and it made her feel better equipped.

She saw now that dreaming about Ivorwood had made him into a sort of doll in her mind, one that would behave in her thoughts the way she wanted. She'd never really even talked to him very much, and without the patina her imagination had lent him, he was only real, and that made him like everyone else. Which meant he surely did unattractive things, like belching sometimes even if she didn't see it, and maybe he was so quiet not because he was a deep thinker but because he didn't have anything to say. Kissing him had not turned her into a fountain of bliss.

So when she'd seen him at breakfast and he'd been as reserved but polite as ever to her, she'd given him a rueful smile and asked for the butter, and that had been the end of it.

Being around Donwell was different and felt

awkward now. And she didn't like being near him and not being able to find out what fascinating thing he was up to. Besides, she owed him something.

She moved away from Diana and, walking along the shore, came closer to where Donwell stood in the water. So engrossed as he was, he didn't look up when she came within a few feet of him. The top of his auburn head entranced her, not because of the interesting way it was mussed, but because it was familiar.

"Donwell," she said quietly.

He started and looked up. "Miss Waverly," he said in a neutral voice.

"I want to thank you for what you did the other night. You saved both me and Ivorwood from being forced into a choice neither of us wanted."

He looked at her steadily. He had such good eyes—his intelligence shone through from their steady brown depths. "You're welcome."

She wished he would say something that might give her a glimpse into his thoughts.

"I'm not disappointed, you know, that…" Her voice was getting wispy, but she needed to say this to him. "That Ivorwood didn't want to kiss me. I realize now that there never really was anything of substance there."

"I see," he said, but he had no other reaction. She'd thought he'd be happy and sweep her into his arms, but she reminded herself that believing she knew what other people wanted would only get her into trouble.

Several moments passed. She didn't know what to say, and he didn't seem inclined to fill the silence.

Perhaps he didn't care for her anymore, after she'd received his admiration so ungraciously and then made such a fool of herself. But she had so enjoyed his friendship—surely if nothing else, they could still be friends? Though she felt such a strong urge to touch him.

"What is it you're looking at?" she finally asked.

"A trout, gone into hiding. It's changing colors to blend in better."

She grabbed the trunk of a sapling and leaned out over the water a bit. "That sounds interesting."

"It is, but, Miss Waverly—"

As she was leaning out a bit farther, the sapling suddenly drooped forward, and she lost her balance and lurched toward the water. He caught her about the waist and steadied her, so that she landed in the water up to her knees with his hands around her waist. He was looking down at her with those intelligent brown eyes that must be hiding any number of fascinating thoughts and plans she wanted to know about. His breathing seemed to have changed.

"Are you quite all right, Miss Waverly?"

"Yes. Only, won't you please call me Eloise?"

"I…" His eyes looked less focused. "Eloise."

From the shore, Diana called to them. "Eloise, what are you doing?"

"Fell in," she called back. They only had a moment before propriety must push them apart.

"I'm sorry that I wasn't ready to hear what you said to me on the roof," she said quickly. "But I hope we'll have another chance to see the stars together without a proper chaperone."

His arms tightened around her. "Are you really saying what I think you're saying?"

"Yes," she whispered.

Warmth deepened his chocolate eyes. "I have to let go of you and I don't want to."

"I don't want you to," she said.

His arms loosened, and she put a proper distance between them even as they held each other's gaze.

"I can only think we've scared away your trout."

"Then stay and help me find something else to fascinate me."

And she did.

◈

It was late that night, and alone in her darkened guest room in Hal's grand home, Lily sat by the window in her nightgown, worrying about Nate and watching to see if a light would show in the woods. With all the guests at Mayfield, she didn't dare go out, but she could keep watch.

The evening had been spent doing needlepoint with the women while the men disappeared for rather a long time over their port. Lily found she could have done without the conversation of Hyacinth, who'd asked slyly at one point if there wasn't some kind of understanding between Lily and the viscount.

Lily had said there wasn't, and what an idea. Hyacinth had said she'd thought it odd, too, but he'd spent so much time talking with Lily today. Lily had forced a laugh and said that he was only being a polite host. All the ladies had agreed he was the best host in the *ton*, and giggled. It had made Lily feel very low.

By the time the gentlemen returned, she was ready to plead a headache, and she left the party for her room. But that had been hours ago, and now it was almost one o'clock. She supposed she was the only one in the manor besides the odd servant who was still awake.

Well, there was one other person who was very likely still awake.

What she was really wanting now was her knitting. She foolishly hadn't brought any yarn with her, and she missed the way knitting calmed her thoughts and kept her fingers busy while something soft and woolly formed. Instead she twisted the end of her long braid in her fingers as she watched the woods and tried not to think of Hal waiting for her.

But that was near impossible. Part of her was thrilled that he'd asked to court her, that he'd dared her to come to him tonight. But the more she thought about it, the less she could believe that he truly wanted to marry her. There was some design in his attentions, and there was no mystery as to what it was: desire. She felt it, too.

She gazed out into the pitchy darkness. She wanted extremely to go to his room. She ached to touch him again, to touch him *more*.

But just as much, she needed to respect herself, and going to a rendezvous with Hal, possibly surrendering her virginity to him—how could she even think of it? It was madness.

Still, she thought of that silly thing he'd said, that he wanted to "uncover the fragile flower of her softness." She didn't want to be a hard, closed-off woman. She didn't want to end up a shrew. Could what was between them open something good within her?

Her eyes, almost unfocused while her tormented thoughts dueled together, now became aware of something in the dark outside the window—a speck of light among the dense line of trees.

She gasped as she realized what it had to be: Nate!

Concern swept over her. True, the light was small, the woods covered a long swath, and he was digging in an area far from where he'd been before. It was possible no one would notice. Obviously Nate was gambling on this, and on Hal being too busy with guests to watch for him.

A large assumption.

She knew exactly where Hal must be right now, unless he'd seen the light already: in his room, waiting for her. And if he hadn't seen the light yet, he might still glimpse it at any moment.

She considered the choice before her, a choice that might allow her to do something to keep Hal from watching for Nate. And going to Hal was something she wanted desperately to do.

She slipped out of her room and moved down the silent corridor to the wing that held his rooms.

And then she was standing outside his chamber door.

Twenty

HAL WAITED IN HIS ROOM WHILE TELLING HIMSELF HE wasn't waiting, that he was going over the estate account book and it didn't matter to him whether Lily came or not. She was just a woman, and blah blah blah his mind went as he ran through figures.

The third time he had to pause to determine what seventeen and six made he pushed the account ledger away, pulled a book off the small shelf by his bed, and went to sit by the window. It was a book he'd been given at the Spanish monastery where he'd stayed for those few days during the war, on the subject of solitude and its value in life. He supposed the abbot would have smiled to think of how tormented Hal currently was; the abbot was much taken with the value of suffering in forging a soul. Hal felt in no way improved.

He knew he was placing a lot of weight on whether she came tonight. Knew that, while he might be able to make her want him, he couldn't make her *choose* him. If she came tonight, it wouldn't be because she was overtaken with lust in the moment or simply curious. It would take far more for Lily, who thought and planned and chose carefully, to come to him. If she came tonight, it would be because she needed him.

~·~

Lily knocked very softly on Hal's door.

"Come," said a quiet voice from the other side, and she slipped into his bedchamber.

He was sitting in a chair by the window; apparently he'd been reading. She realized that she'd never imagined him simply sitting and doing something so quiet as reading, and perversely, the stillness of the scene startled her.

"Well," he said. "Lily. Lock the door."

She did.

He put down his book and unfolded himself from the chair, long legs unbending as he stood, the sight making her extra aware of how different his body was from hers—longer, taller, stronger, male. He was at his ease; he wore no coat and his shirt, tucked into tight-fitting dark breeches, was loose at the collar, the cravat having been hung over the back of his chair. His sleeves were rolled up to his elbows. The candlelight gleamed in the semi-darkness, making his hair shine dark gold.

Behind him and on the other side of his bed stood two tall windows that gave onto the same view that hers did. With the heat of the day still warming the room, the windows had been left open and the curtains, too, doubtless to let in a breeze. If he turned and looked, he would see Nate's light. She couldn't let him turn and focus his attention there. And she knew, returning his gaze as his eyes settled on her warmly, that she didn't want to.

"Hal," she said back, naming him as he'd just named her, a choosing of each other.

They stood like that for perhaps half a minute, looking at each other, weighing, it felt like. Getting accustomed to this choice of being there together.

His room was grand; it was, after all, a viscount's room. She'd been in here before, when she was taking back her journal, but it had been so dark that she'd perceived almost none of it. Now the light of two candelabra illuminated his substantial bed with its wide mattress and dark drapes. It dominated the room and spoke of the weight of the viscountcy. She'd never before thought of a bed as imposing, but this one was.

"Are you going to come closer, Lily? This must be your choice."

She cleared her throat, gathered her courage. "I have to know something first, a practical thing."

His lips quirked. "By all means."

"Do you have these things called…" She blushed furiously but pushed onward because it was one thing to try something for one night, no matter how much she wanted to, and it was another to do something that could change her whole life. "French letters?"

"Ah. You are well informed."

"By Eloise, actually."

His eyebrows went up.

"Eavesdropping."

A rueful smile tugged the edge of his mouth. "I foresee another conversation. But yes, I have them."

So there was not that practical issue to stop her. He stood with his arms at his sides as she moved closer to him, his posture straight, his confident bearing reflecting something of the military man he'd been. His eyes never left her.

"What were you reading?" she said as she came to stand near him.

"Something the Spanish monks gave me. I think they saw me as a good subject for conversion to their ways."

"I don't suppose they'd be pleased to see what you are up to tonight. Or me."

She was trembling. The realization of what she'd come here to do was bearing down on her.

He spread his arms open, the vulnerable, paler insides of his arms and his palms facing her. The sight made her heart lurch, a deep, willful pulling that drew her toward him.

"And this is why," he said, "we are not going to think about monks right now. No man wants to think about other men when he is with the woman he admires."

She stepped into his arms.

"And never doubt it, Lily. I admire you extremely." He lifted a hand to brush ever so lightly over her hair, which was still pinned up, and she saw that it was shaking a little. It touched her deeply, that he might feel vulnerable with her, even if it was only a vulnerability to desire. Wonder stole over her. She wanted this.

He leaned down and kissed her cheekbone ever so lightly. Then her cheek, her earlobe, and the tip of her chin. His slow kisses made her feel worshipped, though his gentle lingering was making her desperate for him to kiss her mouth.

And then he did.

His lips brushed hers, and there was that crippling tenderness again that simply undid her. How did he come by it, this masculine, arrogant, stunning man?

Her eyes were still open, while his had closed, and as his kiss stirred her passion into flame and his tongue stroked moist heat into her mouth, she gazed at his fair eyelids with their thick lashes and the neat line of one eyebrow that was in view. So real, so human, so present to her now. So lovable it tugged her heart. His breath whished softly against her cheek while his mouth worked upon her desire.

He broke the kiss and pressed his lips just beneath her ear, making her shiver with excitement.

"Stop thinking, Lily. I can feel you thinking."

Her lips curled up. Along with the sexual thrill of his touch, something was bubbling up in the region of her heart, making her giddy. "One of us ought to."

"Not now. Not tonight. Tonight is for feeling."

"I *am* feeling," she whispered and let her hands run down the long, taut line of his back, covered only in the loose cloth of his shirt. "And you feel remarkable."

He laughed, a husky sound, and buried his face in her neck. The bristle that had formed on his cheeks and chin abraded her skin exquisitely, and a moan pressed at the back of her throat.

"Only you, Lily," he said and sucked gently, making the moan release, a hitching, helpless sound she ought to have regretted but didn't, "would use a word like 'remarkable' in the midst of lovemaking."

"Hush," she said and hugged him tight against her, his erection pressing hard into her. "I feel *you*."

He growled and canted his hips so that he pressed

harder against her, and dragged his lips down from her collarbone and across her bosom, pushing the neck of her nightgown wider. He tugged sharply at its fine cloth, so that it ripped open. With a dark chuckle he held it wide and let it slide down her body, leaving her naked to his eyes.

"Ah," he breathed, letting his eyes run over her. "So beautiful. As perfectly formed as the flower you are named for. If *I* had a journal, I might sketch you and keep you as an image of perfection to gaze upon. If I didn't want to touch you more."

The cool night breeze lifted the curtains behind him and passed over her body, touching skin no breeze had ever touched before, giving her goose bumps on her bare belly and arms, which were growing warmer every moment under his heated, greedy gaze. She felt unaccountably taller than she had before, and more at ease than she could have imagined, standing naked in a room with a man.

He set his hands on either side of her hips. His palms, large and warm, skimmed upward, tracing her curves as he looked into her eyes. He was still dressed, and standing there naked as if for his use, she knew the desire to surrender to him. He pushed his hands up under her breasts, pushed her breasts up, too, so that they pressed together in all their fullness. Then he bent his golden head and put his mouth against them. The scratchy beginnings of his whiskers abraded the delicate skin. She closed her eyes with pleasure.

The fire he'd started licked down through her breasts and up the insides of her legs and deep inside her. He moved his head to nuzzle her earlobe, tugged it inside his mouth, and drew a whimper from her with gentle suction.

She pulled impatiently at the open collar of his shirt and worked it loose and pushed it down his arms urgently, over the hard curves and density of his arms with their light furring of hairs. He shrugged out of it roughly, his eyes on hers as if daring her to do her worst. She put her hand against the front of his trousers. His shirt lay upside-down, spilling from his waistband. His eyes stayed on her, waiting, as she unfastened his trousers and pushed them wider. When he sprang free of them, she sucked in her breath.

"Shocked now?"

She *was* shocked, or actually, startled. She'd never seen this most male part. And the way it was now… rather like a thick, jutting dagger.

"It's just not having seen such a thing before. I… shall doubtless become accustomed in a moment."

"Doubtless," he said in a husky voice tinged with amusement.

To pay him back for his teasing—and she instinctively knew it would—she reached out and encircled his erection and squeezed gently, a way of meeting the assertiveness of this part of him that was so hard. And hot—she hadn't expected the burning heat. He groaned, moved his hips, and pressed himself into her grip. She loved this power she felt over him.

He kicked aside the trousers pooled at his feet and pulled her against him. Slipping his hands under her bottom, he picked her up and carried her across the room. At no time did he turn toward the windows and their open curtains, though only the tiniest corner of her mind still registered concern about whether he might glance outside.

He deposited her at the edge of his desk, and her naked bottom came to rest atop a pile of papers that were cool from the freshness of the early autumn night.

"Hal," she gasped. She was *sitting* on his papers—papers he might read later.

"Shh." He put a finger to her lips. "Let me love you."

Love? She grasped at the word, probing it, but thought fell away as he eased her legs apart and propped them open, one at the edge of the desk chair, the other on the front of an open drawer. And then he slid has hands along the insides of her thighs and showed her what he meant by loving her: physical affection, his slow, sensual stroking *there*, among the delicate, hidden, neglected little folds between her legs.

"Oh…" she murmured, hardly knowing what she said, and his finger dipped and stroked and paused over that so recently discovered place that felt so incredibly good. Her arms went out behind her to prop herself up and keep from collapsing.

"Oh what, Lily?" he said low, slowing down his stroke so that he drew out the pleasure and the wanting. *Oh*, but she wanted.

He leaned in and kissed her neck. "Is that 'Oh, my Lord Roxham'?" he chuckled darkly. "Because I would be your lord in this, Lily."

"Yes," she whispered, limp with need.

He bent his head and captured her nipple with his mouth. She moaned and shamelessly urged him closer with her bent knees, and he took his hand away and tugged roughly on one of the desk's small side drawers.

She murmured nonsense, wanting him to bring his hand back, to come closer with his muscular, tall body. And then he was fumbling with something, pulling something onto himself, and she knew it was a French letter.

He moved in close to her and dipped his hips, and she felt him at her opening. She pressed urgently against him. He pushed into her slowly. A tight, uncomfortable pinching inside her. This was the end of her maidenhead. She read in his eyes that he knew it, that he was waiting for some sign from her.

"I... think you won't fit."

His chuckle was almost a moan. "I'll fit. Be patient." He pushed a little more, and she knew from the nearly overwhelming feeling of stretching that he was all the way inside her now. The candlelight picked out a trickle of perspiration as it slid down his temple. In his slow, patient entry, she had come to accommodate him, and it felt much better.

He looked into her eyes and smiled a slow, gloating smile that dragged a grunt of laughter from her. She gave no thought at that moment to how he'd acquired such wonderful bedroom arts. She just wanted him and what they were doing together. She wrapped her arms around his ribs and drew him closer, pressing him harder at the place where they were joined.

He uttered a soft curse and began to stroke inside her, slowly at first, and then with a rhythm that filled her and made the dangling handles on the desk drawers rattle. Their skin was slick, their breathing labored as everything grew more urgent. The tightness built in her feverishly, a headlong rush that was as wild and adventurous as thundering across a midnight moor on a galloping, untamed horse.

And then the wondrous surge of pleasure hurtled her free of the ride. There was that peace again, even deeper this time, that joyful, holy falling into nothingness. There was no voice of judgment within her, no cares or plans or shoulds, just sweet, airy peace.

Coming back to herself, wanting only for him to find what she just had, she hugged him against her as he continued to thrust. She wished she could always be with him like this: intimate, inseparable.

He grunted against her, grinding his teeth, panting, every bit of him focusing on the peak he was climbing. He pushed harder into her until they could get no closer, and with a growl he stiffened, then sagged against her, spent and heaving. Despite the almost violence of the last moments, she felt serenity enfold them both.

❧

"I don't want you to think I customarily use my desk in such a manner." His head had been resting on her shoulder, and he turned it a little and pressed his lips to her neck.

He picked her up from the desk—one of his papers was stuck to her bottom with perspiration, and she brushed it away and let it fall to the floor with the other things they'd knocked off, and didn't care about the disorder they'd created.

He carried her over to his bed and arranged her gently before stretching out behind her and pulling her against him. "Really, it's just been the writing and reading and thinking."

"Hmm," she said, not ready to say anything. Lying in his arms was too wonderful.

So wonderful that it scared the wits out of her.

This was Lord Perfect lying beside her, a man who was experienced at all the things they'd just done, no matter how special and unique and wonder-worthy they'd been to her. He'd done all that before. Well, perhaps not exactly in that way. He seemed to want her to know that.

She'd thought, earlier, that he was going to say something unexpected. He'd said, "Let me love you," and she'd thought for a moment that he meant something by it. He'd been so tender and beguiling, so attuned to her, that she'd felt cherished. Known.

But he hadn't said anything more about love, and that was because he didn't love her. And why should she want him to? How could she think of love with a charmer like Hal, when what she hoped for in the most hidden part of herself, the part she tried never to nourish or even look at, was the deepest possible connection of two souls understanding each other?

The stuff of girlish dreams. A fantasy, and definitely asking too much.

"You're not asleep, are you?" he murmured, his breath stirring the hairs on the back of her neck.

"I'm not."

"And so. Splendid, yes?"

A smile tugged the edge of her mouth even though some of the radiance of those exquisite moments was fading. "Is it customary to conduct a review afterward?"

"I don't know about customary. But I'm interested in right now."

"Splendid. Yes."

But. Lying here in his arms was like teetering on the edge of a precipice over which it would be so easy to fall. And that made her afraid, because she'd never felt so good, so whole as she had tonight with him.

He was a rogue. A teaser. An enchanter who craved diversion. She was his diversion at the moment.

What if he were sincere about liking her so much?

He'd been so attuned to her tonight, as if he really did care.

No.

Even if he were sincere, even if he liked her very much, even if he did speak to her of love and have pure intentions, she didn't *believe* he could love her. Not for a lifetime. He was a butterfly, enchanting and insubstantial, drawn to the nectar of ever-new experiences. Not to be trusted with her heart.

Very well. She'd experienced what she'd wanted to try. It had been beautiful, but now that the rushing, yearning sensations had worn off a little, she had to be clear. What they'd just done had been a passing pleasure. She couldn't build anything on it.

Each cruel, sobering thought made her feel heavier inside as it hustled away more of the glow from their lovemaking. But she was a practical woman, a woman who wanted to do something with her life, and she could not, like a drunkard, be led by her body and her emotions onto a path of need and wanting. She knew that pathetic path, of being at the mercy of urges as her father had been, and she would not take it.

And she remembered now that part of what had

brought her here tonight had been concern that Hal might see Nate's light.

The clock struck half past one. She needed to leave this cozy bed and this warm, witty man who was brushing his whiskery cheek playfully against her neck. Nate might well be gone now.

She sat up.

"Lil?" He propped himself on his elbow.

"I… have to go. It's late."

"Right," he said agreeably. If he stood up and turned now, no longer distracted by her, with Nate still out there, it would be bad.

She moved to the window and discreetly pulled the curtain to cover more of it, checking as she did so for Nate's light. She was relieved to see nothing.

"You surprise me," he said, coming over to stand behind her as he knotted the ties on a silky burgundy dressing gown that made a rich contrast with his gold hair. She told herself halfheartedly that only a vain main would wear such a beautiful dressing gown.

"I wouldn't have thought you likely to stand naked in front of a window." He chuckled. "But perhaps, unleashed from the bonds of propriety as you have so recently been, you feel ready for experiences like displaying your bare body to the moon."

He was looking over her shoulder, and she felt the moment that the thought occurred to him.

"Unless there is some other reason you are standing before this window. Unless you are checking for an accomplice who prefers to do his work after midnight."

She didn't know what to say. Covering for Nate had been part of the reason she'd come to his room.

And her doing that would be a good reason for Hal to forget about pursuing her any more after tonight, if he even wished to do so.

"Ah. I see by your silence that I've hit upon something. A pressing reason for your coming here tonight." Something hard had come into the voice of her tender lover, and it tore at her. She wanted everything to go back to the way it had been ten minutes ago.

"Quite a sacrifice you were willing to make for your accomplice. Tell me, did you arrange it earlier in the day, or was it a spur-of-the-moment decision?"

She couldn't have him think it had been only that—it would be denying the sacredness of those moments they'd shared. She turned, wishing for the armor of clothes as she stood there naked before him. She crossed her arms over her breasts.

"It wasn't like that," she said softly. "I can't talk about this, but—I came here tonight because I wanted to. Because I wanted to experience what you were offering."

"What I was offering," he repeated. The candlelight was growing dimmer since two of the candles had already guttered, but there was enough light that she could see his eyes, deeper and darker and different. "Take care, Lily. I'm not a plate of confections for you to sample at will."

His words pricked her—there was some accusation behind them—and she felt confused again. Why was the ground always shifting under her now, so that she didn't anymore know where to stand?

"I... liked what we did together," she allowed herself to admit.

"Fulsome praise, coming from Miss Teagarden. Regretting it already, then?"

"It's not like that!" A wave of heat rushed into her cheeks and the tops of her ears and made her glad for the darkness.

"Isn't it?"

He held her eyes a moment, his gaze heavy-lidded and unreadable. Then he turned away and came back with her tattered chemise and nightgown, and looked into the empty hearth while she dressed. She felt so crushed, so bereft now of all the ease that had been between them. It was that which she'd miss the most.

She wished, foolishly, that he hadn't guessed why she was looking out the window. But she reminded herself that she had been duplicitous and deserved what pains the discovery of it brought her.

He crossed his arms and leaned casually back against a bedpost. "Well, we had a pleasurable evening, Lily. I do enjoy initiating you into the world of sensual delights."

"I wish you wouldn't talk that way," she said as she tugged the torn pieces of her gown together and tied a makeshift knot to hold it closed.

"Then how would you have me term it?" She had the sense that he actually wanted to know what she thought of it.

Wondrous. As amazing as the thin-air panorama of a just-climbed mountain. "It was… a splendid experience. Thank you," she said.

One haughty viscount's eyebrow drifted lazily upward. "Another *learning* experience perhaps?" He laughed.

How could he laugh so easily, just now? She'd described it stupidly, yes, but she hated that he was laughing at her. She'd been touched somewhere deep inside tonight by a man who was a spiritual lightweight, and she'd didn't know how it had happened. She'd never felt less like laughing.

"Don't think we are done, Lily Teagarden. Not by a long chalk."

Her eyebrows slammed together. "Of course we are done. How can you think…" but her words drifted off as she struggled to phrase what it was he thought. Or what she thought he wanted from her.

She must always remember that he was a teaser. Was this all some elaborate game to him? She couldn't think why he would want to engage in such a game— except that there was a powerful attraction between them. Lust had brought her here as surely as it had prompted him to invite her, and if her own desire was also underlain with true affection, well, more fool she.

He just looked steadily at her with a mocking tilt at one corner of his mouth that deepened to bring out the slash of a dimple in the hard plane of his cheek. A dizzying mixture of panic and glee warred within her.

"I'll see you tomorrow," he said, making it sound like a threat, and opened the door for her.

All the way down the corridor to her room, as she crept on bare feet in the darkness, all she could think about was what he meant by those last words and the tone of dark promise in which he'd said them.

❧

Hal sat up in bed for a long time after Lily left, a glass of brandy resting against his bent knee. It was not something he'd done before, sitting in bed drinking liquor. There was something desperate and idiotic about it, but he didn't care.

Normally after making love with a woman, he was happily sated and drowsy. And making love with Lily had been extraordinary.

But he'd been unprepared for the blow to his gut when he'd realized that the main thing which had brought her to him had been a desire to distract him from looking out his window. She'd needed the goal of sacrificing herself before she would allow herself to come to him.

How very Lily.

He refused to be anybody's sacrificial altar.

He slung back the remaining brandy, put the glass on the nightstand, and blew out his candles.

Twenty-one

HAL SAT AT THE LUNCHEON TABLE, CHATTING UP Hyacinth with a fraction of his attention while he watched Lily talk to Fforde at the other end of the table. Despite living but one mile away, the doctor had accepted Diana's urging to join their meal. Diana felt that the poor man worked too hard and was in dire need of a break. Hal could find no drop of compassion in his own heart for the paragon of Highcross.

Lily gave Fforde a sweet smile, and the doctor received it with a smile of his own. Hal found he had to look away or he would be in danger of sprinting down to the other end of the table and escorting the good doctor out the window.

Any other woman who'd shared all that Lily had shared with him last night would have been saving all her sweetness for *him*, or at the very least giving him meaningful secret glances. But not Lily. She wouldn't be coy or eager or even, he supposed as a tar-like gush of jealousy flowed through him, hopeful.

She hadn't come to him last night purely out

of need because she wasn't ready to admit she needed him.

Yet.

❧

Lily was standing in the foyer in front of Mayfield's grand, curving double staircase later that morning with Delia and Eloise. Eloise couldn't seem to say anything that did not contain the word "Donwell." Apparently, the two of them were getting on very well all of a sudden. Lily was puzzled but happy for her, though she could barely pay attention to all the details of some sort of frog-hunting excursion the pair had engaged in, because her own thoughts were so occupied.

After she left Hal's chamber the night before, she'd half expected to be struck by lightning, or to be found out or punished in some way. But nothing had happened, and she'd fallen asleep and woken up as usual. Surprisingly ordinary. And yet she felt changed.

Shame had tried to hound her this morning, but she simply hadn't cared to listen to the voice of judgment, almost as though it had lost credibility with her. What she and Hal had shared had made her feel more open, more alive, and more human than she'd ever felt before. It had been real and untidy and good and true, and she wouldn't let shame dirty it.

But, disastrously, now she wanted more time with him, more of what they'd shared last night, more of everything from a man who was wrong for her.

Through one of the tall windows, she saw a rider galloping profligately across the beautifully kept grass in front of the manor and knew instinctively who it was. She also knew that she was half in love with him. And if she was not to fall all the way, she *must* avoid him. It had to be possible—they were only to stay one more night at Mayfield.

Excusing herself, she quickly made her way up the grand staircase, intending to seek her bedchamber.

She was still moving through the endless corridor that led to her chamber when she heard assertive, pleased-with-themselves footsteps coming toward her. Quickening her pace, she made for the end of the corridor and the turn that would take her to her chamber—and away from temptation personified.

Temptation merely laughed, and with several long strides, caught her by the arm just outside her room.

He was wearing a mud-flecked old black coat with a pair of tan breeches and high, mud-spattered boots. His golden hair was windblown every which way and should have made him look disorderly, but he looked carelessly, deliciously handsome.

"Well, Lily. Here you are."

"Don't you need to tidy up, my lord? You must've left a muddy trail all through the house."

"I used the boot scraper. But if you'd like to help me get my boots off, I won't have to call my valet."

"I'd be happy to ring for him," she said, even as she drank in the way the green flecks in his eyes were glittering at her. "It would be a service to your guests. You look abominable."

A calculating slanting of his eyes, a boyish quivering of his eyebrows, and a hint of that dimple in his taut cheek… something in her gave a little *huzzah*.

He reached a long arm toward her door handle.

"Come here, woman, I want to show you something." The huskiness in his voice sent an eager shiver across the back of her neck.

"No," she started to say, but he wasn't listening, and he pulled her briskly into her chamber and shut the door behind them.

She reached for the door, but he ignored her and deftly propped a chair under the handle. She gave him a withering look and crossed her arms, but that only made her more aware of how they surrounded her breasts, which were suddenly more sensitive. *Now that he was here.*

Dear God, what had happened to her?

"So, you have lost your mind," she said.

He grinned darkly and pulled her against him. "I've been looking at you all morning in that gown," he said against her temple. "What do you mean by showing so much bosom?" His thumb began to stroke the underside of her breast.

"It's exactly the same amount of bosom every other woman is showing," she said and tipped up her chin. No matter that it was *her* bedchamber, she ought to leave now, escape… but she didn't want to. Apparently she'd turned into someone who simply did what she wanted. Perhaps next she would steal from a shop.

"But on you it's more," he said, burying his face in the crook of her neck. His lips shaped themselves softly to the curve and applied gentle suction.

She sighed as if she'd been waiting for him to do that, and bold as brass—truly, she'd ceased to shock herself—she lifted a hand and loosened his cravat and slid her hand into the slot beneath the ties at the neck of his shirt. The skin of his chest was the hard, warm flesh she'd been craving all morning, like an addiction that had hold of her.

But she didn't have access for long, because he turned her away from him and pressed her toward the wall next to the window drapes. A burst of lavender met her as her nose came up against the edge of the fabric.

"Up with your skirts," he ordered wickedly.

"Certainly not," she said.

"Then I'll have to rip downward," he murmured, putting his hands on the fabric at her nape. She didn't really believe he'd do it, but on the other hand, a terrible tease like Hal would love nothing more than to horrify her.

"Oh, very well," she said, letting primness into her voice even though her eyes were already closed in anticipation of whatever wicked thing he was going to do. She reached down and gathered her skirts up to her knees.

A chuckle. Just the murmur of his voice behind her was making her warm and very tingly. "*Much* higher, and just the back portion."

Surely he wasn't planning anything strange? And yet she was dying to know what. She sighed dramatically and pulled up the back part of her skirts, letting the front portion fall back to her feet.

Cloth rustled behind her. She looked over her shoulder and saw he was undoing the fastenings of his breeches. He sprang free, thick, bold, exactly *other* to every part of her body. Oh good.

"Is this—" she gasped as his wicked finger stroked the most hidden part of her, "allowed?"

"Allowed?" He reached around to rub the flat of his flexed palm against her nipple in teasing circles that made her sag against the wall, her forehead against her crossed arms.

"Darling," he whispered in her ear, everything in her standing at attention to his voice and the sweep of his breath against her suddenly sensitive ear, "everything's allowed in my book."

He pressed himself against the naked skin of her bottom, and she pushed back against his hot flesh, desperate to feel more of him. He was fire against her in the hot pinch of his fingers on her nipple and the clever stroking of his hand between her legs. She moaned, helpless in his arms, wanting him to dictate everything.

He took his hands away briefly to pull something out of his pocket. She knew what it was, but she didn't want to think about practical things. And then he pulled her hard against him, holding her hips to himself, and began to slide into her. He was moving slowly, just when she needed all of him, and she tipped her hips forward to take him, to let him have all he wanted from her.

He grunted, a sound of deep pleasure. "Teagarden, you minx."

He drove into her, pounding with a masculine rhythm that overtook her, and she welcomed its sturdy force. Though they both kept silent to avoid discovery, with his mouth just above her ear she could hear his faint groans. Panting, her mouth pressed to her forearm, she rose to the heights with him and gasped into the curtain as she found her release. He pushed into her again and again, using her body for his needs, and she welcomed what he was doing. With a deep, final groan, he hugged her hard to him and sagged against her back.

As they stood there, linked together and absolutely undone, she realized she was unable—entirely *not* able—to resist the pleasure he brought her. And the closeness, too, the brilliant closeness of breathing in his skin, feeling his heat, feeling him with her.

Terrifying.

How was she ever going to not want him when he made her feel like this? When she had the time of her life in his company?

How could she dally like this when she wanted a future of purpose and meaning?

❧

Hal was breathing hard as he stepped back and tidied up. Lily was still leaning against the wall, and he took a clean handkerchief from his pocket and reached around to hand it to her. Without turning, she took it and thanked him.

He stared at the tidy, simple knot of white-blond hair on the back of her head and thought about how he'd never known that he was lonely until he cared for her. He never *had* been, until she came along, with her Fiend and her journal and her astringent ways.

He put his hands on her small shoulders and gently turned her, letting his hands come to rest lightly against her neck. The wary look in her eyes that had fled when he dragged her into her chamber had already returned. But he was a soldier and a commander, and he wasn't afraid of battle.

"*Now* will you agree that we are courting?"

A skittering look, as though she were ambushed prey, flitted across her features. She didn't want to trust him, or even allow herself to like him too much, and he'd have to push her past that if they were to have a chance together.

"I beg your pardon?" she said in a cooling voice meant to remind him she might have surrendered her body, but she hadn't surrendered her soul. He kept his tone light and brisk.

"Courting. You and I. We've been behaving like lovers—let's call it what it is."

She frowned. "Why talk about courting?"

"Because I want to. Because you need me. Who else is going to make you laugh, and make you stop taking yourself so seriously, and get you to say yes to all the things in life you say no to?"

"Those aren't needs. And this is just you being a bossy viscount."

"This is me making sense. Come, Lily. You value reason so much," he said. "This is reasonable: we get along extremely well in many ways."

Her eyes drifted over his shoulder, so different from her customary forthright way, and her hesitancy gave him a little hope.

"In scandalous, hidden ways," she said.

"Exactly. And I'm suggesting that they not be hidden. That we allow others to see that we have an interest in each other." It was taking everything he had to speak so blandly when that was not at all how he felt. She made him feel young, and free, though he wasn't even certain what it was he felt free *of*. Being with her made his whole world new again, and he was old enough not to fool himself about why that was. And savvy enough to know that telling her how he felt wouldn't be in the least helpful yet. If ever.

"Oh," she said. "Well... I... mmm..." Her voice died out in a dry croak. She cleared her throat. "It's not at all a good idea. Everything we've been doing together is not a good idea. We *must*, we have to stop."

He crossed his arms and gave her the kind of stare he'd once reserved for misbehaving corporals. "You mean you've lost your nerve."

Her chin lifted, all pride and starchiness. "I simply understand that it's time to stop playing."

She would refuse to see what had grown between them, how—damn him for sounding mawkish—but how precious and rare it was. She was refusing to see that what was between them would blossom, and he could feel himself rising to the challenge she'd unwittingly laid down for him.

"You're wrong," he said.

And before she could utter even one sensible syllable, he leaned forward and kissed her smartly on the cheek, whipped the chair away from the door handle, and left her standing there with an open mouth and an insubordinate look.

❦

Lily found, as the day wore on and she caught herself repeatedly listening for Hal's step in corridors and pricking her ears for his voice, that she was making no progress whatsoever in turning away from her desire for him.

Which was how she ended up in his bedchamber that night, being rendered senseless again with passion. She'd told herself she'd gone simply to keep him from looking out the window. She did still mean to provide whatever help she could for Nate. But she knew it was only an excuse.

Hal had greeted her at the door to his chamber at midnight. "Come to distract me, have you?"

And she'd smiled and said yes, and distracted him thoroughly. Twice.

She hadn't returned to her room until the clock was striking four; she hadn't wanted to leave his arms at all. But some modicum of sense had prevailed and carried her feet to her bedchamber, where her still-made bed accused her. Like a drunken youth arriving home to the scolds of a mother, she found herself quite able not to care.

Twenty-two

"OH," LILY SAID TO DR. FFORDE—MATTHEW, AS HE'D reminded her to call him when he sat down next to her on the bench. He'd said he wanted to ask her something important. She had a fairly good idea what it might be.

It was after breakfast and the last day of the house party. The Teagardens would leave after lunch, but for now everyone had gone out to the terrace and were dispersed in different activities. Delia and Eloise were across the terrace, talking to Donwell, Hal was showing Rob something to do with an enormous ancient oak not far from the terrace, while Ivorwood, Ian, and some of the others had gone inside to the billiard room.

So it was very quiet where she sat with Dr. Fforde. Matthew. The perfect place for an intimate moment for which she was not ready.

Her one syllable hung in the air, awaiting others, but she couldn't seem to speak, to advance a conversation that might change the way things were right now—more specifically, the way things were between her and Hal.

Of course the two of them couldn't go on sneaking around, teasing and pleasuring each other and behaving like fools with no concern for consequences. They couldn't go on this way, but everything within her didn't want it to change.

What a coward she'd become. Was this what she wanted for herself, a life of pleasure?

She drew on that inner hardness, that voice of moral authority that was the only thing she felt must guide her.

"Yes, certainly you may ask whatever you wish."

He took her hand. She could feel the moment that Hal, still talking with Rob by the oak, perceived the change in her conversation with Matthew Fforde, but she made herself ignore the awareness.

"Lily, it can't have escaped your notice that I've paid special attention to you in recent days. That is because I've recognized in you someone who values many of the same things I do."

Chilling fingers of conscience dragged at her shoulders. Matthew Fforde was a good man and he deserved the full attention of any woman he honored by his addresses. Even if that woman didn't deserve them.

"You do me great honor, sir."

Hesitancy tugged at the edges of his mouth, a vulnerability that reminded her she'd not discouraged his attentions, which had led to this conversation. His brown eyes looked kind; she liked them, liked the seriousness in them.

"I am hoping that *you* will do *me* the very great honor of becoming my wife."

Across the terrace Delia gave a bark of laughter in

response to something Eloise had said. A bumblebee was buzzing near Lily's arm, and though she generally found the sound drowsily pleasant, just now it was making her incredibly irritated. She ought to be thinking about Matthew Fforde, about the future he was offering her, yet she was letting her attention be drawn to a bee.

A fiery annoyance surged in her; she had no answer for Matthew, and that was because she had no idea who she was anymore. She'd been weak and let pleasure run away with her like a horse on a gallop. It had run off with her sense as well.

Dr. Matthew Fforde, waiting patiently and kindly for her response, was an antidote to all that had been going on in her life in the last few weeks. With him she would be on a reasonable, productive course. She would not be tempted to do unwise things. And not, she could only suppose, be pulled into linen closets for trysts.

She liked him. He'd not spoken of loving her, and perhaps he didn't require love from her, or perhaps he assumed that it would grow.

She could say yes to him. It would change her life.

But how would that be fair to him, when even now she was thinking about Hal, and trying not to notice that his conversation with Rob allowed him to watch her from a distance?

"I…" she began, emotions roiling within her like a skein of yarn growing hopelessly tangled, each knot tightening as she tried to undo another. She had no idea what to say and hoped desperately that instinct—or some latent wisdom—would guide her into what was right.

He smiled a little. "You do not have to reply this very moment, Lily. Perhaps it's better, unless you disagree, that you take a little time to think over such a large decision. A day or two?"

"How kind," she said, feeling as though her voice came from very far off. She was relieved at this reprieve, and yet she must still make the decision. "And how reasonable."

He laughed softly. "I do prize reason, Miss Teagarden. If you will permit me, your reasonableness is one of the qualities that first drew me to you."

He got up and bowed his head graciously and left through the terrace doors into the manor. And all she could manage was to think that she'd clearly deceived the man well, because she'd done so many unreasonable things in the last week that she'd lost count.

She got up and, waving breezily to the others in a way that didn't invite company, made for the path that led toward the lake. What she suddenly wanted more than anything was time alone, away from the splendor and customs of Mayfield and especially from its master.

The quiet of the day soothed her a little, the rhythmic sounds of a lark calling to its mate and the soft rustle of the leaves as a breeze sighed through the trees. How she missed the quiet of her yarn house, the tasks and the serenity and the solitude.

She reached the lake and wandered around it aimlessly for some time, listening to the soft lap of its water and trying to imagine what it would be like to be married to Matthew Fforde. To be with him for hours every day, to do the intimate things with him that she'd already done with Hal. To give up her shawl business and accept Hal's offer to pay for the school, and to go on to the life of significant charitable work Dr. Fforde offered her.

Her mind was blank and unwilling to work with these thoughts, as if it were in revolt.

She sat down in the grass by the side of the lake and picked a few buttercups and twined them together into a chain. Absentmindedly she formed the flowers into a bracelet so that the glossy yellow petals of the flowers faced out in a row. She was holding her arm out to look at it, and acknowledging that she was avoiding the decision she needed to make, when a shadow came across her.

"A new kind of jewelry to go with the shawls?"

Hal. She stared at the lake, telling herself she must not look into his golden handsomeness. He was for her a kind of Medusa, and the sight of him enchanted her, turning her not to stone but into someone she'd never meant to be.

He ignored her lack of greeting and sat down next to her.

"You like to create things," he said. "The shawls give you a lot of satisfaction."

She did love making them, but that could never be her main reason for creating them—they were a means to an end. "I suppose."

"There's nothing wrong with doing something just because you like it, Lily. Everything in life doesn't have to be productive, or worthwhile, or morally upright."

"Well, I've certainly been testing that idea out this week."

He laughed a little, but it wasn't his usual wicked

chuckle, and she finally couldn't resist temptation anymore and turned to him. But he wasn't looking at her, he was looking away, out across the lake.

"He asked you to marry him, didn't he?"

"Yes."

"And you thought about me and told him no."

"I said I'd think about it."

He continued to stare out over the lake, a gorgeous viscount in his impeccably tailored dark green coat and tan breeches, his cravat snowy white against a little end-of-summer tan that still colored his skin.

And then he looked at her, his eyes dark with serious intent, his jaw seeming more chiseled, any trace of those playful dimples gone, so that he was almost a stranger to her, commanding and hard.

"Marry *me*, Lily. You know we are good together. Say you'll marry me."

Her heart leapt a chasm at his words. He wanted to marry her! He was serious, very serious. Now, in this moment, he wanted her and only her.

But she reminded her leaping heart that what Hal loved most was novelty and thrill. That she'd led him a merry chase, perhaps the best one he'd ever known because, angry and frustrated as she'd often been with herself and him, she'd doubtless been more resistant to his charm than any woman he'd ever known.

She felt a little ill. She cared for him, and she'd shared so much with him. But she couldn't trust her future to him.

And she hadn't needed a second proposal today to make her even more muddled.

"Hal," she began gently, "you do me great honor. I never expected this."

"Why not? I told you I wanted to court you."

"But I thought it was a game to you."

His brows slammed together. "It wasn't a game."

He was waiting for an answer. She would have to say words to him that would hurt her to say, but she must.

"Then I thank you, but I cannot marry you."

Silence. She endured his gaze on her, his eyes heavy-lidded.

"Then you mean to go north with Fforde. You will run away."

The hard note in his voice sparked something unreasonable in her. Why could he never see things her way?

"It wouldn't be running away—if anything it's running *to* something, to the kind of things we all should care about: discipline, valuable work, selflessness." Her heart thudded sickly in her chest—she didn't want to say more. But she must, so that nothing might remain between them. "And how can you accuse me of running away when your whole life has been nothing but going from one diversion to another just to avoid being bored?"

Hal looked away from her again, out over the lake. Did she have any idea how her words cut him? She would never see him as anything but a wastrel. He must accept that. All the things about him that attracted women were a mark against him, because they made her unable to believe he had any depth of character.

He could feel her looking at the side of his face, but the last thing he wanted right now was to look at her; it only twisted his gut harder. He was already churning with jealousy that Fforde had proposed to her.

He acknowledged, with a bitter twist of his mouth, that his plan to bind her to him with sensual intimacy had been fatally flawed because she would refuse to see pleasure as valuable, and she would judge herself unworthy for enjoying it. But how the hell could he have stopped himself from trying? He wasn't made of stone.

And now her knight in shining armor had offered marriage, had beat him to the punch, to the loving blow he'd been working toward that might have bound Lily to him in all the ways he needed her to be—but above all, in love. Damned Fforde; he'd probably never even sullied her with so much as a kiss.

He forced evenness into his voice though he wanted to shout at her not to turn her back on what had grown between them. "And what about the linen closet and my bedchamber and all that we've shared?"

Her lips took on a tightness that said she'd pushed all the things they'd done out of her mind as soon as they were over. Probably put them in a mental refuse bin. He shouldn't want to probe this—it would only be excruciating—but he would hear her articulate it.

"We both know that was just…"

"Yes? Just what?"

"Obsession! I can't resist you. But that's not love. It's unhealthy and out of control."

Inside, he flinched. "Do you love him then? Fforde?"

Her cheeks reddened. "I don't owe you an

accounting of my feelings. But I believe I could learn to love him. He is a kind man whom I respect."

She couldn't have been plainer. "I understand. You can't allow yourself to consider me because you could never respect yourself if you accepted me." He stood up and turned to go.

"Wait," she said. "I'm sorry."

That he certainly didn't want to hear. "No need to be sorry. It's only the truth."

He turned and walked away.

Twenty-three

THE TEAGARDENS' DEPARTURE FROM MAYFIELD WAS uneventful, save for the significant amount of time that Delia and Eloise spent in taking leave of one another as the carriage stood ready to depart.

Lily sat next to Ian and tried not to look at Hal as he stood in the courtyard seeing them off. Hal was somewhat distracted by his brother and sister-in-law, who were departing as well, and Lily was grateful for the bustle and nearly ready to strangle Delia by the time they were finally able to leave.

As their carriage pulled away, her siblings called out their thanks, waving heartily, and Hal returned their courtesies. He never once looked at her, and she hated how that felt. Everything else aside, he'd become a friend to her, but of course she couldn't expect him to seek her when she'd hurt him. Turning down his offer might have been the right thing to do, but ever since he'd walked away from her at the lake, she'd felt horribly bereft and out of sorts.

Her spirits were not improved when Rob told her he'd invited Matthew Fforde for dinner two nights hence. She still wasn't ready to accept his offer, yet she knew that she'd never have another chance to so perfectly satisfy every hope she'd ever had for her future. She would use the time until he came to sweep away the emotions of the last days and prepare herself to accept this kind man. She really did like him. All would be well.

She'd meant to send a note to Nate as soon as they reached Thistlethwaite, but a storm blew in soon after they arrived, howling and beating rain against the windowpanes, and it became obvious he wouldn't be able to dig that night. She was glad for the respite this meant—he wouldn't be in danger, and she wouldn't have to worry. Which only freed her mind to dwell on Hal and how much she missed him. She resisted this by busying herself in making arrangements with the house-keeper, reading a book of sermons, and helping Delia alter another of the dresses from her London Season.

Buck was delighted by her return, and she spent the evening by the sitting room fire, brushing burrs out of his fur while Rob went over account books and Ian experimented with a small flute. Delia, predictably, was eager to revisit their stay at Mayfield.

"As long as I live I shall never forget dancing with the Earl of Ivorwood," she said from the sofa behind Lily, where she had draped herself in what she called a "Grecian pose," which meant lying as languorously as possible, as if she'd just partaken of ambrosia.

"Doubtless it will remain a golden memory for him as well: the girl who would not speak when spoken to," Ian said in between bars of a lively tune.

Delia threw a small pillow at him and turned to her

sister. "What about you, Lily? And dancing with the most handsome viscount ever?"

"I'm sure I won't forget that either," she said. If only she could. Surely in time she would.

"But don't you hope—" Delia said, leaning close to her. "That is, the two of you looked to be in such deep conversation at the ball, and at other times, too. Don't you think there's a chance he might wish to court you?"

Lily could feel both her brothers' eyes on her as well. "I have no reason to think the viscount would court me." Not now, he wouldn't. Not since she'd told him she couldn't respect him, that she couldn't allow herself to love him. Leaving Mayfield hadn't helped relieve the emotions pressing on her, and every time she thought of their final conversation she felt ill.

"Besides," Rob said, "Matthew Fforde is coming to dinner tomorrow, and I doubt it is because he wishes to see me."

"Oh. Dr. Fforde," Delia said with an air of gloomy acceptance.

That night Lily stayed up as late as she could so that she wouldn't have trouble falling asleep. But still she lay tossing and turning while lightning flashed outside her window. Eventually she threw back the covers and got up and went into the dark dining room and drank two glasses of brandy quickly, like medicine. She lay down again with the bed spinning, feeling as though she didn't know herself anymore. She missed Hal terribly.

The next day early, she sent a note to Nate. She wrote that Roxham would doubtless be on the alert for him, and that she would watch for him all night from her window if he didn't tell her what time he would dig. He sent a terse note back saying that he would dig near five in the morning. She meant to be there.

Determined to be productive in the meantime, she went to the yarn house and boiled up a pot of oak bark to make some brown dye and spun some yarn. The storm had blown in cool, bright weather, the very best kind for working, but she couldn't seem to settle to a task and kept starting new things while leaving other tasks unfinished, which annoyed her.

In the afternoon she took Buck and went out to visit the sheep, who were happy to see her. But all the while, doing these familiar activities that used to make her content, she felt dull, as if there were no purpose behind them.

She used to know exactly what she wanted and who she was, she thought, as she brushed a gentle hand over Rosemary's soft head, but now she did not. She felt like a rushing river of emotion. Of lust for Hal. Greed for more time with him. Envy that she wasn't carefree like Delia or Eloise. Anger at her father for being weak. And heaven knew she'd been deceitful countless times in the last weeks.

A veritable crop of vices.

She'd never felt so fallible in her life, so imperfect, so untidy in her thoughts and deeds.

But what she also felt was… human.

❧

The moon was low in the sky when she slipped out of Thistlethwaite very early the next morning. Autumn had truly settled in, and she'd put on an old black mourning gown to help hide her and wrapped a dark brown shawl around her against its chill.

She moved across the grass, the dew soaking her half-boots, and soon she was on the Mayfield side of the woods, near the pale glimmer of Nate's light. Very softly, she gave the call they'd agreed on. A pause, and he responded.

She moved away from the tree line and settled into a leaning position against the rock where she'd hidden before and tried to filter out the faint sounds of his shovel pushing into the ground while she trained her ears toward Mayfield. Her eyes fruitlessly combed the dark lawn, her ears strained for any noise.

Though the other times when she'd come she'd been anxious about being caught by Hal, there had also been an element of playfulness, of each of them trying to best the other. Now it was different. She didn't care about besting him anymore, and it wouldn't be amusing if he came upon them. The time dragged by heavy and slow, as if coated in mud.

After perhaps an hour, she heard the signal she and Nate had agreed on. Had he finally found what he was looking for? She crept toward the woods to find out.

❧

Unable to sleep, Hal had walked down to the lake around four, which seemed, lately, to be the hour past which he could not sleep. He'd gone there and gazed at the moonlight on the water and appreciated its lonesome beauty and wished Lily had been there to share it with him. Which was idiotic because the last thing he wanted now was to see her. And yet he could think of nothing else.

She had, like the bracing autumn wind, scoured him clean of everything else, so that he felt empty. It was an emptiness that couldn't be filled with card games or chatter or whiskey, though he'd tried. Every hour dragged as if it were a strange new experience, and he felt murky and slow. Eloise had asked him that afternoon if he were sick. John had reminded him that only two days remained to the wager over the Woods Fiend, and teased him about how he would lose his new hunter. Hal had made the appropriate noises while realizing that he didn't much care who owned that horse.

He could hardly stand himself.

He was just passing the half-completed folly—he supposed he ought to find some other work for Giuseppe and Pietro and simply deem the folly even more of a ruin than it was supposed to be—when he saw the light in the trees.

Perversely, it stirred a response in him as nothing had in the last two days. The Woods Fiend was a man Lily knew, a man she was helping, and jealousy surged, pushing his steps toward the wood.

As he drew near he became aware of the low murmur of conversation near the light, just inside the edge of the trees. Sunrise was not far off, and he could make out two figures crouching by the light of a lantern. He inched close enough to see.

Lily and a man were leaning over something on the ground.

"What the devil is going on here?" Hal said.

Lily yelped and the two sprang apart. Hal saw a box the size of a bread loaf lying on the ground between them, next to a hole at the foot of a large old beech tree. As the lantern picked out the man's features, Hal saw that it was Nate Beckett, the farmer who lived on the other side of Thistlethwaite. The man Lily had been talking to after church.

"Er," Lily said in a thready voice.

His blood boiled hotter every moment. Why was she here, why had she been here those other times, with Beckett? Upright Lily, who was going to marry Fforde?

He fixed his gaze on Beckett. "You are trespassing."

Beckett held his gaze. "Yes. I'm sorry about that, my lord. It was necessary."

"You *needed* to be on my land?" Hal flicked his eyes downward. "To dig. For this box, I presume. Which, being that it's on my land, rightfully belongs to me."

The dark shine of Beckett's eyes flickered in the lantern glow, but he said nothing, doubtless aware of the egregiousness of his behavior. No doubt Beckett was also frustrated at having been caught, now, when he'd finally gotten what it was he wanted. Too bad.

Hal flicked a quick glance at Lily, not lingering. "And you," he began, but she cut him off.

"I'm sorry. I know this looks bad. But Nate had a good reason to dig in your woods. Something was buried here years ago that belongs to his family."

Why was she defending Beckett? Were they lovers? He forced unruly anger down and kept his eyes on Beckett.

"Why should anything belonging to the Beckett family have been buried on Mayfield land?"

"Because it was your great-uncle who buried it, my lord," Beckett said. "Something meant for my great-aunt."

So it had to do with that old rumor about Great-Uncle Edmund romancing a farmer's daughter. "You're hoping for money, aren't you?"

Beckett made no response, but Hal could feel Lily looking at him imploringly. He melted not a whit.

"If it is money," she said, "it belongs to his family. And it's not as if you'd need it."

Ignoring her, Hal bent over to examine the chest.

"It's locked," Beckett said.

"Evidently. Give me the shovel."

"I'll do it," Beckett said.

"The shovel," Hal repeated. Beckett handed it over. Hal was more than happy, at that moment, to slam the blade hard against the old lock, which fell free at his first strike. He nudged the lid open with his foot, and they all leaned over to peer into it.

The lantern light caught the shine of gold. Hal picked up the small object, and as he brought it closer to the light, the hairs on the back of his neck stood up. It was a heavy man's ring set with a large, square ruby.

He knew what this was. He'd never seen it in person, but he'd gazed at it all his life.

"This belongs to me, actually. It's always gone to the second-born Waverly son. What do you mean by suggesting it's yours?"

"Hal," Lily began, but he cut her off.

"Did you know this was here all along?" he demanded.

She didn't say anything for a moment, a hesitation that spoke of guilt. His anger surged higher.

She cleared her throat. "I didn't actually know what was in the box."

"Never mind, Beckett will explain."

Beckett crossed his arms. He was a sturdy, dark-haired man, and in the dim light he looked formidable—though not as formidable as Hal felt, with righteous fury swelling his chest.

"I knew something was here because of a letter that was recently found, a letter written by your great-uncle to my great-aunt. He wrote of a gift he had for her, a gift he would bury in the woods, at the foot of a beech tree they knew. That's the only reason I've been digging here."

"You expect me to believe that my great-uncle gave away a family heirloom to your great-aunt. Why would he have done that?"

"I believe it was to be an engagement ring. I have the letter at home if you'd like to see."

"What nonsense."

❧

Lily watched Hal, unable to take her eyes from his face. She'd missed him so desperately since they'd parted that even to see him now in this cold, angry state answered the deep yearning she had for him. He wore no coat or cravat but only a white shirt open at the neck and dark trousers.

She ached for him to sweep her into his arms, but he'd never looked less like he wanted to touch her. His tone, his posture—everything about him was distant and closed to her. She couldn't bear it. And for Nate's sake, she needed to get him to listen with an open heart.

"Hal, I know that most people have always thought your great-uncle was killed while trying to rescue Anne Beckett from the Woods Fiend. And now that Nate has this note from him, we know that was very likely what happened—but that this also wasn't the whole story, because the young woman he was trying to save was his sweetheart. A woman who was very nearly your relative. He wanted her to have that ring."

She searched his face in the gleam of the lantern and the weak, predawn light, and wished for more light to illuminate those familiar angles and lines, that expressive flesh that she'd come to know with her hands and lips. She saw there... nothing.

He kept his eyes from her and disciplined his features in a way she never would have expected; he was the viscount now, remote from other mortals. Nor had there been anything hard or ungracious in his voice. Whatever was there, whatever emotion he was feeling, he'd tamed it so that his voice held none of the resentment or anguish he must be feeling. It was a side of him she'd never seen before.

If he felt her eyes on him, he didn't turn to her. His attention was fixed on Nate. He held out his hand, the ring on his open palm. "Very well, I agree it is yours."

Nate simply stared. Lily was incredulous, too. Was he going to surrender it, and without a fight?

"My lord," Nate said after a long pause, "I did not suppose you could be so willing to believe me in this."

"You might be the greatest liar the world has ever

known, Beckett, but if Lily says you speak the truth, I believe you, and I will make no claim upon it."

Lily's heart beat faster. What did he mean, *if Lily says you speak the truth, I believe you*? He still trusted her, even though she'd rejected him and worked against him? How could he trust her so much, when she'd never been able to trust him—and told him so? And how could he be willing to surrender the ring when it had meant so much to him? Was it truly because of her?

"I had not supposed you could be so gracious, my lord," Nate said.

Lily wanted to shout that she hadn't either, but she felt askew, as if rushing to keep up with her shifting awareness of Hal. He was the same man he'd always been, but it was as though she was really seeing him now, like a painting that was suddenly more compelling for having a new frame.

"I don't know what to say, my lord," Nate said. "My thanks are inadequate."

"You are welcome," Hal said.

A glimmer of dawn light penetrated the trees, falling across his chest, making that part of him glow with all the warmth and familiarity of home. She'd thought that putting her trust in him would leave her vulnerable, but now she saw she'd been wrong.

He and Nate shook hands.

"Beckett, Lily," he said and before she could say a thing, he was walking away from them, having taken control of the situation and resolved it. She realized that her mouth was gaping, and she shut it.

Gathering her wits, she quickly took leave of Nate and ran after Hal. Dawn was breaking on the horizon, a flat, bursting light spilling larger every minute, starting a new day.

Striding fast on his long legs, Hal was well ahead of her already. She called softly to him to wait, mindful of the need to not make noise that could draw attention from anyone who might be awake, but he kept going. She gathered up her skirts and ran, and reaching him, grabbed his shirtsleeve. He rounded on her.

"What do you *want*?"

Morning light gilded the clean lines of his jaw and cheek like an angel bathed in heavenly light. He wasn't an angel, though he'd accused her of seeking saintliness—and he'd been right. But when she'd found the sacred in his arms, she hadn't fully known what it was. And now she knew how human and muddled she was, and she was glad, because it was real.

"I—I'm sorry," she said.

"For what? For conspiring against me? I would have thought you'd be triumphant to see a hardworking man like Beckett win out over a viscount."

"Stop it, it's not like that." He arched an eyebrow at her. "Very well, yes, it's true that once I would have felt that way, but I don't now. You didn't have to do what you just did. That ring meant something to you."

"It's just a piece of jewelry."

She shook her head. "It was significant to you, and valuable. Probably the only family heirloom you ever wanted. And you could easily have taken it and walked off and hidden behind the power of the viscountcy. No one would have disputed your claim."

"Beckett would have."

"You know he wouldn't have stood a chance. The ring belonged for generations to the men in your family you most admired. It was buried on your land. But you let Nate have it because you believed it had been given to his family."

And she'd never been prouder of him.

"*Nate*," he said, still talking in that cold voice she hated. "So what's between you two, Lily? Are you lovers?"

Inappropriately in this tense moment, she laughed, a thin, slightly hysterical sound. His look turned thunderous.

"Nate is like a brother to me. I spent countless hours in the Becketts' kitchen when I was young. Our families are old friends. But I didn't know he was the Woods Fiend until I saw him that first night with you. And then when I found out what he was doing—that he was digging for an engagement gift your great-uncle had given his great-aunt—I couldn't let you catch him."

"So you interfered to help him."

"Yes." She huffed out a small breath, aware of how her motives had not been so pure as she'd wanted to believe. "At first I was angry at you over what happened four years ago with my journal, even if I didn't want to admit that it still bothered me. Deep down I was angry that you'd never noticed me, and I wanted to pay you back."

He crossed his arms, so shut off from her that he might have been a stranger. "So you can admit it."

She pushed on, needing him to understand it was different now. "Yes, you were right when you said I was angry. I was angry about many things, but I didn't want to acknowledge that. Being angry felt out of control and wrong."

"It's not wrong to be angry about injustice. The way your father treated you after your mother died was weak. He imposed on you."

"Yes," she said, her voice deepening as she admitted it out loud. "He did, and I hated it, and hated that he seemed to choose to be feeble. He left me to contend with problems that were too much for me."

"Bravo," he said softly.

She wanted to ask him what he meant by that, but she'd betrayed him, and right now she owed him a full explanation. "At first I didn't guess that the engagement gift might be your ring. And then I found that I was having the time of my life trying to get the best of you."

Something flickered in his eyes. "Were you?" he said and, though his voice was soft, it scared her a little, as if he were turning harder before her eyes, so hard that he was impenetrable to her. She rushed on to explain.

"When I realized it might possibly be your family heirloom, I dismissed the idea because it seemed like too grand a gift."

"Did it ever occur to you, Lily, to simply talk to me about Beckett and what he felt he needed to do? Am I an ogre?"

"It was Nate's secret. I couldn't share it with anyone."

"And you couldn't have asked him if you might talk with me about it? As close as we'd gotten, you couldn't talk to me?"

It hadn't occurred to her, of course, because she hadn't believed she could trust him, even though everything they'd done together—the talking, the touching, the fighting—had told her that he knew her, that he wanted to know her more, and that he cared about her. But she'd rejected him and hurt him, and she was very much afraid she'd thrown all that away.

"I…"

"Didn't trust me. Couldn't imagine I might do something good."

"Yes." She looked down at her feet, so ashamed of how freely she'd judged him, how righteously she'd found him wanting. He was such a threat to her heart that she'd needed to. But that need to judge him was gone now; it had been replaced by need *for* him. She couldn't have picked a worse time to recognize it.

"I know you are a kind person," she said, the words coming out husky. She needed him to see that she understood him now. That finally she'd seen the world through his eyes, a view he'd been trying to show her all along. "I should have tried."

"You're right, you should have. But you were too busy trying to save the world."

"Yes," she said, her heart in her throat. She looked up at him, needing him to know how sincere she was. "But I feel differently now."

Her words seemed to confuse him, and then his eyes narrowed. "No you don't. You've simply been swayed into thinking I'm a worthy man because I treated Beckett fairly. Don't let it sway you. I have loads of money and jewels. It was nothing to me."

He was being deliberately cruel. It wasn't just the

personal value of the ring he'd surrendered. It was the way he'd treated Nate, a farmer, a nobody as far as a viscount was concerned. He'd treated him as an equal. Only a very *good* man would do that.

He turned and starting walking again.

"Hal, wait!" He stopped but didn't turn around, and she moved to face him. "You're right. I didn't want to believe that you might do the right thing. I… needed you to be someone I couldn't admire. I was wrong."

"You, Lily Teagarden, owe an apology to a wastrel like me?"

She was seeing the hard core at his center, and she could hardly bear it. "I deserved that. But I don't think you're a wastrel. And I am more sorry than I can say."

"Fine," he said. "Apology accepted. Now go home. The sun's up and you've no good excuse to be standing here alone talking to me."

That was true, but suddenly there was so much to be said. Didn't he feel that, too? Didn't her apology mean anything to him? Or was everything ruined between them?

"But… I hate how it feels, you being unhappy with me."

He sighed and lifted a hand and cupped her cheek. "I'm not unhappy with you, Teagarden. Truly. We enjoyed each other, but that was a time outside of time. You were right: we are too different."

He started walking again, and she didn't follow him, aware that, now that she so much wanted to, she didn't have the right.

Twenty-four

MATTHEW FFORDE CAME TO DINNER THAT NIGHT, AND Lily, exhausted from what had happened early that morning, nonetheless forced herself to face him. At least now she knew, with no hesitation, that she couldn't marry him.

They spoke together alone in the sitting room after dinner, her siblings having discreetly made themselves scarce. She was very sorry for the disappointment in his kind eyes when she gave him her answer. Some of that was her fault. But they'd been little more to each other than good companions and hope for the future, and she knew now that she couldn't build a life on that.

As she watched the door close behind him, the room almost dark with evening settling in, she thought how all this time, all these years, she'd been wanting to do good deeds, not allowing herself to slip up and waste time or lose her focus on her goals. It had all been in a sense empty. Not that the desire to do good was wrong, but it had grown out of something askew; it hadn't come from love.

She who was going to serve the world knew nothing about love. She was a mere beginner; she had so much to learn. She wanted to learn, more than anything, and she knew that this desire to learn was right, a good beginning. The person she wanted most to discuss this with was Hal, but she didn't know how to begin. Besides, she thought it very likely that he no longer wanted to hear what she had to say.

Ian came back from a trip to Highcross village the next day and reported that Hal had made a public announcement that he'd caught the Woods Fiend—and that their specter had only been a foolish young man from another village, playing a joke. Hal had said he'd scolded the youth for the trouble he'd caused, then offered him a position at one of his other estates. Everyone was now having a good laugh over how they'd been fooled.

"Quite magnanimous of him, wasn't it?" Ian said. "Offering the young scoundrel a job when he might have thrown him in the stocks instead."

"He ought to be properly thanked," she said, carefully keeping emotion out of her voice. "Shouldn't we ask him to dinner?"

"Can't. He's left, for Spain I think. Doesn't his cousin James have a vineyard there?"

Her heart fell with a thud. He'd gone. Mayfield had been vacant all those years, and he'd come back and brought it to life and woken her up to so much, and now he was gone. All the way to Spain.

So that was it. She'd had a taste of something wonderful and refused it. Wasted her chance. *No* had been her watchword for so long, a reflex she hadn't known to question. And now she didn't want to live out of a reflex anymore, and it was too late.

It couldn't have been more clear that he didn't want to see her again.

But how would she ever forget him?

The days dragged by as though weighted, despite her best efforts to fill them. Helen came back, and the shawl business picked up where it had left off. Lily threw herself into her old routines, carding wool for hours and spinning until her fingers were numb. She knitted four new shawls, but she was unhappy with all of them and unraveled each soon after it was done.

She met with Anna and Mary Cooper and allowed herself to be delighted by how much they'd learned so far. They responded to her warm praise with renewed enthusiasm and brought their friend Eliza Cartwright to join them. Hal had promised to provide funds for the school, and she was certain he would honor his promise, but she'd have to wait to receive whatever help he would give now that he was gone, so in the meantime she meant to continue raising funds herself as well.

She stopped by the Beckett farm and found a laborer fixing the damaged gutters. Mrs. Beckett invited her in for tea, clearly eager to tell their amazing news: Nate had found a valuable ring and sold it to Lord Roxham for a large sum.

"Can you imagine?" Mrs. Beckett enthused. "Well, it is beyond imagining, really. And we have such plans for the money. There are some debts that must be paid, but then Little Billy can go to school and study to be a surgeon. So much is possible!"

Out walking with Buck some days later, Lily wandered onto the Mayfield property, where the Italians were at work finishing the folly. She asked them as best she could whether the master was coming back to see the completed folly, but they just shook their heads uncomprehendingly.

She meandered daily among the woods and meadows for hours, the kind of time-wasting thing she never used to do.

"I wish he were here to walk with us," she said to Buck one afternoon as they poked around at the edge of a meadow looking for something to use as a dye. The sky had been gray all day, and the chill October wind bent the branches down low over the dying plants. There was little of anything with color around to be found, but she aimlessly tugged at spent raspberry canes and picked at the bark of a fallen tree.

Buck just barked at her, as if to ask why they were lingering there. A gust of wind sprinkled them with drops of water left on the leaves from a noontime rain. "Very well, I suppose it isn't a nice day for a walk."

They moved on, making for home. As they were drawing near to Thistlethwaite, Delia came running out waving the post, which had just arrived.

"A letter from Eloise! She's in London, and she writes that every time she's worn the shawl we gave her, she's gotten lavish compliments. And now she has seven friends—imagine having seven friends!—who all want shawls. So they're sending orders to Mr. Trent."

"Oh," Lily said. "Well, that is very good news."

"Good grief, Lily, where's your enthusiasm? With

the Woods Fiend gone and new orders coming in, you can have everything the way you want it now."

If only Delia knew the irony of her words. But she was glad for the shawl orders, because if anything could help her through the restlessness that Hal's departure had brought her, surely it was work.

"Shall I tell you why I've been so invested in the shawl business, Delia? What I hope to do with the money that's earned?"

"I always supposed you just liked to save it."

"I *have* been saving it—because I want to start a school for all the local girls."

"Oh! What a lovely idea. Why didn't you ever say?"

"I suppose I didn't think anyone would like the idea of my doing it."

"Well, that's silly. We already know you like to help people. Though why you don't also like to dance and laugh with gentlemen I will never understand."

A faint smile nudged the edge of Lily's mouth. "Sometimes I do like those things, too. Very much. Does Eloise say anything else?" she asked, trying to keep eagerness out of her voice.

Delia returned to her letter. "Let's see. Eloise bought three new gowns, one poppy, one yellow, and one green. Freddy and Louie got into Diana's best perfume and put it all over one of their dogs."

"Oh, dear," Lily said dispiritedly.

"I'm sure the dog will be fine," Delia said. "Oh, and she writes about Hal, but we knew this already, that he's gone to stay with their cousin James and his wife, at their vineyard in Spain. Though Eloise writes that she thinks he's going to spend some time in a monastery as well." Delia looked up from the letter. "A *monastery*? Why on earth would he go there?"

Lily was surprised, too. But not astonished, or incredulous, as she would once have been. "To have some quiet, I imagine. People do, you know."

"I suppose, but I shouldn't have thought Hal would want *that* much quiet."

"He's not *only* a handsome man, you know."

Delia gave her sister a penetrating look. "I knew it! You do care for him!"

Lily had been so used to denying it, but now she was finished with being who she was not. She sighed. "Yes, I do care for him. More than any other man I know."

Delia's smile slipped. "You must be very disappointed that he's gone."

"I am."

Delia put a hand kindly on Lily's arm. "He cares for you, too, I'm certain he does. And surely he will come back."

"I'm afraid that's rather too much to hope for," Lily said. She smiled a little. "But I do have the shawl business."

Delia sighed. "At least you didn't accept Dr. Fforde. He was dull."

"Oh, Delia, what are we going to do with you?"

"Take me to London, if at all possible," she said, giving Lily's arm a squeeze. "You could do with a visit there, too. I'm sure it's wonderfully distracting."

"Perhaps," Lily said. Rob had been talking of their going, but she hadn't had much enthusiasm for it.

Delia gave her the other piece of mail, a packet

from Mr. Trent, and went back inside the house to reply to Eloise's letter. Lily took the packet over to a stone bench at the far end of the garden, Buck following her, and sat down. Mr. Trent's packet contained a long list of orders and a note from him addressed to the responsible person in charge of the Thistlethwaite shawl business.

It read in part:

> *And so, with the unmasking of the Woods Fiend, orders have been coming in daily for new shawls. A list is attached. By far the largest order is from Viscount Roxham. Puzzling though it may be to waste such beauty on those who have so little need of it, the viscount has ordered fifty shawls, which are to be sent to the Millhouse Foundling Home in London.*

Tears filled her eyes. She sniffed inelegantly to discourage them, but they spilled down her cheeks as if they'd been stored up for years and were finally being released, and they fell on Trent's letter and made the ink run. She let her head drop into her hands and sobbed as she couldn't remember ever doing.

Sitting by her knees, Buck sniffed at her hidden face and whimpered a little.

"Oh, Buck," she said in a husky voice, emotion pressing hard on her chest. "I miss him so."

The dog nuzzled her neck, and she hugged his comforting, furry body. She cried some more.

Finally the flow of tears abated, and she took a deep, shaky breath.

"He was thinking of me," she told Buck in a quivering voice as she petted his soft head and ears. "He wants me to recognize the pleasure the shawls can bring those girls. He wants me to see that beauty is valuable, that something good comes from enjoying it."

She wished it hadn't taken her so long to see what had been trying to make itself known for so long: she loved Hal, loved him deeply. And she knew now that some of the very things that she'd most resisted about him were the things she needed if she was ever to grow as a person.

"But I was so unkind to him. I hurt him, and now he's put me behind him, as well he should. I must learn to do the same regarding him. But it will be very hard."

She wiped the last of the wetness from her cheeks and stood up. "Come, we must tell Helen about all this work to be done."

❧

Hal sat in his tiny cell of a room, his bare feet flat on the stone floor. His body, clad in only breeches and boots and a shirt with the collar left loose, was resting but alert in the old wooden chair, his mind wondering what he was doing here. But it was only a thought, he told himself. Brother Pablo had said that distracting thoughts would always come, and if Hal didn't hold onto them, they would also go. And for the last three weeks in San Sebastian, that was exactly what Hal had been doing—letting distracting thoughts go.

Here in this plain, quiet place with days of vacant hours, he'd come to find that he could sit still. He'd

never been so satisfied with so little, and it was exhila-
rating. Perhaps he would stay another month, or into
the winter—the idea gave him hope for how he might
get through the coming months, missing Lily as much
as he did. She was not for him, and he was doing his
best to root her out of his being, one thought at a time.

Outside the room's small, arched window, a
bird twittered under the clear Spanish sun, the heat
of summer having softened into the warmth of
October. At his cousin's bodega, the grapes pressed in
September were already fermenting in barrels. On his
way to San Sebastian, Hal had stopped in Jerez to visit
James and Felicity. They were over the moon at their
recent discovery that Felicity was increasing, and while
Hal wished them every happiness, he'd not been in the
mood for the exuberance of lovers, and he'd kept his
visit short.

The monastery bells sounded, four clangs in the still
air. He was meant to be thinking about some words
Brother Pablo had given him: "*Consider the lilies of the
field, how they grow; they toil not, neither do they spin.*"

A small, pained laugh escaped him. If there had ever
been a lily that toiled and spun, it was Lily Teagarden.

She would be back at work on her shawls now.
He knew that she'd turned Fforde down; Delia had
written to Eloise, who had let him know. But Fforde
had never truly been what was standing in his way
with Lily; it had always been, as she'd said herself, that
they were too different. And that Lily couldn't see him
as a man worthy of her love.

He'd gotten over caring so much about that last
part; being at the monastery helped—a little, when

it didn't give him more time to think of her. And to wonder what she might have said if he hadn't walked away in a black mood of pain after Beckett found the ring. But he knew leaving had been the right thing. She'd been impressed by his magnanimity, but that wasn't enough. It wasn't love, and love was what he wanted.

Letting go of this desire for her love was a matter of disciplining his mind, and he reminded himself rather idiotically that he'd always relished a challenge.

A soft knock sounded at his door.

"Come," he said.

Brother Pablo stepped quietly into the room on his sandaled feet. Hal had noticed that everything Brother Pablo and the other monks did was purposeful, as though they were choosing each thing when they did it. Raking leaves, singing in the chapel, eating dinner silently; everything to them was a prayer. With the quiet and the lack of diversions, Hal had had no choice but to practice as they did.

"The day is beautiful," Brother Pablo said. "Would you like to walk in the garden?"

Hal agreed, following him down the loggia. The heels of his boots rang out, making what seemed like the only sound in the place. Brother Pablo's sandals made no noise at all.

"So, my son," Brother Pablo said, which made Hal smile. No one had called him son in decades. His own father hadn't been much for affectionate expressions—or for any kind of affection at all. None of them—Everard, Hal, John, or Eloise—had had an example of the kind of love that cared nothing for achievements or appearances, the kind of selfless love Lily had shown for her family. A kind of love he'd come to understand a little. He made a note to make certain to write to Eloise and let her know he was thinking of her, and to write John as well.

"How goes your quiet time?"

"Well enough," Hal said as they sat down on a stone bench. Near his feet, yellow crocuses bloomed with their orange stigmas, which the monks gathered and sold at the market as saffron.

"And how are you doing with distractions?"

Hal considered his life in recent years. The constant travel, the army, the parties—all of it had been on some level a way of creating diversions so that he wouldn't have the quiet to hear himself. Whenever things had become boring or dull, he'd turned away from them so he could find new things with which to entertain himself. Lily, of course, had started out as a magnificent diversion. But then everything had changed.

He nudged the edge of the stone bench with the tip of his boot. "I have only one distraction now."

"Ah."

For a man who spent his days in silence, Brother Pablo was very good at getting others to talk. "I think it's time you told me why you came."

"I wanted the quiet."

"You wanted escape. You crave escape."

He did. And he'd wanted to escape from Lily and the woods and the people of Highcross, from everything that could remind him that she would never truly give him her heart. "I wanted to marry a woman who wouldn't have me."

"And you hoped to find answers here."

"Perhaps."

"Here is an answer then: you are wrong for each other."

Hal felt his jaw tightening, but he "invited" it to relax, as Brother Pablo had taught him to do. "How can you know that? You don't even know her."

"Tell me about her, then."

He thought about Lily, who was likely sitting somewhere quiet at that moment, knitting for a purpose she believed in. "She wants to improve the world. She is hard on herself, and sometimes on the people around her. She is also a delight to be around, but she doesn't believe that it's important to laugh and waste time."

"I see. So you wanted to waste her time."

"No. I mean—yes, I did. Not waste, really. More like she needs to be extravagant with it, to not always be focused on doing something productive."

"Does she need this? Or is it merely that you can't bear for her to tell you no? You are rich and important, and your every wish is fulfilled the instant you express it. Yours is a life of ease and pleasure."

"It doesn't have to be. Not *only* that. There can be balance between her way and mine."

"That seems unlikely. You will both be happiest if you give her up."

What the devil sort of talk was this from a monk?

"Excuse me?"

"She is simply one more distraction for you."

"That's not true! I love her. I want the best for her."

"Then leave her to her life of virtue."

Hal thought of Lily and how she inspired him. "But I'm not certain that *is* what's best for her. And I know she's made me understand things I didn't know before. What if we are just the right sort of challenge for each other?"

A smile played about the corners of the monk's eyes. "Then you don't need to be here. Why aren't you with her?"

And Hal realized that there was something he'd been avoiding: the hope that remained though it pained him to keep it alive. He'd rather ride into battle than face rejection from Lily one more time, but he realized in that moment that he believed in what he and Lily had shared more than he'd ever believed in anything, and he couldn't let it go without a fight.

Twenty-five

THE TEAGARDENS HAD COME TO LONDON. AS THEIR carriage brought them through the crowded Town streets on a cloudy late October afternoon, Delia stared out the window in awe.

"Finally," she breathed adoringly. "We're finally here."

Lily smiled. "We finally are." The whole way to London, Delia had chattered excitedly about the hotel where they'd stay, and about how fine the shops would be, and what it would be like to stroll in Hyde Park. Rob, too, had been uncharacteristically ebullient; Marianne Preston and her family were already in Town, and Lily was fairly certain that the two would soon be engaged.

Delia smiled. "I thought for certain that you'd insist on staying at Thistlethwaite to work while we were gone."

Lily wasn't quite as excited as Delia about coming to Town, but she'd realized a change of scene would be good for her. With Helen back, there was no reason Lily shouldn't have a brief holiday. For once, she wanted one.

"Nonsense," Lily said. "I wouldn't have dreamed of missing London."

"And think of the balls!" Delia gave Lily a stern look. "You're not going to stand in the corner talking to the dowagers, I hope."

"Certainly not," Lily said with the ghost of a mischievous smile. "I shall dance with every gentleman who asks me."

Delia laughed. "Then you shall end up very winded."

And in fact Lily was rather worn out by the end of their first week, having danced almost constantly at the two balls they attended. After each ball, flowers had come for both ladies, and Delia had teased Lily that she'd received the most. Ian had helpfully pointed out that was merely because Lily had danced with every man who asked her, and so she'd improved her odds. Lily had laughed but knew she welcomed the change that the social whirl provided. She would forget Hal, she told herself several times a day. Or more reasonably, she would move past what they'd shared.

Tonight the Teagardens were attending a dinner party hosted by the Prestons. Mrs. Preston had taken care to invite several of the gentlemen who'd shown marked attention to Lily and Delia. Lily was in a side room talking with one of them—Mr. Grant, the second son of a baronet and an avid Latin scholar—when she saw a familiar brown-haired young lady enter the room.

"Eloise!" Delia cried, rushing over to her. No one had said that Eloise would be invited, or anyone else from her family, and Lily's heart began to beat in great thuds. Donwell came in behind Eloise.

And then through the doorway that was suddenly so fascinating came Hal.

Since she was across the room and a little hidden behind Mr. Grant, he hadn't seen her yet. She watched as he bowed with great warmth to Delia, and let herself fully enjoy how handsome he was, feeling that nothing was so beautiful and special as what we love. His skin was tan and his hair sun-kissed, the look of someone who'd just been to a southern clime.

Would he, knowing Delia was there, look for her? He didn't seem anxious to do so—he was already caught up in conversation with Delia, and Ian had come over as well. Hal seemed entirely content to talk to her siblings, and she knew she had no right to be unhappy about that after the things she'd said to him, but she was. Her chest felt tight.

She wanted to go over to him, but she suddenly felt terrified that he might not want to speak with her. Or, almost worse, that her presence would have no effect on him at all.

She tried to focus on Mr. Grant, who was discussing his recent trip to Rome, but it was impossible because all she could think was that there were a good dozen people in the room, and she might not even have a chance to speak to Hal. And what would she say if she did?

Finally, long minutes later, she felt Hal's eyes on her from across the room. She looked at him, and he inclined his head at her in greeting, his expression oddly sober. And then a gentleman came up and spoke to him, claiming his attention.

Was that to be their only contact? After everything

that had happened? And yet she couldn't seem to make herself approach him.

Dinner was announced shortly thereafter, and they were seated at opposite ends of the long table. Lily had no idea what she conversed about with her dinner companions as the meal progressed. Eloise, aglow next to Donwell, caught her eye and smiled hugely, and Lily could only guess Hal had said nothing to her of what had happened between them. Of course he hadn't—what could he have said that wouldn't have been far too much?

She was feeling very low. Hal was not going to seek her out, and she couldn't blame him. How could he want her company after what she'd said to him the last time? The party now seemed loud and jangling, and she only wanted to go back to their hotel and be alone, but she could hardly leave on her own.

Giving herself a stern talking-to, she sat up straighter in her chair and forced herself to be interested in Mrs. Acton, who was discussing the opera.

And then it was time for the gentlemen to depart for their port, and Lily still hadn't come near Hal, and now she was starting to be impatient with both of them. They were neighbors after all, and they ought to be civil to each other. She would seek him out when the men returned and greet him properly.

As the ladies moved into the drawing room, Eloise came and linked arms with Lily and led her toward a window seat.

"I never properly thanked you for what you did at Mayfield, in bringing me and Donwell together."

"Oh," Lily said. "I don't know that I can take any credit. I seemed only to cause dismay."

"Nonsense. If it weren't for you, I never should have realized what a wonderful, dear, irresistible man he is."

"Then I'm very happy," Lily said, genuinely pleased.

Eloise leaned closer. "And as you are such a fine matchmaker, perhaps you would consider turning your talents to my brother?" Eloise looked toward the doorway as she said these astonishing words. The gentlemen, apparently not interested in much time with their port, were already rejoining the ladies.

"I know he said he would never marry," she continued, apparently oblivious to Lily's blanching face, "but he's been strangely out of sorts for weeks, and I can only think his advanced age is starting to wear on him. He may even be lonely, poor man."

"I've hung up my matchmaker's hat, actually," Lily said, grateful that her voice betrayed none of the emotion she was feeling as she considered the painful idea of Hal courting anyone but her. "But I'm certain your brother wouldn't have any trouble finding a wife."

"Oh, look," Eloise said cheerfully. "He's coming over."

Lily's heart seemed determined to make her feel ill, sending sickening flutters to her stomach. She breathed deeply and considered getting up and walking away with a blithe smile, but she told herself not to be a coward.

Eloise bounced up and said, "There's Donwell. Do excuse me," and she was gone.

And then Hal was standing before Lily. Though there were two score people in the room and a young lady had just begun the opening bars of a melody on the pianoforte, the space between the two of them felt as silent as a chapel.

"Lily," he said. She looked up into his eyes and tried to guess what he was thinking but failed.

"Hal. We meet at last."

A flash of humor in his eyes. "Are you angry that I didn't come to you before now?"

"That would be unreasonable of me."

A ghost of a smile teased the edge of his mouth but didn't make it to his eyes. "It would. May I sit with you?"

She made room for him on the window seat. A little waft of his familiar, beloved scent came to her as he sat. Their words were mild, conversational, but her pulse was racing at his nearness. *Why* had he come to her? Could it be possible that he still cared for her? She must not feed hope, or she would be crushed when all came to nothing.

"How was Spain?" she asked, so grateful that her tone was mild and polite. Quite an accomplishment when everything in her wanted only for him to gather her into his arms.

"Warm, very pretty."

"And your time in the monastery? How long did you stay?"

"Three weeks."

Hal thought perhaps that he wasn't going to be able to do this, to sit here with her and make small talk while his whole life hung in the balance. She kept asking him polite questions, and perhaps that was because she didn't want to leave room for him to say something she didn't want to hear.

"Were you surprised to hear I was at a monastery?" he said. "I suppose you laughed."

"I did not. I thought it very fine."

The silence stretched out between them. So much to say, and also nothing.

"How are Parsley and Sage?" he said. "No longer esteemed haunted, I hope."

She laughed a little. "Yes. You arranged that quite well, the misbehaving young man from another village. Everyone had a good laugh about how we were all tricked." She'd been looking at the girl playing the pianoforte, but now she turned to look at him. "And the Becketts. That ring made all the difference for them."

He merely gave a nod. The Becketts had been done out of a connection to the Waverlys when his great-uncle was killed, a connection that, whether his family liked it or not, would have been very advantageous to them.

He knew himself to be hesitating because her dismissal of his proposal had been so painful. But somehow he'd lost a little of the need to avoid emotions that were unpleasant, and this had given him a new perspective.

"You were more than fair with him," she said, "giving up such a valuable piece of jewelry."

He would take this chance. "Lily, I was furious that you'd worked against me with Nate, but what I did, I did because of you."

He thought—he was almost certain—that the edge of her mouth quivered. By God but everything seemed to hang on the most subtle of signals.

"Eloise wants me to make a match for you," she said. Her voice sounded husky. *Was* it husky?

"There's only one match I want to make, Lily," he said, lifting his eyes to hers. He held out his hand, his whole heart and self waiting to know how she would respond.

Her eyes held his. She lifted her hand and put it in his, a wordless yes.

"You came back to me," she said in a soft voice that made all the tightness in him begin to relax. "I was so unhappy that you left. And so ashamed over how I'd judged you all that time. Can you forgive me?"

"I don't know that there is anything to forgive. Some of the things you said woke me up, in a way."

She shook her head. "I was hard. A hardening woman. And you saw things about me that I didn't want to see."

He could feel a dizzy smile slipping over his lips. "Perhaps when two people are just right for each other, they see one another other as no one else can."

"I missed you so terribly," she said. "Only I didn't know until then how much I would. I'd come to trust you and care for you, and I hadn't even realized it."

Her blue eyes held everything he wanted for his future. For their future. "I think you were right to be leery of me as I was when you met me again. But loving you has changed me. I do love you, dearest Lily."

She squeezed his hand. "Isn't it a wonder," she said, "that after all the wild things that happened between us, the simple feel of your hand in mine could bring me such incredible bliss?"

"*You* are a wonder, Lily Teagarden. You've made me know what bliss truly is."

Her beautiful smile melted the last remaining bit of unhappiness in his heart. "I love you, dearest Hal."

"For a lifetime," he said.

"For a lifetime."

❧

It was August again, sunny but not too hot, and Hal and Lily were entertaining family on the terrace.

Lily sat at a stone table on the terrace drinking lemonade with Delia and Eloise, while Hal, Donwell, and Ian bowled on the lawn with Louie and Freddy, Diana and John having gone for a walk.

"Lily, are you quite certain you are comfortable out here?" Hal called to her from the bowling green, where she'd encouraged him to go.

Lily smiled at her husband, who, as she'd moved into the ninth month of her confinement, had become something of a mother hen. Which was why, though she'd been feeling some mild contractions of her muscles since the middle of last night, she'd yet to mention them—she didn't want to worry him.

Ever since their wedding in November, he hadn't let a day go by without delighting her anew with his inventive, playful, wonderfully mischievous love. Just last week he'd surprised her with a candlelit dinner on the roof of the west tower, at which he served her himself—and then proceeded to make gentle love to her there, right out in the open under the stars. And to think she'd once considered him shallow and uncaring. She hadn't yet stopped wondering at her incredible good luck.

"Just lovely, darling," she called back, then had

to take a deep breath as another muscular squeezing tightened across her belly.

Delia and Eloise, who had turned their chairs to watch the bowling, called out encouragement to Louie, whose ball kept rolling in the wrong direction.

"Let's go into the village later," Delia said to Eloise. "I want to see how things are looking inside the new school now that all the painting is done. I saw Mary and Anna Cooper yesterday, and they are very excited for the start of classes in September."

"I want to come visit the school, too," Lily said.

"Oh Lily," Delia laughed, still watching the bowlers. "You know that Hal hasn't let you get in a carriage for the last month, never mind walking that far. Eloise and I can go have a look and report back to you."

When Lily didn't make any reply, Delia finally turned to glance at her quiet sister.

"You look a bit hot, or something, Lily," Delia said from across the table.

"Would you like some lemonade?" Eloise said over her shoulder.

Eloise, who'd been giddy ever since Donwell's recent return from a six-month voyage to South America, spoke somewhat distractedly as she gazed across the lawn at the men. Lily had suggested to Hal that it might not be long before his sister and Donwell were engaged, and Hal had replied that he only hoped that Eloise would be half so happy in her married life as he was in his. Lily had told him that married life was making him mawkish, and he'd smiled wickedly and showed her just how entertainingly mawkish he could be.

But now another squeezing in her belly left her unable to answer Eloise's question, and both Eloise and Delia were looking at her.

"Hal," Delia called out after watching her mute sister for several moments, "perhaps it's time to send for the doctor."

He was by Lily's side in a trice, kissing her and gently scolding her for not telling him that her time was close, and calling for a footman to fetch Dr. Peters, who'd replaced Dr. Fforde. Matthew Fforde had left for the north three months earlier, with a large contribution from Hal and Lily that would ensure the doctor could spend his time caring for patients and not worrying about funds.

Against Lily's feeble protests, her husband carried her up to their room and gently laid her on the bed. His brow was creased in anguish, and Lily, having just come through another contraction, reached up and cupped his cheek.

"My darling husband, all will be well."

He sighed and squeezed her hand. "Yes. Yes, of course it will." He smiled at her, and it was her favorite smile, the one that caused those irresistible dimples to form and lit sparks of mischief in his eyes, though the sparks were muted now. Unspoken between them was the awareness of how life would hang in the balance over the next hours.

Hal watched his wife with his heart in his throat.

"These past months with you have been the best of my life," he said, knowing that the words were inadequate but needing to say them anyway. The thought of the pain she must undergo was agony to him, never mind the danger that always hovered during childbirth. "You've made me so happy, dearest Lily."

She smiled her love back, reminding him there was no need for words between them.

Dr. Peters arrived then, and Hal moved to the edges of the room, out of the way of the doctor and Diana and Delia, and only coming closer now and then to murmur words of encouragement to his wife. He supposed that Dr. Peters found it strange of him to stay, but he could never have left Lily to bear so much alone.

Long hours later, Lily was safely delivered of a son who was both healthy and loud. Hal knew such relief mingled with joy that he felt dizzy.

The baby was carried carefully across the room to be wiped clean and fussed over by Delia and Diana while Lily lay propped up in bed, exhausted but serene. Hal knelt down beside her.

"He's beautiful," Hal said. "You are beautiful. The whole world is beautiful."

She smiled. "You sound like a fool," she said gently.

"I am, a happy fool in love with you and everything else. I feel surpassingly fortunate and grateful."

"So do I," she said.

The others slipped away and Lily watched as her beloved husband brought their son to her. He lay nestled in her arms with his parents smiling over his head.

She kissed the top of her son's head. "Perfect," she whispered.

"I always wanted to be perfect," she said quietly to her husband, "but I never really knew what that was until I got mixed up with you. And then I discovered that the only kind of perfect I want to strive for is to be perfect in love."

He leaned forward to kiss her with infinite tenderness. It was only a moment before their son began to fuss.

Hal smiled ruefully, gently rubbing their baby's downy head. "He has impressive volume."

Lily sighed, but her lips were quivering in a smile. "I suppose he'll be full of mischief as well. He'll need a weighty name to balance it out. Ethelred? Eadwig?"

Hal chuckled. "You really are much more mischievous than you look, my darling. And you know we've already agreed. Welcome to the world, Sebastian Everard Waverly."

About the Author

Emily Greenwood worked for a number of years as a writer, crafting newsletters and fundraising brochures, but she far prefers writing playful love stories set in Regency England, and she thinks romance novels are the chocolate of literature. A Golden Heart finalist, she lives in Maryland with her husband and two daughters.